# Rajasthan Suite Memory

# Mughal India

# Rajasthan Suite Memory

Dyan Dubois

 SALT RIVER

BEYOND BORDERS
is an imprint of Salt River Publishing
Phoenix, Arizona
**www.SaltRiverPublishing.com**

FIRST EDITION 2016
18  17  16      3  2  1       III  II  I
ISBN 978-1-946051-01-1

Cover photo by Andrew Johnson, used with permission: Lake Pichola,
Lake Palace Hotel and Aravalli Hills, Udaipur, Rajasthan

SR

**Publisher discount available**
SaltRiverPublishing.com/estore/

# CONTENTS

# Rajputana

Map of Rajasthan

# CHAPTER 1 – LAKE PALACE HOTEL

Rajasthan, land of bone dry fingers severed by sand rivers, begged for monsoon rains. Four years of severe drought echoed over the sand, whispered to the rising storm: Bring relief, water – not dust. Sardar Singh felt words without sound reverberate across the desiccated vista – his hopes, his fears. He watched the sky grow yellow with rainless wind.

Sardar Singh hailed the boat taxi at the Pichola Lake dock at dawn when the world moved with hurried step to outdistance the day's heat. He studied lake-bank muck, now fifteen feet below where sun had danced on gentle waves. He considered himself privileged to work at the Lake Palace Hotel, to have a job, but his farmer's heart beat for the land.

He felt the rhythm of early dawn to dusk, working the dark lava fields, feeling the earth sift through his fingers. In spring his heart grew buoyant when yellow mustard flowers brightened the land. He traded pulses for wheat and rice, watched green sugarcane fields to the east grow tall on irrigation water he needed.

Earlier in his cramped house in Udaipur, while his wife, their four daughters, elderly parents, and a lone uncle slept, Sardar inhaled prayer in deep, slow draughts. Farmer Sardar stood, bested by drought, between his family and starvation. Now a hotel waiter, he feared he might not stave off the inevitable of fourteen years of diminished rainfall. His salary provided some lentils and rice, and vegetables when the dry earth would cooperate. Allotted water, trucked into the city every other day, eliminated his crops. Without a crop he had no means to set aside a dowry for his eldest, Asha. He worried: Who would have a girl of twenty?

Today he didn't shave – the water ration almost used up – adjusted his trimmed moustache, tucked streaked gray hair under the waiter's red cap, and left his saffron turban draped on its hook. He smoothed the white tunic under his red cummerbund, straightened the tight churidar leggings, aware his job depended on neatness and affability. He pleaded, "Lord Shiva, hide the fear festering in my heart. I must stand strong for my family. Bless us with rain. I will work to win your favor. I will bring life back to my fields. This I swear."

In the rising sun, diamonds flickered on gentle waves. Sardar felt something akin to joy. This could be the day, he thought. He heard the cough and sputter of the approaching motorboat that crossed the lake to pick him up every morning for work.

"Many visitors at the hotel coming today?" the boat driver said. He pulled up to the cement dock.

"No, very slow," Sardar said, climbing in. "A group from Germany canceled. It is now too hot for foreigners. Yesterday the temperature reached 34 degrees. That makes any white face a pomegranate. Who can blame them?" He wiped the perspiration from his forehead and watched locals frolic and bathe in the sluggish brown water. He checked his watch. "They better hurry. Management ordered they must finish bathing by now. No guests should see them."

The boatman ignored Sardar's concern. "Yes, yes, these foreigners come from far. I hear them speaking. They think I am not understanding. They walk down from the gate, excited. One said to see white palace, like a swan on quiet waters, admiring her own reflection. They sit in my boat. The beautiful white palace with its ghostly reflection, where is it? They ask me, complain that photos showed blue waters, the palace like a graceful bird rising. They see the gray foundation exposed like a scab. They curse. I am wishing they would not speak words that hurt my soul. They should go home."

"Well, my friend, let us be happy any of them come at this time for they are the food that feeds us. You take their comments too much to heart. Let them say what they want. We know the beauty we have."

"What, Sardar? They are the food? No, they are eating the food, pulling it from our burnt fields, out of our hands, out of our mouths, food that should feed our families. Something must change."

They neared the hotel dock. The driver pulled back on the throttle, causing a small wake that rocked the boat. "You are correct in this, Sardar, we must be having more faith. It is only the end of April. Monsoons may yet come and change our lives. We will dance in the rain, you and me, faces up to the sky, drink to our farmer's life. No more foreigners for me. I go back to the fields. For now I must be driving this boat and you serving the guests. We are having work. When the rains return we rejoice in our crops. For you, all will be forgotten – and forgiven. For me, I am not forgetting."

Sardar Singh nodded in agreement, stepped on the wooden pier and roped the ferryboat to the post.

"Sardar Ji, before you go, I heard a story of interest."

"Yes?"

"Another guest saw something and grew scared."

"Where?"

"In Sajjan Niwas Suite."

"Does management know?"

"No. The sweeper fetched a desk clerk to calm the lady. He did not make a report. You remember the trouble caused last time. We all want to keep our jobs."

"Was it the same as last time, screaming?"

"No. This time a woman on the bench swing in the bedroom. When the guest saw her, she fainted. Her husband caught her before she hit the marble floor."

"That's luck! An injury, we have to report. I am glad her husband reached her."

"The woman insisted on leaving that very day. They had booked for two more days."

"We do report that to management." Sardar Singh felt his chest deflate, heard a sigh drag fragile joy into shadow.

The boatman whispered, "Yesterday a couple arrived earlier than expected. The booking agent in Delhi made a mistake. The desk clerk gave them Sajjan Niwas at reduced rate, offered them extended booking for same price, as soon as they were stepping in. That pleased them. They have the suite for five days. Desk clerk told staff only, management not knowing about the other problem. We close our lips."

"Well, so many lips make wide gaps. Let's see if our new guests remain pleased. If this goes against us, we could all lose our jobs. I will make their stay a pleasant one, even if I have to camp on their doorstep with a loaded rifle. Pray for blessings, friend. See you on the return."

Sardar Singh approached the front entrance. Two young girls straightened their blue-violet saris with gold trimmed hems to cover their dusty sandals. They greeted him like a guest.

"Namaskar," he said and smiled, thinking these poor girls, no hope of dowry, their fathers farmers of failed crops like me. He felt his chest constrict. Sardar heard their namaskar crushed by the clip of his rigid leather heels striking the marble floor.

The desk clerk looked up. "Sardar Ji, we have guests in...."

"I heard. From which country?"

"Their passports are American. The woman is white, her husband a non-resident Indian, a Punjabi Sikh."

"That's not good! How can I calm a Sikh? They are as fierce as Rajput warriors."

"Let us hope you will not be having to. So far the suite's been quiet."

"Yes, but they have four more days, correct?"

"Correct."

"A long time, especially at this season when guests are few. I shall do everything I can to make their stay first class. Are they early risers?"

"No. They asked for bed tea at eight a.m."

Sardar Singh checked his watch. "Let me serve them morning tea. I should know soon what kind of man is this Sikh from America."

"Yes. Good idea. I myself have not seen them. The namaskar girls yesterday said they were polite."

"Everyone is…at the entrance," Sardar Singh said and turned to take his position at the carved wooden door to the Jharokha Café to greet early breakfast arrivals.

Sardar Singh left his post shortly before eight, skirted the edge of the lily pond where two large black and white ducks dove under the lotus flowers, only their white tail feathers visible between the large shiny green disks covering the pond. He hurried to the far corner of the palace and stood tray-in-hand at the door to announce: "Bed tea, sir, madam."

"Wait a minute," a man's voice said. Sardar kept military attention, arched back, head high, chin tucked. "Come in, please set it on the table."

"Yes sir, as you wish, but may I suggest your private verandah? Most pleasant in the morning." The woman emerged from the air-conditioned bedroom and greeted him with a smile.

Sardar, embarrassed that the foreigner looked directly into his eyes, cast his gaze down and said, "Good morning, madam. I am Sardar Singh, at your service."

"Thank you." She pulled her pale hair into a coil anchored at her neck, a much smaller coil than his daughter's, Sardar thought, and introduced herself. "I'm Ciprianne. This is my husband, Jaswant." Sardar Singh made a polite bow, unsure how to react to such informality. "I don't think we should have tea on the verandah. We would disturb the ladies."

"Where, madam?"

"Out there, that is the door to the verandah, right?"

"Yes, it is specific to your suite, that verandah. Possibly some tourists went astray and mistook yours for theirs. Let me first check." Sardar looked around, saw no one. "No one is there, madam. Sound travels in these marble corridors."

Jaswant stepped from the curtained sitting room to the gleaming patio. "This is quite a view. Wonderful!"

"Yes, sir. Have you been here before?"

"No. This is our first time. We live in America, California. I grew up in Punjab, never visited Udaipur before this trip."

"You are Sikh, correct?"

"Yes."

"We are brothers, Rajasthani warriors and Punjabi Sikhs. Warrior-farmers, both. We tend and protect our land. Now Punjab feeds all of India. We are pleased to have you and the missus with us. Anything you like, please ask."

Ciprianne walked over to the table. "They were out here, two of them, in that marble canopy thing."

"That is a jharokha, madam."

"And one was standing below it. They woke me up with their laughter. When I came out, they smiled. How'd they get up there anyway? The jharokha is several feet above the verandah floor."

Sardar Singh faltered, started a reply, but Jaswant cut him off. "There's a door at the back. The jharokha's where the palace ladies would sit, out of view, to enjoy the scenery and catch the cool breeze off the lake."

"Yes, sir, correct," Sardar Singh said. "Over two-and-a-half centuries ago, Maharana Jagat Singh II completed this palace, originally called Jag Niwas. Now the Lake Palace Hotel."

The palace on the other natural island we call Lake Garden Palace. Maharana Jagat Singh I finished constructing it, but Maharana Karan Singh began the project. We call that one Jag Mandir. Once a famous summer resort and party palace, it housed the Mughal Prince Khurram for some time. He's better known as Emperor Shah Jehan, builder of Taj Mahal in Agra. Some call Jag Mandir a floating light of heaven on earth."

Sardar felt pleased to see the Sikh shake his head in agreement, but the woman seemed uninterested. He worried she would be difficult.

"Good tea – must be Assam, my favorite." Ciprianne said. "Those barren hills we see from here, Sardar, did they ever have trees?"

"Yes, madam," Sardar said, thinking this woman asked too many questions.

"The valley settlement, looks like discarded cardboard boxes tossed on cracked earth like garbage. Who owns that land? The people? The royal family?"

"Madam, that village belongs to the royal family. Palace workers live there."

"Looks like a slum."

Sardar looked away from the view. He felt heat rising up his neck. He thought this foreign woman has a viper's tongue. "Our Maharana remodeled Lake Palace, opened it as a hotel. Gave land for the workers' village. Later the Taj

Group, businessmen, took over, expanded the property to what you see today, a first-class luxury hotel. Film people made a James Bond here. Do you know which?" Sardar hoped the woman wouldn't answer.

"Octopussy," Jaswant said. He smiled at Sardar. "I recognized it. Is our suite original, the murals and décor?"

"You, sir, have the Maharana's favorite suite. Yes, very historic. Paintings in the sitting room are of the ruler, Maharana Raj Singh I. Murals in your bedroom depict him and others, unchanged since the palace was completed, except for minor restoration.

"Excuse me, sir, madam, I must be returning to my station at the Jharokha Café. Please come, enjoy our cuisine at your leisure."

"Yes, thank you. We'll be down soon." Jaswant pressed many rupee notes into Sardar Singh's palm.

"Thank you, sir, not necessary." Sardar felt the weight and stifled a smile. He knew his family would have buffalo cream tonight on their black dahl.

"Consider it an exchange for the history lesson."

"Please inform me of any requests, or concerns. I am Sardar Singh, at your service, sir." Sardar gave a crisp salute, right hand palm-forward at his temple.

"Out of curiosity, how full is the hotel at this time?"

"Sir, you have come at our low season. Few come in this heat. We have ten, possibly more. Take care. The temperature will reach 34 degrees today. Foreigners do not fare well this time of year. You almost have the palace to yourselves."

"I'm surprised," Ciprianne said. "With all the laughter I would have thought you had more guests."

"Sound travels over water and marble in mysterious ways. I must be going. Enjoy your tea."

Sardar Singh crossed the sitting room in two long strides and pulled the heavy wooden door closed after him. Reverberations bounced off marble screens in the corridor.

"This is the life, Jaswant! I love it! I never thought I'd find myself in such a beautiful place!"

"Well, I had to bring my lady back here in this lifetime, at least once."

"Oh! So you're the Maharana reincarnated or something?"

"Well, let's just say this place feels very familiar."

"You! I could put you in any luxury place in the world and you would feel at home. See what privilege does to you? It's your mom's blood in your veins, the granddaughter of a Punjabi maharaja. Have you thought about those poor people living in that cardboard village over there?"

"Look, my mother cared for the peasants, fed them, gave presents to their children, as did her mother. You've read too much Karl Marx. You're only for the peasants, Ciprianne. Rich people can be good, too. Plus, how about the way we live? You don't seem to mind it, wealthy by world standards, spoiled.

"But you're wrong. I don't feel at home in luxury. I don't feel antagonistic to it either. You missed my point. As soon as we landed at the airport and got the taxi to the old part of the city, I felt at home. The sights, little kids leading huge water buffalo, the sound of hawkers in the bazaar, incense drifting from temples – home.

"Listen, Cip, how about stopping at that flower vendor's to buy flowers for you?"

"That was sweet, my love."

"Did you realize I bought tuberose, the same flowers that young woman in the mural near our bed holds in her hand?"

"I hadn't noticed."

"Well, look when you go in."

Ciprianne laughed. She saw the exasperation fade from Jaswant's face. Tiny lines in the corners of his eyes ran like wispy pencil marks to touch the silver in his temples. His cheeks expanded with a smile.

"Well, don't stop now, honey, manifest jewelry for me."

"Look at that village over there. Can't have it both ways. It's your choice. I have my eye on the pearl armband the maharana's wearing in that painting. I wouldn't mind having that – for me."

"You always have an eye for jewels. In another life you were the thief of Baghdad. Great taste, sticky fingers. And I said for me."

Ciprianne studied the delicate carved marble lace screens of the jharokha. "How beautiful – ornate cages, though, in a way. Couldn't the women go where they wanted?"

"Not really. The maharana considered them prized possessions, not to be viewed by commoners."

"Prized possessions? That's disgusting – more like prized cattle."

"Different time, different place. They wanted for nothing, had a beautiful palace home, eunuch servants, excellent food, fine jewels, silk clothes, and protection."

"I don't like the connotation, women as property."

"You liked it then," Jaswant said, his smile mischievous. She loved when he gave her that look.

"Well, Jaswant, you have an infinitely better memory than mine and longer range. Your imagination's fertile." Ciprianne ran her hand along the entwined white marble lotus plants, traced a stem to the palace wall. "You can't really climb in from the verandah, can you? I'd like to go in there, so you can take a photo of me in the jharokha."

"Good idea. I'll go around and open it from the inside."

Ciprianne watched Jaswant enter the sitting room, yank open a wooden door that led to a shallow recess. He struggled, shoved, then slammed his shoulder into the jharokha door, but it wouldn't budge. After several attempts to force it, Jaswant returned to the verandah.

"I can't open it. It's jammed. I'll ask Sardar Singh to get someone in here to fix it. How about a photo in that one on the next level up? I see steps on the side."

"Okay. But don't shoot into the sun. I don't want to look like a shadow."

"Trust me. I'll take a great photo."

"You'd better."

"Go up, lean against the pillar. Good! Turn your head, chin lower, hold it." Ciprianne posed, flinched. "Cip, you turned away just as I took the shot. Okay, again. Now look past me at the lake."

"Jaswant, did you hear them? The laughing ladies?"

"No. A shadow fell across you in this shot. Freeze. Okay, got it."

"You didn't hear the ladies, that laughter, just like earlier?"

Jaswant turned to look around. "Oh, must have been them. See that couple on the flotilla out in the lake. Sound travels over water."

Ciprianne got closer for a better view of the couple seated at a white linen draped table. "That barge? A hundred yards out in the lake? How could that couple sound like several women laughing?"

"Oh, probably a mixture, their conversation, the locals over there on the left, bathing, other guests. Anyway, I'm hungry. Let's go lock the suite. It's hot out here. I'm dying for an iced coffee."

Ciprianne said, "I could see you all dressed up in a silk tunic, pearls on your turban, a gold upper arm bracelet full of rubies and diamonds, like the maharana in that portrait. How very royal – but it ain't this lifetime, baby!" She passed the tuberose bouquet, breathed in the sweetness. "Umm, smell those. What heaven."

"We'd better pull these curtains or the sun will cook the flowers by afternoon. Sweet heaven to foul decay. The air conditioner's no match for this heat. Cip, I'm worried you're no match, either."

"I'm okay. I can take the heat. You think I'm weak? Well, maybe in one area, but otherwise, no."

"I didn't mean anything like that. You overreact."

Jaswant looked across the lake, avoided meeting Ciprianne's eyes – the sadness, the pain so visible, raking her lower lip as if she could prevent memory from surfacing, scrape it away, dispense with it. He'd seen that look too much in the past year. On this trip he planned to put an end to the past, her look of desperation, the look he saw when she miscarried and the doctor said her body couldn't retain a growing embryo.

He dragged himself back, focused on the scenery. In the distance he saw City Palace, a mother-of-pearl mirage shimmering white, pink, and lilac, dancing in wavy bands that edged up parched brown hills. He pulled the last curtain, thwarted the sun, reduced it to a halo around the window edges and they walked out.

Jaswant took Ciprianne's hand in his, surprised how cool and clammy her hand felt. "Feeling okay, Cip?"

"Yeah." She pointed. "I love those gardens, paisley designs, so many colors. The jasmine's overpowering, like a perfume store, makes me dizzy. And the sunlight through the marble screens, patterns everywhere, worse than a strobe light. Wow, this hallway's chilly."

"Cip, it's hot. Sure you're okay?"

"I'm fine."

Jaswant studied her. She stared at pink plumeria blossoms falling into the lily pond, cocked her head to the pigeons cooing, watched them strut, heads moving forward and backward.

"They look like damn maharanas surveying their domain, don't they, Jaswant? Arrogant birds. Life for the royals, all this wealth – a posh prison for women. It's...."

Sardar Singh interrupted them at the café door. He ushered them to a table dwarfed by a large arched window that faced the city.

"The view is finest from here: that's City Palace."

"Do you have another? The glare's too much," Ciprianne said.

Sardar Singh stood still. He knew this to be the very best table in the café. What would it take to please this American, he wondered. Her face looked like a fiery moon to him, a rare occurrence he witnessed years back, red-edged full butter-cream moon – a bad sign. The drought started with that harvest moon. He faltered, regained his thoughts.

"We have buffet or à la carte, English and Indian. Your choice."

"Buffet for me," Ciprianne said. "I love dry roasted chickpea curry. I saw it over there."

"She'll have chai, iced coffee for me." When Sardar walked away Jaswant said, "Cip, since when?'

"What?"

"You hate curry for breakfast. They have waffles and eggs. You don't have to eat Indian."

"Since now. I plan to eat five rotis with it."

"Suit yourself."

"Love those sarees on display, bright oranges and yellows, trimmed in heavy gold thread. Don't you, Jaswant?"

"Yes, very fine work. Cip, Fort Chittorgarh's near here. An air conditioned taxi ride, about an hour, I think. Let's go."

"What's so great about it?"

"History, a famous story. In the 1400s a sultan heard of Queen Padmini, a legendary beauty. He wanted to see her. No foreign man could, especially a Mughal – she being a chaste Hindu queen. The sultan swore he wouldn't attack the fort if he could look upon her. That was all. He would spare the people certain death in exchange.

"King Rawal Ratan Singh agreed but stipulated the Mughal could only look upon her reflection, not upon her. The sultan agreed. Queen Padmini agreed. She stood by the lake. Her image bounced from one mirror to another and then to the lake's surface. Even with such a distorted image, the Mughal fell deeply in love. He reneged on his promise and attacked the fort. The battle raged; many Rajput warriors died. The women realized their men couldn't defeat the Mughal invader, the fort would fall. Each placed a handprint on the chamber wall, a sign of defiance, better death than disgrace, and walked into the fire. Queen Padmini and thousands of women. Dead."

"That's a true story?"

"Yes, in our history books. Let's go see the fort. There's a saying..." Jaswant hesitated, called Sardar Singh over. "The saying goes, Queen Padmini was so beautiful that when she swallowed you could see the water go down her throat."

Sardar Singh repeated the verse in Hindi, stretched his neck, stroked down its length.

"I don't get it," Ciprianne said.

Sardar Singh spoke to Jaswant in Hindi. They nodded in agreement.

Jaswant translated, "She was so fair, so luminous, so, well, pure, that you could see the water go down."

"That's odd."

Sardar Singh said, "Madam, the queen, fairest of the fair, most beautiful of ladies, a brave Rajput, came from a line of noble warriors. She chose death over disgrace. She is most famous in our history. We Rajputs are known for bravery. Many forts in Rajasthan record noble acts. At Mehrangarh Fort in Jodhpur, you see handprints of queens who committed jauhar, death by fire. Please, madam, excuse me. Guests waiting."

Ciprianne whispered to Jaswant, "Same as sati? Like when you kill yourself because your husband dies? I get the queen, but because your husband dies, you die? Wow, that's not right."

"Not right for you, not right for modern India, but in the old days a woman depended on her husband for survival. If he died, the wife starved. The thought 'die with honor, die on your husband's pyre' meant a noble act. The wife, often younger, abandoned. Who would care for her for a lifetime? The British outlawed it. You still hear of it from time to time, in remote areas, even today."

"God, that's revolting. I'm going for the buffet." Sardar glanced over to see Ciprianne with two plates piled high with curried vegetables, a mountain of papaya, mango, lychees and dosas. He thought: That could feed my entire family. Americans don't know hunger. That woman doesn't know India.

"Cip, it's a buffet. You can go back whenever you want."

"I know. I love sweet and sour together."

"Those mangoes, they're from Punjab. I recognize them, but not our finest – Sandhuris. Sandhuris are smaller and yellow-orange. You massage them, break up the pulp, suck it from a small hole in the top. Sweetest fruit imaginable."

Sardar Singh approached. "Shall I arrange a tour for you today, sir?"

"No, thanks. Not today. Sardar, ever had Sandhuris?"

"Yes, once a traveler brought some to my father, from Patiala. Sweetness of the gods. Nothing beats mangoes from Punjab, which you must be knowing."

"Absolutely."

"Sir, shall I book a walking guide?"

"No. We'll do fine."

"Very well. The maids will attend to your room as soon as you depart. The guard mentioned you did not lock your room last night. Please do. With some eighty rooms, one gets lost, may enter a room by mistake. The women who entered your chamber, the ones you heard laughing, caused themselves embarrassment. They sent apologies."

"I didn't hear them, Sardar, only my wife." Sardar avoided looking at Ciprianne. He hoped she would not bring up the laughing ladies again.

"Tonight, entertainment, a traditional puppet show and tribal dance in Lily Pond Courtyard at seven. Please, enjoy your stay. I am at your service." Sardar nodded and hurried away to greet more guests.

# CHAPTER 2 – SAJJAN NIWAS SUITE

"Large glass chandeliers, hanging from second floor, you must see, this way, please. Guests now dine where Maharanas greeted, and dismissed, foreign rulers. In old palace, a museum, marble rooms with interior courtyards. Large shade trees fed by aqueduct system and fountains cooled even hottest days. Today no water in fountains because of drought.

"Listen, you can hear blind sitar player sing ragas in the cool courtyard. Enjoy. Look at rooms. Many artworks. We meet downstairs in thirty minutes."

The guide noticed Ciprianne braced against the wall outside the miniature paintings room. He rushed to her: "Madam, water?"

"I feel dizzy. Get my husband."

The guide turned to see Jaswant run up the corridor, dappled red and green by the colored glass in the marble filigree. "Your wife, sir..."

"Come with me, Cip."

Jaswant led her to the hallway that wrapped around the outside of the building. He stopped at a small recess and pulled her to an opening in the stone wall. A cool breeze dried the perspiration from her skin. She shivered.

"It's cold here. How?"

"They cooled the buildings, used cross ventilation, water fountains, shade trees. This'll revive you. I knew we shouldn't have come out midday. Sorry, Cip. I'll take you back."

"I guess life could have been good here, even in this tremendous heat, if you could cool off. It's slow and quiet, but good... for the royals. Life in that mural in our room looks pleasant. I want to go back. I need a nap."

The namaskar girls shyly smiled and greeted Jaswant and Ciprianne at the front entrance. Sardar Singh rushed to greet them, gave them a clipped salute.

"Is everything satisfactory, madam, sir?"

Ciprianne pulled her damp kameez away from her back, "It is very hot."

"May I order tea and biscuits for your courtyard?"

Jaswant smiled and said, "Thank you, Sardar Singh, but we would like it in our suite. The missus needs an air-conditioner."

"Yes, as you wish. Your room is in order."

They walked down the decorated corridor to their suite. Ciprianne stopped to inspect a mirrorwork peacock set in the wall. Running her fingers over the mirror chips, she turned to Jaswant and said, "How do they get it so smooth? There's no ridge where the glass ends and the plaster begins."

"I saw it done as a child. The trick is to set the mirror into damp plaster. As it dries, gently rub it with cheesecloth until the residue is removed. The plaster and glass form a flawless edge. Rajasthanis are famous for it. Mirrorwork."

They reached their suite. Jaswant stopped. "Cip, did you hear that?"

She leaned closer, whispered, "What?"

"I heard a man's voice in our suite." Jaswant turned the key a half-turn. Before he completed the rotation, the large door swung open. "Hello? Namaskar? Strange, it wasn't locked." He crossed the sitting room, checked the verandah door. Locked. He flung open the bedroom door with a quick movement. The musty air-conditioned smell seeped into the dim sitting room.

"You act like you're tracking something," Ciprianne said and pulled the curtains for a lake view. "The heat's gotten to you, too."

"No, it hasn't!"

"Strange," Ciprianne said and turned to face him.

"What?"

"The portrait, the one of the maharana, it's been moved. It was above the desk in the corner. Now it's above the settee – and the miniature of Krishna and Radha are above the desk."

Jaswant walked over and inspected the paintings.

Sardar Singh knocked loudly and stepped in the half-opened door with the tray. "Tea."

"Come in," Jaswant said as he stood, perplexed, in front of the painting. "Sardar Singh, where does this portrait belong?"

"Why, sir?"

"It hangs above the desk with the blue lamp, correct?"

"Yes, I see. The new cleaning woman decided to rearrange things. I shall speak to her." Sardar replaced the portrait in its rightful position. "Not a problem, sir. Sugar, milk?" He poured two cups of tea.

"Both," Jaswant answered in a distant voice.

"Sir, may I check the air-conditioner in the bed chamber? It should be turned up."

"Go ahead."

"Everything is in order, sir. For security reasons, make sure your door is properly shut."

"Have someone check it. I think the wood swells; it doesn't lock well. The door was open when we arrived."

"Yes? I shall have it checked immediately. These heavy wooden doors take some getting used to, even by our staff."

"Check the jharokha door, too."

"Yes, sir."

"I thought I heard someone in here when we reached the door, Sardar."

"Sir, the suite directly adjoining yours is now rented. It is those guests you heard. Marble walls, sir, they play tricks on the ears."

"I guess."

"Sir, the manager extended my hours of service today; in fact, I shall remain here tonight. I am at your service, anything you need, ask for me only." Sardar Singh tipped his head, crossed the Persian carpet without a sound, and pulled the front door firmly closed behind him.

"Now you're being weird, Jaswant. You laughed when I was hearing things. You're not laughing now."

"I know," Jaswant said and smoothed his mustache to the sides.

CViprianne finished her tea and left Jaswant to read a magazine while she took a cold shower. She turned the gold-plated handles full force and stood letting the cool water beat down on her head. She heard giggling girls. The laughter grew louder and louder and bounced off the shower's marble walls. She felt a cold finger trace a channel down her arm. She leapt from the shower, grabbed a fluffy towel to wrap around her, and ran to call Jaswant.

"Honey, did you hear that?"

He made no reply.

She shouted, "Jaswant! Jaswant?"

A chill made her shake. She arrived in the sitting room, dripping water on the carpet, to see no one. She bolted out the front door to the garden.

Her shocked husband turned to see her and gasped. "Cip, there are people out here. What are you doing?"

"What are *you* doing?"

"I came to meet our neighbors."

"And?"

"And... it's empty. I asked the gardener. The suite isn't rented."

"Oh!" Ciprianne rubbed her face and began to cry.

Jaswant led her back inside, covering her partially visible rearview with his body.

"What's the matter, Cip?"

He shut and bolted the door. Ciprianne blurted out: "Jaswant, I'm hearing things. It happened again. In the shower, I heard laughing, girls laughing, like it was right in the room with me. My body went cold. I felt an icy finger touch me! It slid down my arm. I ran out. You were gone. I felt someone following me. I ran outside for help, for you." Ciprianne trembled. "I'm scared."

"Honey, I'm sorry. I think someone's playing tricks. Maybe the new maid. I will speak to Sardar Singh when we go for dinner. For now I need a cold shower and to stretch out."

"The bedroom's not very cool yet."

"We won't wear clothes."

Ciprianne listened while Jaswant showered but heard nothing other than water splashing. She lay down and studied the painted walls. On the left, between the window alcove and the eight-foot gilt frame mirror, a young woman stood with her hand resting on a tree, feet balanced on a rocky terrace, sari falling in neat accordion pleats to her gold anklets. She stared into the room as if she had stopped by to say hello.

Her round face and small even square teeth packed corner to corner created a mischievous smile. Dark upturned lashes almost touched her full eyebrows that met on the bridge of her nose. The painting seemed very much a portrait of a particular person, with no stylization of features as in the religious paintings in the suite of Radha, Lord Krishna's consort. Her gold bangles, jewel nose ring, and pearls dangling from her forehead meant she was no peasant girl. She must have been a favorite zenana woman, possibly even a maharana's wife, Ciprianne thought.

Ciprianne studied the whimsical face. She felt a chill and reached for a sheet to cover her nude body. She couldn't grasp it. It slipped from her hand like rainwater. She felt fuzzy, as though she had drunk too many drinks. She floated, gently bobbed up and down over gentle waves. Through half-closed eyes she saw the woman in the mural tilt her head. She spoke. Her rhythmical words matched her hand movements. The room came alive with her gestures. Monkeys on the far wall screeched and ran up painted trees. A wind caught the branches and shook them. Dislodged cranes spread their huge wings and soared up to the cloudy sky.

Ciprianne jerked her head around to face the woman. "What did you say?"

"Namaskar."

She stepped forward and rested her back along the tree's trunk. "You are invited to our terrace, but if you come like that he will not let you in. You know how particular he is. You must wear the silk sari."

"I don't own a silk sari!"

"We kept them in the cabinet behind the mirror for you. Take the peacock blue one with gold embroidery, his favorite. Remember?" The woman straightened up and took her pose next to the tree and carefully placed her hand on the trunk.

Jaswant opened the bathroom door. "Cip, where's the toothpaste?"

Ciprianne tried to reply, but her mouth moved like soft putty and couldn't hold the shape of a letter long enough to sound it.

"Honey, are you ill?" he said, pulling the covers up to her neck. "You're shaking."

Ciprianne looked beyond him to the mural. Her eyes watered. "Jaswant, something is wrong with me. I started hallucinating. That woman, over there, the one on the wall, spoke to me. I spoke to her. It seemed so real. Oh, God, it seemed so real!"

"Cip, I'm worried you got a heatstroke today. I shouldn't have taken you out in the heat. You'd better stay in bed, rest. Here drink this bottled water. You're dehydrated."

"Yeah, my brain's boiled. Lie down and cuddle with me. I feel so strange, like a rubber band stretched out too far, about to collapse. I don't have a center."

"Should I call a doctor?"

"No, stay here beside me. Does it look like she's watching us?"

Jaswant studied the mural for a minute to soothe his distraught wife. "Yes. It's that style of portraiture only. Go anywhere in the room and she will appear to watch you. I've seen that technique displayed in museums. It was popular after the Renaissance, I think."

"She didn't watch me when I stood by the closet."

"The angle's too oblique. Try another spot."

"Well, she didn't watch me once when I sat on the swing."

"Once?"

"Well, the first time, when I studied the brass animals in the chain, she watched me then. At first I didn't notice her, but when I sat on the wooden seat and began to swing, wondering if the chain would hold, I saw her looking at me. I thought I imagined it, of course. I figured the shift in her position, a slight one, had something to do with the reflection off the water, and my movement."

"I'm sure it was. We're surrounded by the lake. That creates a lot of light patterns."

"That could be, but now the curtains are drawn."

"Cip, I'm calling for nimbu pani, our version of lemonade. It has sugar, salt and pepper in it. It's like Gatorade. That'll fix you up."

"Don't leave!"

"I'll fetch the gardener to get it. He's just outside."

Jaswant pulled on his trousers and undershirt and walked to the sitting room door, left the bedroom door wide open, at the cost of losing the somewhat cooled air, so Ciprianne could clearly hear him. He reached the front door as someone knocked.

"Yes?"

"Sir, I am Sardar Singh here."

Jaswant opened the door. "Ah, could you get us a pitcher of nimbu pani? I'm afraid the heat, my wife doesn't feel well."

"Most certainly, sir. Shall I call a doctor?"

"Not yet."

When Jaswant returned to the bedroom, Ciprianne had put on her green cotton salwar kameez.

"Feeling better?"

"I'm not sick," she snapped. Turning to the gilded mirror, she scratched along its edge where it met the plaster wall.

"What are you doing, Cip?"

"Looking for the opening."

"That's a mirror!"

"Do I look stupid, Jaswant?"

"Well, yes, you're scratching the plaster of historic murals in a five-star resort. I'd call that stupid! We'll have to pay for it!"

"I'm looking for something," she said tugging at the frame. Bits of plaster fell to the marble floor and exploded into fine chalk.

"Ciprianne, this is crazy! Stop it!"

Ciprianne started to reply. They heard a knock at the front door. "Go."

Jaswant rushed to the sitting room. Sardar Singh entered carrying a silver pitcher with cold beads of sweat rolling down its rounded contour.

"Thank you."

"My pleasure, sir. May I be of further service?" Sardar glanced around the room, relieved everything remained in place.

Hearing his deep voice, Ciprianne walked out. "Sardar Singh, I need your help. Come help me open the mirror."

"Madam, the mirror does not open. I believe you have opening mirrors in your country. We do not in this palace."

"I think you do. Come help me."

Sardar Singh looked at Jaswant, who shook his head side to side. Sardar followed Ciprianne into the bedroom. She scratched the mirror's edge.

"Please, madam. These walls, they are priceless. Please I must ask you to stop."

"Come over here and help me," she said as if she had not heard him.

She wedged her metal nail file into an edge and scored the plaster the length of the mirror on one side before Sardar Singh grabbed her hand.

"Sir," he called in alarm, "please stop your wife!"

She wrestled her hand free, jammed her nails into the crevice and yanked as hard as she could on the mirror's frame. With a small avalanche of plaster chips, the mirror swung open.

"See! Here it is. I knew it!"

Sardar Singh stepped back stunned while Ciprianne reached into the cavity and withdrew several neatly folded saris, each trimmed in gold thread.

"This," she said and held up a very finely woven peacock blue silk sari, "is the one I am supposed to wear!"

Jaswant put his arm around his wife who stood like her existence at the moment seemed as fragile as the tuberose flowers wilting in the vase by the bed. She swayed.

Sardar Singh took command of the situation. "Madam, what an excellent find you have made, a closet as yet unknown. The City Palace Museum will be most pleased with this, a display of authentic saris. Thank you."

Jaswant's mouth dropped. "You're not upset, about... about the damage to the wall, to the mural?"

"Oh, sir, madam. It is hardly scarred. The palace painter will repair this small bit of lost paint easily. Please, do not speak of this to anyone. The curator of the museum, is, well, he is the authority, and for you, a foreigner, to have found something he overlooked, would, well, you must understand. His honor, and reputation...."

Jaswant started to reply, but Ciprianne cut him off. "Sardar Singh, I found it because *she* told me where to look." She pointed at the mural woman. "Sardar, we will be glad to pay for any damages. Let us settle this, here and now."

"Sir, there is no need. Please allow us to offer you a complimentary dinner at the Neel Kamal tonight. It is our pleasure. This matter is closed, forever."

Jaswant stood speechless for a couple of seconds. "Thank you."

"And sir, madam, as a show of appreciation, I will shift you to the Sarva Ritu Suite. You will find it most comfortable and elegant, Waterford crystal chandelier, carved silver headboards, ornate carving of...."

"No! I want to stay here in this suite."

"Ciprianne, we must leave. You damaged this suite, and they have to repair it. They are extremely generous. Thank you, Sardar Singh. We shall pack up now."

"No, we won't," Ciprianne said, and glared at her husband. "There's hardly any damage, none to the mural itself, only the blue border is chipped. That should take about twenty minutes to touch up. I'll do it myself if they give me the supplies! I am not moving out because you think something is wrong with me. Nothing is. These saris prove it!"

"Madam, it was only a suggestion – for your sake. You are most welcome to remain in this suite if you choose. You are correct, the work will take little time."

"I want to stay."

"It is settled then. I have to leave. The restaurant opens at six o'clock hour. The performance is from seven to eight. I imagine you will be wanting dinner after the performance?"

With consternation Jaswant said, "Thank you, but we'd rather eat before," and followed Sardar Singh to the front door, hoping to speak to him privately. Sardar exited so quickly Jaswant had no opportunity. When he returned to the bedroom, Ciprianne was investigating the hidden closet.

"Imagine me finding a hidden treasure. And you thought I was nuts," she said with a timid laugh.

"Cip, you are not yourself. That was rude. You're lucky he's a gentleman."

"Rude? There's a difference between being direct and being rude. I was direct."

"You were rude."

Jaswant realized there was no reasoning with his wife. "What do you want to see tomorrow?"

"The art school, and shops. Let's go early, before it's so hot."

"Okay. I want to get a Rajasthani tunic like the one the maharana is wearing in the portrait."

"You do?"

"Yes, it's very stylish. I'm sure the tailors can make it in a day. I like the cross-over lapel look."

"I'm not the only one being affected here."

"What do you mean by that?"

"It seems you're getting clothes for a party!"

# CHAPTER 3 – IMPENDING STORM

With much trepidation Sardar Singh approached the night manager's desk. He knew Mrs. Jaswant Singh was in danger – but more than himself? He doubted it. She would not be physically hurt, never happened before, yet he felt, in the balance of justice, her mental duress minor compared to losing his job, his family's lifeline.

The American can go home to a rich country, want for nothing. Sardar knew he alone stood between starvation and life for his family. He worried: no one before this woman had spoken to the mural inhabitants. They had taken her into their confidence. Why?

Sardar Singh marched to the manager's desk.

"Sir," he said in a most respectful tone, "the lady in Sajjan Niwas Suite, a Mrs. Jaswant Singh, an American, made a discovery." He held up the saris. "She discovered a hidden compartment behind the full-length mirror. These she found."

The manager looked at Sardar Singh with an incredulous smile. "Is this a joke?"

"No, sir."

"How?"

"She scratched the plaster around the mirror. It opened a hidden door."

"She what? Is she mad?"

"It would appear so, sir."

The manager took the uppermost sari, the peacock blue one, into his hand and caressed its soft volume into a wafer. He stroked the fabric right to left and back again, held it in the afternoon light.

"It slides like a waterfall in one direction and rises like morning sky in the other. This is very fine." He tugged at the gold paisley border until he caught a single thread. Flicking it between his fingers, he bit it. "Spun gold, pure. Very ancient work." His eyes welled with delight. "Sardar Ji, a matter of most delicate nature. I must handle, a delicate situation. You understand?"

"Yes, sir." Sardar Singh imagined his wife wail, seeing him return without his uniform. He blinked to dispel the image.

"You must speak of this to no one – not even your wife!" The night manager placed the saris in a canvas bag. "I require your silence. I am handling this through proper channels, my own way, a way that protects you and me. Upper management should not assume you had anything to do with theft."

"Of course not, sir. The American didn't steal them. Public disgrace, in front of her husband, she does not deserve."

"Naturally, Sardar Ji, my thoughts exactly. Consider this matter closed."

"I told Mrs. Singh the saris would go to City Palace Museum for display."

"Very good! And they may, if upper management chooses."

"What of the Maharana? Is it not his decision, his property?"

"No, Sardar Ji, the company purchased the palace in total, everything."

Hearing this, Sardar Singh feared the booking cover-up would come to light. "Sir, may I mention one point?"

"Yes."

"You are responsible for your employees, correct? Your job depends on us doing our work as you require, as upper management desires."

"Naturally," the manager said. "Why?"

"The Americans took that room for five nights, not the two they intended. Your assistant, yesterday, allowed the booking at reduced rate. The previous guests left earlier than expected."

"So?"

"He protected you, sir. The previous guests in the suite encountered some difficulty, sir, and left abruptly. They expected a refund on their credit card for the unused nights. They accused management of poor service, wanted to write a complaint. Your assistant handled it. He offered Mr. Jaswant Singh additional nights, upgraded him to Sajjan Niwas Suite, so the ledger would appear balanced. The names changed only, not length of booking. They are getting the suite for rate of lesser one."

The manager stroked his trimmed beard and said, "Well, let this be the end of it, Sardar Ji. We have all done our jobs to the best of our abilities. This is not a matter for the chief officer. It ends here, with our silence. What do you say?"

"Thank you, sir. I believe it the wisest course."

"Indeed. Sardar Ji, this Mrs. Jaswant Singh, what can we do to make her stay pleasurable, and quiet?"

"Start with flowers. She enjoys tuberose. Fill the suite. Tonight I provided them complimentary dinner."

"Excellent! Tomorrow, a day excursion, compliments of the hotel, a good bottle of scotch for Mr. Singh, breakfast on the flotilla, an evening cruise. Keep them busy, Sardar Ji. We don't want them bored or unhappy. They must know how we deal with guests! We are a five-star property! Sardar, your attitude does you credit. I shall speak to my superior about a promotion for you. Captain of the Jharokha Café, perhaps?"

"Thank you, sir. I would like to ensure their stay, first class. I shall remain at the hotel day and night until they leave. I will attend to their every wish."

"Commendable! Take the extra cot in the boatman's quarters. Your diligence serves you well!"

The manager, with a grin, dismissed Sardar Singh, disappeared into his office, and locked the door behind him. Sardar leaned into the door to hear "event of the season, not even a rupee" and wondered at the meaning.

Ciprianne enjoyed the complimentary dinner more for the wine than the food. She commented drinking her dinner was a lot more fun than chewing it and smiled at her husband. She called to the waiter. "I, celebrant, celebrate, oh, whatever, tonight with this Australian wine. A hand-painted concubine invited me to her party for a dead maharana."

Jaswant shook his head and winced at her mischievous smile. The waiter refilled her glass. "I am serving you, madam," he replied and bowed, backing away.

"Cip, in seven years of marriage, I've never seen you drink so much! Please stop."

"Poor sunstruck me. Is she sick? Is that what you ask yourself, or is it the wine? You married a crazy person, Jaswant. Feel sorry for yourself, not me."

"I am at a loss here."

"You're at a loss! How pathetic! Last time I checked, your mind was intact. That's more than I can say for mine."

"There's nothing wrong with your mind that cooler weather and rest cannot fix. I want to cut our stay short, head to Kullu Manali, tomorrow. We can fly to Delhi and..."

"Forget it! You've never run away from anything, and neither will I. I'll face her and tell her to leave me alone."

"You'll face a painting?"

Ciprianne burst out laughing. "Sure, I'll face a painting, face the music, face the music in the painting, whatever. I'll deal with it, whatever the hell it is. Then we'll leave."

Ciprianne watched Jaswant look down at the pigeon-blood ruby ring on his left hand, his wedding ring, and bite his lip. He smoothed his mustache with the linen napkin. "Alright, but promise me this."

"What?"

"I'll be with you when you do."

Ciprianne felt the heat of rude humor drain from her face. She knew Jaswant always stood up for her; she could count on him. She wondered, could he count on her? The thought saddened and sobered her. She saw anguish in his eyes. She realized he had never looked at her that way, not after the car wreck that broke her ribs and totaled the car, not after the third miscarriage at five months when they lost their son, a huge disappointment to him – nothing compared to this look now. This desperation shook her.

"Jaswant," Ciprianne said trying to appear composed, "this, well, it's gone too far. I am not going to confront a stupid illusion. Something strange did happen. It must have been some brain chemistry thing. You're right. I got dehydrated, I guess. I have an active imagination, but I know reality. I know paintings don't talk. It was a fluke – those saris. Bet a maid hid them, planned to come back for them. Let's enjoy our stay, honey. You wanted some shirts stitched? Let's do that first thing tomorrow morning, before it gets too hot. I'd like to get a silk suit stitched. Maybe we could look at the art school, take a boat tour in the cool of the evening. Okay?"

Ciprianne saw Jaswant exhale after seeming not to have breathed for minutes – a good sign.

"Cip, we'll do whatever you like."

"Good," she said, nibbling at her dinner. "Folk dancing starts soon. Want dessert?"

"If they have gulab jamuns."

"They even have black forest cake! The pastry chef trained in Europe, according to the blurb on the menu."

Jaswant smiled. Ciprianne felt reassured. She knew his purpose, this trip, a honeymoon of sorts, was meant to cheer her up. Since the miscarriage, she had been gloomy. They both wanted a baby very much. She feared she could not carry one to term although her doctor had never said that. The late-term miscarriage horrified them. She couldn't forget what she had seen that terrible morning.

Her neighbor had found her and called the ambulance. Jaswant met her at the emergency room. She screamed and cried for her baby boy, said she was cursed, before they gave her a sedative.

Why couldn't she control that part of her life, she wondered. She worked hard at everything in her life – her profession, sports, health, and her marriage. Bridging cultures hadn't been easy, but at no time had she failed to accomplish what she set out to do, except in this most fundamental part of her life: childbearing. She feared this failure would seep into other avenues and wick like India ink into the fibers of her being, darken her hopes and dreams, make her lose everything most dear. She looked at Jaswant, wiped her tears, and apologized for the outburst.

Jaswant felt his chest constrict. With every mouthful of dessert Ciprianne ate, he watched tension ripple through her like a tiger crouched to attack. He looked away. He prayed for sweetness to return, calm her, bring her back to him.

"Ready to go, Cip? The performance starts in a few minutes."

"Okay, but we could practically watch it from here."

"We must throw our lot in with the other guests, all twelve of them, make the performers feel it's worth their effort. Playing to an empty house, no performer likes. You know, I'm glad we've come now, even if it is hot. We're treated like royalty!"

At the performance, Jaswant watched the narrator, whose English, a recitation of sounds that obviously made no sense to her, faltered and bumped along stressing the wrong syllables, breathing in the interior of words to the point that it didn't resemble English but some distant, archaic drumbeat punctured by Hindi words. Jaswant wondered if any of this made sense to Ciprianne and the other guests, who sat with foreign decorum and unreadable expressions. Musicians seated right of the stage played tablas and accordion, Jaswant happy they did not speak.

Actors manipulated the puppets. With a flick of the wrist a peasant girl pursued by an evil snake became a turbaned man who chopped off the snake's head and saved her. Another flip, his tunic became her dress, his dark turban, her hair. Jaswant clapped hard to compensate for the audience, small in number and unused to this form of theater. He encouraged Ciprianne to do the same. The peasant girl marionette took a bow, exited the stage, and with a flip of the puppeteer's wrist hurried back as the turbaned warrior to take his bow.

With the tablas even louder, tribal dancers appeared, tipped their heads towards Jaswant and swirled into view encircling the small audience. Women in bright skirts, oranges, reds, greens and yellows, spun like dervishes, silver anklets jingling to the pounding rhythm. One danced forward, tossed a silver metal bowl onto her head, then another and another, each smaller than the first, until a ten-foot-high stack teetered while she danced to a frenetic drumbeat crescendo. The music stopped. She tilted her head forward and caught the bowls one by one, bowed, and balanced the stack in one hand.

Jaswant approached and placed two hundred-rupee notes at her feet to demonstrate the custom. Others followed.

The floor became littered with notes. A small boy ran out to scrape them up. The audience clapped and cheered. The actors bowed. The narrator ended the performance with 'gudthank'.

"Did you enjoy the entertainment?" Sardar Singh said, approaching from the corridor.

"Ah, Sardar Singh, yes, very good. First class!"

"I am most pleased. Anything tonight, sir, ask for me. I stay here only."

"Thank you, Sardar. We're low on bottled water."

"I shall bring it immediately, sir."

Ciprianne took Jaswant's hand in hers. "Honey, let's look at the pool. I want to swim in the morning. Where is it?"

Ciprianne skipped over the waxing moon shadows cast through marble screens. Light shimmered on lake water. Jasmine permeated the dense night air. "Smell that? Wonderful."

A huge shade tree swayed in the evening breeze. Bull frogs rumbled by the lake's edge and jumped when the couple drew closer. Ciprianne and Jaswant walked to the far end of the palace, in lovers' silence, oneness, breathing in the night's sensuality. Ciprianne made a silent wish. She would conceive tonight and carry their healthy baby to term. She implored nature and all the gods and goddesses to bless her.

"I thought it would be bigger, a lap pool," Ciprianne said when they stopped.

"Well, I'm sure the princesses did little more than cool their toes."

"Look, fairy lights shine from the upper-story jharokhas. If I had been a princess here, I would've been content on this island. You do feel a sort of magic in this place."

"Really? I didn't know you would even consider that. I'm glad you enjoy it. You would have been safe, that's for sure. An advantage of the lake... and Rajput warriors."

"I hadn't thought of the lake as protection."

"Well, no one could sneak up unannounced, could they? And I'll bet today no one can cross the lake without permission, otherwise there would be vendors here trying to sell us all manner of trinkets right now."

"What if we wanted to suddenly go in the night, to the city, or something? Would we be able to?" She dropped Jaswant's hand from hers.

"No. We'd have to find a boatman, and if we did, he wouldn't take us because the hotel management wouldn't allow him."

"It's a pretty prison then? Sardar would help us."

"That's right, princess, you've discovered what all the maharanas' women knew: Nothing happens without the boss's consent on this island. Why worry? We didn't pay for this elaborate hotel to leave it in the night anyway, even if Sardar would take us."

Jaswant grabbed Ciprianne's hand in his and led her back towards their suite. She felt reluctant, an unexplainable fear surfaced. She squeezed his hand.

They reached the alcove of their verandah. Jaswant saw their door ajar. Ciprianne froze. Jaswant shoved her back, away from the entrance and stormed in.

"Sir, your bottled water only," Sardar Singh said in explanation. He turned on the small lamp in the corner. The dim light from the stained glass shade barely illuminated the table. "And for madam, a fresh bouquet of tuberose."

"Thank you. I forgot. Kind of you, Sardar Singh."

Ciprianne said, "Wow, I taste divinity candy every time I smell these flowers."

"Anything to make your stay enjoyable, madam," he said with a slight bow.

"One thing. Could you make that painted woman quit talking to me?" Jaswant felt the night's ambiance shatter and fall to the floor like broken bits of glass. He watched Sardar Singh's face go buffalo-cream white, his jaw quivered. "Just kidding, just kidding. I know she only talks if I have sunstroke!"

"Good night, Sardar Singh. Thank you," Jaswant said and followed him to the door. "We'd like bed tea at nine tomorrow morning."

"Yes, sir. Please, let me lock your door for you properly tonight." He set two locks and pulled the door with force. "Good night" he called from the other side and walked away at a brisk pace, his footfalls growing indistinct in the distance.

Ciprianne sat on the ornate carved wood settee. She followed the wall's border design with her finger, traced the colored glass mosaic pattern. She came to a small ridge where a blue translucent flower touched green serrated leaves of the adjacent orange blossom. She picked at it with her nails.

"Cip, what are you doing?"

"Trying to feel the seam. I can't feel where the glass meets the plaster, not even a tiny ridge. Talk about decorative arts! Tiffany would be jealous!"

"Rajasthanis made art with colored glass and mirrors long before the West thought of it, and with primitive tools."

"That's him as an old man in that painting?"

"Must be."

"And the mural in our bedroom, when he was young?"

"I assume, yes."

"They don't look the same."

"Age does that, and weight."

Ciprianne opened the bedroom. "In this he's younger, stronger, in his white tunic, a sword tucked into the cummerbund. Look at those strings of pearls on his chest. His upturned mustache touches the edge of his turban. Wow, he's looking out with cool disdain. In his older years he looks more opulent, yet kinder, like life had been good to him." Ciprianne felt a sensation like warm breath at the nape of her neck. She shivered.

Jaswant studied the painting. "Same person."

"He looks different in the oil painting out there, Jaswant. His turban and beard... look, even his style is different. I don't think they are the same person. In fact, I'm sure of it."

Jaswant turned to compare the painting in the sitting room. "The older maharana's more relaxed. He has come to understand and accept life. See how his hand rests on the sword. It's an ornament now, not a weapon. He's looking into the distance, not at the viewer. He's not aggressive. They are one and the same man, Cip. Only time separates them."

"How could that complacent man be this forceful younger one in the mural? It's too much of a change."

"Battles are over, that's all. He has everything he wants in old age."

"Wasn't life good for him in his youth? He was royalty."

"Well, I don't know much about Maharana Jagat Singh, if that is who he is, but I would assume life was good all along. He did, after all, have a pleasure palace. Of course, deciding which female to bed might have posed undue hardship, I suppose."

"I disagree. Something in his face when he was young says he had troubles."

"Too little time, perhaps?"

Ciprianne laughed at Jaswant's wistful sigh and said, "Well, I'm not falling into the same trap."

# CHAPTER 4 – PORTRAITS

Ciprianne entered the bedchamber. She felt her heart jump a beat when she saw the swing. She stopped mid-step. Jaswant bumped into her. The swing moved back and forth. He rushed to the window, yanked the curtains back, pulled one window full open, re-bolted it.

"A bit open, Cip. I saw the swing, too. Nothing to worry about. It's breezy tonight."

Ciprianne looked outside. Moonlight surged like spilt milk on the waves. It gathered and dispersed and oozed along the shore. What had seemed beautiful to her earlier now seemed an omen, light foamed against the marble below, her own fortress. She turned to Jaswant without a word.

"Silly people. They must pay a fortune for electricity, and still they leave a window open when the cooler is on!"

Ciprianne took a deep breath, felt her shoulders relax. "Unlocked, you're sure?"

"Yes."

She studied the window ledge. She leaned out to look twenty feet down. Now the moonlight skipped on dark miniscule waves like thousands of votive candles, stirred by the slight evening breeze. She turned back to see Jaswant put his hand on the swing. He lit a candle on the nightstand.

He looked so alluring, she thought, his dark eyes with candlelight dancing in them, hair surrounded by amber light like a halo. She sensed something beyond the earth, beyond the mundane world, in him tonight. It filled the room. Light radiated from Jaswant and reflected off the brass animals making them look as if they climbed up the heavy chain in steady progression. Their hooves moved the air in swirls like water flowing around a river rock.

Ciprianne felt the room shrink, walls draw closer and compress Jaswant with her illuminated body into a narrow glass box. Mural girls danced, breasts exposed, pleated saris tucked loosely below their navels. Tuberose filled the room like vapor curling from a hookah. Ciprianne's head swayed. She felt her body list side to side. She opened her eyes to see bright yellow-orange marigold garlands mimic her movements, a gift from the namaskar girls, draped on the bedposts.

Ciprianne slumped on the bed. She avoided the mural woman's gaze. The blue-skinned god Krishna embraced Radha, his eternal love, in a verdant garden. Her eyes followed the dark forest that stretched along the wall to a bright border of fully-opened pink lotus flowers. White cranes ascended huge gray monsoon clouds, spread their wings, sliced a ray of light free from the heavy, dark sky. Ciprianne heard a peacock cry mayur, mayur.

"This room's stuffy. Let's go on the verandah for a little while. Want a scotch, Cip?"

Ciprianne shook her head, blinked. "Umm, in a second. I feel a bit…tired." She walked to the window. Heat lightning exploded like bombs in the dark sky. She turned to look at the mural – same sky. "Lighting's really great. I'll get amazing shots, be out in a few. Start your scotch, honey, I don't want one."

"Don't be long. This view's the real deal."

Ciprianne moved bedside lamps to better view the dancers. She heard Jaswant's ice cubes clink against glass, crackle when the scotch hit, the heavy wooden door groan along the stone floor. She positioned her camera, clicked a rapid succession, dancers and lovers, Krishna and Radha. Ciprianne stretched out on the bed to shoot the ceiling. She watched dark clouds skitter across the sky. A gentle breeze, the breath of a whisper, crossed her cheek.

Tension slipped from her muscles like a forgotten memory. Contentment filled her. She felt the perpetual knot between her brows release. Her grip loosened. The camera's weight fell away. She closed her eyes, felt her body drift and bob along on gentle waves, rising up, sinking down, like her breaths. She heard flute music. She remembered the scent of divinity candy, could almost taste it. Her mouth watered sugary sweetness. She felt small hands touch her cool skin, knead her face in delicate circles, glide down along her cheekbones, up over her nose bridge, descend into eye hollows, and trace her lips. She couldn't imagine her face, only the face created by the sculptor's tracing. She saw herself...not herself.

A soft voice said, "Devi, wake up! Join us."

Ciprianne slowly opened her eyes to see a young woman leaning over her. Her dark kohl-lined eyes looked familiar. She tossed her jasmine flower-braided hair to the side and massaged Ciprianne's cheek.

"Tickles? Remember? Our game. You always said the braid tickled more than the peacock feather. I could never fool you! We've waited a long time for you, naughty girl. You promised you would return soon. Will you not speak to us? In all your travels have you forgotten your sisters so easily? Shame. Shame. Never mind, you are home now. All is well. He awaits you, most happy you have returned. Many gave up hope... but not I. Maharana's army searched for you for weeks. Rumors spread: you drowned, you ran off with a lover. No matter, you are home, safe now. Why do you wear rough weave peasant's cotton?"

Ciprianne looked down at her clothes, back up at the woman. "I have no memory of these clothes. Please, bring my sari."

"Yes, you must look the most favored queen when you greet your husband. He took others in your absence, yet never forgot you. You hold his heart. A sadhu last week foretold your return. We said prayers, lit lamps, sprinkled holy Ganges water to lure you home, bless your arrival. The holy man warned your return would bring danger to the Maharana's door. An old enemy would approach. My brother confided to me he longed for your return as much as feared it."

"I bring no enemy! I am alone, as you see."

"I shall declare it so. Oh, my favorite sister, to have you home with us in Maharana's Udaipur palace, such a blessing. Devi, I shall send word that you have come. Tonight we feast and dance like before. The Maharana and hunting party just returned from shikar. We shall dine on wild boar marinated in kachri, kababs, aubergines, Khamiri green pea rotis, all your favorites. The thought makes me tremble, such a celebration after so long. Cook will make your favorite sweet, jalebis, when he hears you have returned. No one will stop you from licking sweet syrup from your fingertips. We shall outshine the sparkling desert night, dance until dawn puts her stars to sleep!"

"Do we leave now?" Devi said.

"Not yet. Your jewelry?" Devi looked down at her peasant cloak. She surveyed her brown bare hands. "No matter. I shall send for your belongings. I hid them. Shall I tell the servant to prepare your rosewater bath?"

"Yes." Devi reached up and tried to run her fingers through a thick, matted cascade of dark hair. She pulled a clump forward to study it, a tangled creature.

From the brass tub full of floating fragrant pink rose petals Devi looked out the window to the distant hills. Transparent blue sky dotted by wispy cotton clouds. She wondered: Will my husband take me back? No one mentions the reason for my absence. Why would I leave such luxury? I was drugged by poppy juice, abducted?

The servant girl, hardly twelve years old, washed her hair, massaged her neck. Devi drifted. Her hair, longer than her arms, pulled her down into sweet water. She recalled her husband forbade her to cut it. Of all his zenana, only she had hair of such length and luster, he told her. She saw him, how he had woken after a night of love, the morning light glowing in his dark eyes. He brushed her hair back to admire the ruby and pearl earrings he had given her. He twirled the tip of his mustache up, saying a Maharana's mustache must never turn down. He kissed her along her neck, ended at the hollow in her throat where a pendant of sea green emeralds, pigeon blood rubies, and iridescent Basra pearls rested. She bolted to attention when the servant scooped up her hair and wrapped it in a silk towel.

Someone thwacked the door and shouted, "Ready?"

Devi said in a lazy voice: "No. She's got to henna my hands first."

"Devi, are you preparing for a wedding? Your husband waits. The ladies long to greet you. Henna another time."

Devi smirked. She admired herself in the mirror watching the servant comb her hair. She wondered at her face, different somehow. The eyebrows? The lips? She couldn't decide. She doused her body with jasmine attar, pulled the sari top over her head, wiggling it down over her breasts. The servant folded the sari's length of crimson silk into even pleats cinched at the waist. Devi motioned for the henna paste and ordered 'a quick design only, my feet.' She closed her eyes.

Devi awoke to a brusque hand rubbing her forehead. She opened her eyes and shrieked.

"Cip? What's the matter?" Jaswant said leaning over her. She looked up at him. Ciprianne scooted up on the pillows, gathered them, grabbed her knees and held them close, rocked like a little girl. She flexed her feet several times to wake up.

"Jaswant! You're here?"

"Naturally. Sorry I startled you. I heard you mumbling."

Ciprianne rubbed her eyes. "Wow, what a dream! So vivid. I've never dreamed like that before. I felt sensations, smelled fragrances, talked to people. Someone washed my hair, mine but not mine, long and black." Ciprianne looked down at her clothes. "Silk, I wore a silk sari."

"Easy to arrange. You don't have to dream it. We'll go shopping in the morning and get you several."

"I had sisters, Jaswant, lots of them. My favorite said she missed me. I had been away a long time."

Jaswant laughed. "Well, honey, I can't do anything about that. Lots of sisters can mean lots of trouble. Lucky for you, you have only one."

Ciprianne felt slighted by his cavalier attitude. She stood. The room spun in the candlelight. She staggered to keep her balance.

"Are you alright?" Jaswant steadied her with a strong grip.

"I feel like I've been sculling too long."

"Jet lag. Drink a lot of water. It'll go away. You'll get your land legs."

"Where'd you go, Jaswant?"

"The verandah. I waited for you."

"Sorry, I forgot. I need to go to the bathroom."

Ciprianne felt apprehension that her footstep might not make contact. She balanced herself against the sink. The tube of toothpaste deflated as soon as she touched it. A great ooze of paste climbed onto the bristles and swan dived into the basin. She put the brush to her mouth but felt no pressure, as if she brushed someone else's teeth. She closed the door. She spotted faint orange squiggles around her ankles, paisley designs that radiated onto her feet. With a nailbrush she scrubbed and scrubbed. The pattern melded into the redness of her roughened skin.

When she came out, Jaswant had disappeared. She gasped and ran to the sitting room where she found him pouring another glass of scotch.

"What's the matter, Cip?"

"Nothing. I didn't see you at first."

"There are only three rooms here. You shouldn't get so undone, especially on holiday. I want you to rest, enjoy yourself. Forget everything. We're here to enjoy."

"I know. I'm having a good time. Come to bed, Jaswant. I can't be alone in that room."

"I never intended to leave you alone. You were to join me, remember?"

"Right." Ciprianne faltered. "Don't let me fall asleep like that again."

"Five minutes? Want me to monitor you? You hate that. I've heard you and your friends, those stories of husbands checking on wives. Not in our marriage, Cip."

"Jaswant, I didn't mean that. Well, this place, I love it, but something's going on. Someone wants to communicate with me – from the past."

"Ghosts?"

"Possibly, but not like in the movies."

"The mural lady?"

"Yes... and others."

"Which wall?" "No wall. One's not in the mural. She's me, an Indian me."

"You're Indian in your dreams? My mother would rejoice. How about me, am I Indian in your dreams, or did you turn me into a white American?"

"You're not in my dreams."

"Cheap shot, Cip. I brought you here. You could, out of courtesy, invite me into your Indian dreams. My homeland, you know."

Ciprianne exhaled a weak hah. "I'll try."

In bed, with Jaswant's arm wrapped around her, she relaxed in the warmth of his chest and wondered how she could sleep but not dream. She worried something would drag her back. She didn't want to go. She told herself she would stay up all night. She feared the dreams. She feared herself. She concentrated on Jaswant's caresses and made him her world.

The following morning at breakfast Sardar Singh spotted the couple and smiled. He felt red heat rise to the crimson cotton turban pleated over his ears. He rushed past waiting guests to reach them. "All first class last night?"

"Fine, Sardar Singh. Good show," Ciprianne said. The madam's weak smile caused him to wonder. "My husband and I disagree on something though." Sardar Singh felt his breathing stop. "The painting of the Maharana, the young man in the mural, is not the same older man in the sitting room portrait. Right?"

"Correct, madam. The mural shows Maharana Raj Singh I. The sitting room portrait shows Maharana Jagat Singh II. He built this, his summer palace, in 1743. Half a century separates them."

"Right! I knew they weren't the same." She smiled at Jaswant and pretended to lick her finger and put another point on the board.

"Most visitors would not notice – or care – madam."

"Maharana Raj Singh I, in the mural, great diplomat and warrior, patron of the arts and learning, saved our people from drought and famine. He built Lake Rajsamand by damming three rivers. Madam, you may find this odd, he had many queens, such was the custom for royalty, but he liked jewelry as much as any of them."

"No, I don't find that odd, the zenana thing."

"And your room... did the AC work well enough?"

"Too well," Jaswant said. "We overslept. We wanted to go to the bazaar before it got too hot. You didn't come by with bed tea?"

"Yes, sir, I knocked. No one came. Good sleep is a gift. Not to worry, shops have small ACs and turn them on when tourists approach."

"And raise the prices?"

"Our shopkeepers are not like those in Delhi. Rajasthanis have pride. You will get a fair price, even with the missus. You must be looking for what?"

"Jewelry."

"I recommend one man. His shop third down on left side of City Palace bazaar, has AC. He recently lost his father, a friend to me. The son runs the shop by himself now. Recognize him by his head, shaved, out of respect for his father. He is having large supply of necklaces, bracelets, earrings, gold and silver."

"Any antique jewelry?"

"Yes, yes. Tell him Sardar Singh sent you for best service. Please enjoy. I am bringing your drinks. Buffet is very fine today."

Sardar Singh sighed with relief when the Americans waved goodbye. His fears subsided. He assumed the niggling spirits of the suite must have found the company pleasing. Saying his prayers to Lord Shiva with renewed faith, he grew confident his family would survive, he would return to his fields to reap bountiful harvests, see his daughters properly married, especially his eldest, Asha. He could finally atone for his sin against her, dispel the pain he had carried in his heart for these nineteen years.

He watched the morning sky grow dull, an approaching storm. This rain, he prayed, would bring the cracked dry earth back to life. He inhaled the prayer deep into his lungs, all of Rajasthan breathed with him: Let the rains come!

# CHAPTER 5 – LEANING IN

Sardar Singh hurried to finish his café duties to catch the ferry home until his evening shift. He stood in the kitchen counting the silverware when the front desk clerk ran in, breathless, to find him.

"Sardar Ji, come quickly. Problem in Sajjan Niwas Suite."

Sardar Singh rushed past the clerk, skirted guests in the corridor, ran to the suite, the clerk following close behind.

"Look, Sardar Ji. What kind of people are these?"

Sardar Singh entered with caution to survey the room. Stunned, he looked at a sight he could not imagine. He knew at a glance the Americans had nothing to do with this mayhem. They had left only twenty minutes earlier. In so short a time? he muttered. No, not even in a day, even two. Sardar's prayers vaporized in the heady aroma of the suite, a mixture of sandalwood incense, rose water, and jasmine. It choked more violently than an assailant's hand. He gasped for breath. He knew how to fight, but not this. He closed his eyes, shook his head to dispel the image. His disbelieving eyes opened.

He yanked back the heavy curtain, stood in silence, stared at the view outside, morning light tangled in small whitecaps whipped by the coming storm that made the scene inside eerier. The carved wood settee, now a brass tub full of rose-scented water. Water pooled on the marble floor, a golden reflection of brass, and wicked into the edge of the Persian carpet. When Sardar Singh pulled back the carpet, he discovered pink rose petals crushed beneath its weight. Mud spilled from an earthen pot left a partially dried trail on the polished wood table. Sardar Singh leaned in closer to inspect. He swiped his finger. He sniffed.

"Henna paste! Wipe it off before it stains!" he shouted at the clerk.

He approached the bedroom with apprehension. He pushed open the heavy door little by little, mumbling a prayer. On the wall opposite the door, the finely dressed Maharana had stood surveying his domain from the balcony of his palace. Now empty.

"He's gone. How?"

With the eyes of a falcon, Sardar checked for further abnormalities. The zenana girl with the impish smile of square teeth – missing. Dancing girls as before, frozen. Krishna and Radha in the garden eternal – thankfully, Sardar thought, stationary lovers.

"What to do?" Sardar Singh said aloud, stomping back and forth across the suite. He collapsed on the chair in the sitting room, head buried in his large hands, veins popped up, blue snakes on a brown sea. "What to do?"

The desk clerk, seeing Sardar so distraught, spoke up. "Sir, I believe the sweeper did this. He must be punished! I am reporting this immediately!"

"You will not!" bellowed Sardar Singh. "He had no way. He had no reason. He wants to work as much as we do.

What would he gain from such disgrace? His family would starve. You cannot report this."

"Sir, if we do not blame someone... The Americans. Let them pay. Americans are always being very rich!"

"Don't be so stupid, man. Why would they? How could they?"

"Sir, the suite is theirs only. They had time. Many witnesses say the woman acts strange. We could report..."

"Shut up, you fool. Do not place blame where it is not due!"

"We will lose our jobs. On our heads, this tragedy falls."

"Let me think. The Americans went out for the morning, shopping. The day's heat affects the lady, but they must remain away for the entire day. I shall send someone to find them. A free tour of the surrounding area in our air-conditioned car. That should work," Sardar said, talking to himself. "Arrange lunch at Fateh Prakash Palace. Take them to all shops. Let the shopkeepers know the hotel will pay the difference in their bills. Make them feel they get cut-rate prices. Special guests, after all. Ah, Monsoon Palace tour. I must keep them away all day, whatever it takes."

"A painter from the art school can repaint the figures," Sardar said to the clerk. "Take the ferry, return with a painter, no, several painters. Tell them keep silence on this matter. We shall not disgrace our guest, poor woman with mental troubles, American."

"How to pay?"

"From the café cash register."

"We report it?" the clerk said with apprehension.

"Of course. It would be stealing if we did not. We term it 'necessary expenses.' "

"Management will not believe."

"Quick, bring the Jharokha chef here. He's my trusted friend. I can depend on him. That makes the sweeper, chef, you and me witnesses."

"I am not wanting any part of this, sir."

"Nor do any of us. Do your duty, man."

The front desk clerk stiffened and walked away. Sardar heard him grumbling under his breath.

Sardar Singh and the sweeper straightened the room and helped servants carry the tub out. The gardener proposed an idea for it, an urn for his flowerpots. Sardar Singh agreed and stipulated he take it to the farthest courtyard by the swimming pool. When the gardener dumped the water on the lawn, white pigeons rushed over, strutted and cooed in the rose water, before the thirsty earth swallowed it.

Sardar Singh's mind raced at the turn of events. Had the couple not seen anything? They seemed relaxed at breakfast. Could they pretend that well? Could the mural figures escape and the tub appear in such a short time between the couple's departure and now, hardly an hour later? His head swelled with questions. His temples throbbed from the pressure. He rechecked all the window locks and doors, none showed damage. He commanded the sweeper to admit no one to the suite. The thin man straightened his sloppy, dirt stained turban, nodded in agreement and placed his broom across his chest like a bayonet.

Sardar Singh returned to the front desk to await the painters' arrival. He checked his watch, paced the marble floor, trying to look composed. He knew the wildness in his eyes frightened the namaskar girls by the way they pulled back from his advance. They huddled in the shade of the front entrance, whispering as he paced, afraid they were soon to lose their jobs. They straightened the marigold necklaces, made sure they were not bruised, lined them in the dampened tray, and waited to greet the next guest. Sardar Singh turned from them, lost in thought. He walked as if he could stamp out impending loss with forceful footfalls.

Surely, he thought, the marble palace would record his plight, have mercy on him. He had given so much to it, his honor. He feared for his young daughters, his aging parents, his devoted wife. Why would the gods send him this? What had he done to deserve such a destiny? He recoiled. He knew as soon as the words surfaced in his mind: his destiny, his punishment, came the reply. Not parched earth, not fallow fields, this – humiliation – would scorch him beyond what he could handle, reduce him to a famine of spirit, take from him the one thing that had sustained him: hope for redemption. The gods laughed at his folly, laughed at his attempt to save himself from the worst aspect of himself. This he understood – no act goes unpunished, not even a regretted attempt. He stormed out the entrance, looked across the lake to the city growing yellow in the dusty haze, sure the wind carried with it a curse upon his head.

The storm had reached Udaipur. Dry wind kicked up the lake, frothed it into a frenzy. Women ran, gathered their drying colorful saris from the rocks. Parrots whizzed by on turbulent gusts, some careened into jharokha turrets, helpless against the wind. In the distance Sardar saw the coughing, choking ferryboat struggle against the waves, tossed side to side. He rushed to the dock to receive the boat with the painters. His tunic flapped in the strong wind. He bent forward to shield his face from flying debris. He grabbed the boat's mooring rope, lifted his head to see the frightened passengers, and gasped.

"Sardar, steady the boat. Grab my wife's hand. She's sick. Hurry, man, help her get out!"

Sardar Singh grabbed Ciprianne's white twitching hand in his and pulled her up. She swayed into him, unable to get her footing. He caught her in his arms and set her upright, at a distance. A strong gust hurled her into his chest. Stricken with embarrassment and fear, he passed her over to her husband's grasp when he stepped onto the dock.

The boatman yelled, "Unleash the rope. I must return for the painters."

Sardar Singh, realizing the futility of the mission, yelled, "No matter now. Tie your boat. Come to shelter. At least you should be safe."

The boatman crawled onto the dock just as a stiff wind slammed the boat into the mooring post. The impact threw him forward. His boat screeched against the dock.

"My boat!" he shouted over the howling wind. "It will be bashed to rubble if I keep it here. I must anchor it farther out."

"How? Who will bring you in?"

"I swim."

"Madness!" Sardar shouted.

"No matter. Throw me this ring," the boatman said tossing a blue life-saver ring towards Sardar Singh.

Sardar Singh grabbed the ring, surprised how unwieldy it was. He watched his friend edge out into the storm, cut the engine and toss a metal anchor into the heaving brown water. The boatman untied his turban, laced the length through his sandals, secured it around his chest, and jumped into the water. Sardar Singh watched his friend bob up and down in the waves. He sputtered and gasped. He flailed towards the pier, a rat swimming to safety.

His strokes failed to move him forward. He disappeared. When he resurfaced, Sardar Singh grabbed the ring, leaned back and launched it forward with all his strength. The lifesaver fell short. He reeled it in, hurled again, and it reached his friend's grasp, barely. The boatman wrapped his arms through it and held on grimly. Sardar Singh pulled with such force a small wake followed the blue ring. He wrenched his friend up out of the waves onto the first step of the dock's cement foundation.

"Gods bless us," Sardar said.

The boatman had no breath to reply – or time. Sardar Singh dropped his grip, chased after the Americans. The hotel guests stared at the man who ran through the foyer, water gushing from his shoes. He made no apology when he bumped into a woman in the corridor beside the lily pond. At Sajjan Niwas Suite, he tripped and slammed into the closed door.

Trying to compose himself, he wiped rivulets of water and dust from the folds of his turban that inched down like brown worms onto his forehead. He knocked.

"Who's there?" he heard the American's deep voice shout.

"Sir, Sardar Singh here."

Jaswant opened the heavy door, barefoot, his hair dripping.

"Nasty storm. Come inside."

Sardar Singh walked in like a man walking to his execution. When he raised his head he saw the sitting room. No tub. No henna mud, no splashed water, not even a damp carpet. He felt his face contort; a spasm in his forehead made him wince. He knew for certain the gods pursued him, played him like cat and mouse.

"Everything first class, sir. Missus okay, pukka?"

"Yes, all fine except the weather. I imagine you have no control over that."

"No, sir. I do not. We desperately need rain. A dry storm, false promise, brings only misery. It remains to be seen. I think we are not lucky today."

"I remember times from my childhood when the Punjab sky turned yellow for days with choking dust from Rajasthan. Herders with their cattle came north to graze, so the animals wouldn't starve, a dark, sickly sky following them like a brown shadow. Twenty years ago – and here again today."

"It happens, sir. Desperation. This – the fourth year I have not farmed because no rain. Most difficult. I hope the missus is not unhappy with her stay?"

"No, no. She enjoys everything, even the dust storm, her first."

"Management would like to keep you happy. Would the missus enjoy an Ayurvedic massage, our gift to her? I can book this afternoon."

"Let me ask."

Jaswant walked to the bedroom door, rapped his knuckles on the dark wood. The door swung open. Sardar Singh positioned himself to view the mural. He glimpsed the Maharana standing as regal as ever in his jeweled turban. Sardar sighed with relief. He jumped back from the door when the American whirled to face him.

"My God. She's gone. My wife's gone! She was showering. How could that be? Sardar, check the windows."

Sardar rushed to the window alcoves but found them all locked. He grabbed the verandah door and yanked. Locked. He unbolted the latch and ran out. He heard Jaswant yank on the inner door of the jharokha, kick the heavy door, retreat, slam into it with force, over and over.

Sardar Singh yelled, "Sir, stop. I know where your wife is. You cannot get there from that door!"

"Tell me, man!" Jaswant shouted back, careening around the corner like a wild boar.

"She's been taken, by... the Maharana." He pointed to the mural. "He has her."

"Are you mad? What's going on here? Call the police!"

"Sir, you may never get her back if we do not act. There is no time!"

"You're dead if you don't tell me where she is, now!"

Sardar Singh stepped back, rushed to the window alcove, to the right of the Maharana's image, studied the mural wall. "Here, sir, look!" he said pointing his finger. "She entered here."

Jaswant rushed over. He saw wet footprints, Ciprianne's footprints, on the floor in front of the mural. Sardar Singh rubbed across a painted cliff overhanging a painted river.

Jaswant studied the mural for a second in astonishment. His eye caught a flash of movement, a tiny thing. He blinked. The tiny thing moved. He leaned in, got on his hands and knees to look more closely. He saw two figures, a man and a woman, move along the river's edge. He recognized Ciprianne's blue salwar kameez.

"My God! That's Ciprianne! Someone has her?" he said with incredulous desperation. "How do we, how can we, Sardar?"

"Sir, do as I do. I think we can."

Jaswant watched Sardar Singh thrust his foot into the wall; he melted into the mural, bit by bit. Paint squiggled to accommodate the force as if an unseen painter rubbed a brush across the scene. Jaswant narrowed his eyes, looked closer. Sardar Singh floundered on the ledge above the river, trying to stop himself from falling in.

Jaswant heard a faint cry for help, or thought he did. He thrust his hand forward to grab Sardar Singh's bright red cummerbund. The motion propelled him headlong towards the cliff. A shower of stones plummeted into the fast-moving river below. Jaswant flattened on the rocky ground, steadied himself on the ledge.

He gasped. "Sardar, we made it! We're here, above the river."

"Yes, sir. I cannot swim," he said, crawling away from the edge on his belly. "We must hurry. They go to the palace on the hill, see – way up there."

Jaswant shielded his eyes from the sun. Beyond the river, up a lone mountain sat a white palace skirted by dark green forests. "Why Ciprianne?"

"Sir, it's a mystery to me. I must tell you there have been odd occurrences in the suite for years, but never anything like this, never!"

"Like what, then?"

"Silly things, girls giggling, swing moving. Nothing like this. But since you and the missus came... Sir, some of us have grown worried. It appeared your wife was... wanted. It was like she knew the place already. We never considered danger would come, believe me. I would have risked my job and told management if I had ever thought there was real danger to anyone."

"Who wants her?"

"The Maharana!"

"The mural Maharana?" Jaswant sat up on the rocky path. "Sardar, we joked about this place feeling familiar, the palace I mean. A joke, right?"

Jaswant surveyed the terrain. Ahead marshy grassland stretched out along the river's edge. White cranes stood in shallow water, their images reflected in the stillness. The afternoon sky, full of creamy white thunderheads piled one on top of another, with huge swollen gray folds, threatened rain. "Which way, Sardar?"

"We track your wife, retrieve her before nightfall. Follow me." Sardar Singh said in a grave voice.

Jaswant looked down to see prints in the soft earth along the rocky ledge. He looked at Sardar.

"Tiger, sir. Huge one, and a smaller one. They track your wife. Hurry."

# CHAPTER 6 – LOTUS FLOWER

Placid inlet water captured an exact copy of the trees, clouds entangled in finger reaching branches. Ciprianne recalled how she loved bathing with village women in the cool water. In childhood she and her brother splashed for hours, wove crowns of herbs for their hair, skipped rocks, braided ropes of riverweeds. She smiled at the memory – at its lie: she had no brother. She had never been here before.

She looked at the swarthy man walking in front of her on the path. "Why are you taking me here, where are we?"

"He commanded. I obey," he said half-turning to face her. He avoided her gaze. Ciprianne thought his face in profile looked like a melting candle; a great nose slid down the mountain of his face, rested on his lips.

"Well, I should like to go back there," Ciprianne said, pointing to the distant cliff where they had met.

"You come with me. We go to hill palace. That is my master's order: 'Meet her at the river and bring her to me.'"

Ciprianne stopped in her tracks. The guard continued for a few paces, turned to face her. She jumped from shock when she saw his pockmarked face, caverns of scars left from illness. She felt repulsed... and sorry for him. He wore his suffering for everyone to see.

"Come along, lady. Two hours more. By sunset we reach the peak."

"I don't want to go! I want to return to the river."

"No. You do not know the way. You would not survive. I have orders."

"It is only a walk, a short journey. I can do it."

"Longer than you think, far more difficult. We are being watched – and followed."

"Who follows?"

"What follows."

"No riddles. What do you mean?"

"The tigress and her cub. They track us. Make large circles ahead, and behind," he said pointing. "They wait for dark, attack if we rest. By nightfall they will spring; we won't see them."

Ciprianne wanted to laugh and challenge the guard, but she remembered a strange sound, a low growl from a long distance. The guard had yanked her from where she stooped by the river to drink. She had felt the sound vibrate in her chest. Now she understood. She drew closer, followed the man walking, drawn sword in hand, and studied the terrain.

They rounded a clump of trees that hid an eddy choked by pink lotus flowers. From there the path swung wide from the river to cross large boulders heaped one on another and between them, battered trees, evidence of a flash flood, stuck like skewers in clods of displaced earth.

Ciprianne saw in the distant hill a thin silver ribbon waterfall catch the afternoon light and shine orange as it dropped to the valley below. Beyond that the forest fused in deep blue shadow.

"We go up. The path, narrow, steep. Many chances for tigress to attack. You walk in front." He studied the river trail for prints. "Clever animals, good trackers, have taste for Rajput flesh – good, strong meat! She comes from behind."

Ciprianne made no argument. The rocky path hurt her sandaled feet, but she hiked as fast as she could.

"Guard, why does the Maharana want to see me?"

The guard snorted with disbelief. "You know."

"I don't. I am not sure what is happening. I feel this is a familiar land, yet that cannot be. I remain lost and unlost at the same time, here and not here."

"Familiar? You grew up in the valley by the river, over that second ridge. Your home, until he called for you. I served you as chief guard of the zenana. The Maharana sent me to fetch you. He knew you would come with me."

"How did you serve me?"

"With honor."

"In what way?"

"Your personal guard. As his prize, you deserve better than walking like a commoner on rough ground, no palanquin to carry you, but after what you did, I say you earned this, maybe more. A queen gone bad."

"A queen?"

"His favorite. You know that. Some believe number one wife drove you away, but others say, well..."

"What?"

"Keep walking. Nightfall comes. No time to talk."

Ciprianne tried to recall a time as queen but could not. She realized her predicament.

"Sir, guard, whatever your name is."

"Rama."

"Rama, I understand now. You have the wrong person. I am no queen. I want to return. I want to go home."

"I knew you. Your escape almost cost my life. I lived with one thought: spend my life searching for you, or lose it in dishonor. I deliver you to Maharana and earn back respect. After that, do what you like. Leave or stay, I don't care. If he grants your wish to leave, I will walk you back to where I discovered you by the river. It is as he commands!"

Ciprianne considered her options while she followed the path's S-curve into the forest. A breeze came up from the valley floor. Acacia trees rustled and swayed. Monkeys overhead screeched an alarm, swinging from branch to branch, their white bellies shining like ghosts in the dim light.

"They speak of the tigress. They fear her. Next to human flesh, the sweet meat of the white-belly monkey satisfies her best."

Ciprianne realized she had not eaten in hours, yet she felt no hunger.

"Tell me what I did to deserve this."

"No, we are forbidden to talk, so great the insult to our ruler. Rajput women display better natures. You acted not a Rajput Maharani, but a common.... Your family suffered. You caused your father great sadness. After he found what he found, he looked everywhere for you. He did not believe you had died. He tried to cross the desert to the Sindh, to find you, but he died. Could a daughter shame her family more? Your mother, hearing of her husband's death, built her funeral pyre, and people say, walked into it, calling his name. Some say you caused a curse to fall on your lineage. A gypsy told the Maharana the females of your line would be barren, and your brother would die in battle. It came to pass. No one knew what had happened to you."

Ciprianne swallowed hard to stifle a welling in her chest, lava from a long dormant volcano, ready to explode and sear her heart. Her mind raced back to a distant day with her father. She recalled the tenderness in his voice:

"Dear child, my most precious jewel, the Maharana has chosen. He honors us. Devi, you he wants as wife."

She looked at her father in disbelief, the garland of herbs falling from her lap. "Father, how can that be? I am your daughter, not yet a woman. What could he want with me? He has many wives. Let him be content with them. I want to stay here, with you. Tell him to choose another. I will not go!"

"He requested you. I cannot decline the honor, however much I would like. He will send for you."

"No! I will not go!"

"You are young and headstrong. You do not realize the honor he bestows. We are peasants, farmers. Our daughter, a queen! We will want for nothing."

"He has many wives, many children who bear his face. I want to stay here with you, to hunt. I am very good with the bow, aren't I, Father?"

"As good a hunter as any man," her father said. "But no one refuses and lives. I cannot disobey. You will see. When the time comes, you will be ready."

"I will never be ready! I will not live like a caged bird in a garden. Let him take a peahen instead!"

"Devi, do not talk so. If anyone hears, we could all be executed! Think of your family. We will be cared for, protected, with you as queen."

"Will I live with you?"

"No. At the palace with the others."

"I will only consent if I can remain here with you, dearest father. You cannot cast me out."

"I never dreamed it would come to this. I knew you would one day marry. I thought it would be to someone like us, a village boy, a farmer. I had spoken to our friends for their son. But, no matter, it is all done, passed. We must accept this honor."

"Why me, Father, a village girl? I know nothing of their ways."

"Your beauty and spirit. Many speak of you."

"What do they say?"

"They say your skin glows because the goddesses blessed you, your dark eyes are keen like the hawk's, your courage equal to any warrior's. Too many things. We pay a price for them. I should have blackened your cheek when you were born to ward off the evil eye."

"I am a good hunter. That is true, yet many girls are prettier."

"You have Rajput valor, easy to see in your strong face, the fierceness in your eyes. When you saved your brother from the wild boar's tusk at the Festival of Lights, villagers spoke of it. More than the village heard the tale. Since that time I knew the Maharana watched you from afar. On festival days did you not wonder that we attended the palace grounds, simple farmers? He commanded me, so he could see you.

You blossomed. He liked more and more what he saw. Last year he made an official request to me. My heart sank. Your mother and I wanted our friends' son, Jaswant, for you, a fine boy, strong and honest."

At the mention of his name, Devi blushed. Jaswant had taught her wonderful things: rope knots, animal traps, tracking. Jaswant, the only villager who could use the bow and arrow as well as her. But to marry him? The thought stunned her.

"Father, say I am promised to Jaswant from childhood!"

"No, I cannot. Even so, you cannot. Maharana requested you. It is too late. Any girl would dance with joy. But look at you. Your face says you lost your bow and arrow, mouth like a downturned sickle. Devi, this means a life of ease for you, for us. You cannot refuse! What shame on us all, you would bring."

"Father, will the Brahmin cast our charts?"

"Yes, naturally."

"And if there is some terrible problem with our stars, what then?"

"That is for the Brahmin to say."

"I pray he finds me unfit, our stars unhappy!"

Devi harbored that wish with every prayer, with every circle she paced around the temple, with every marigold she placed on Vishnu's statue, yet a year later she wept to hear the Brahmin's proclamation: the auspicious day for her marriage to the Maharana had arrived.

"Father, the Brahmin must be wrong!"

"No, daughter."

"How could we be destined when I have no affection for him?"

"You are young. Affection builds when a man and woman are together."

"What did the Brahmin say to you?"

"He said both your planets are in strong houses for ruling. You would be a fit partner, with robust health and a quick mind for justice, and a kind nature. Venus gives you blessings in love. The one thing, a concern, the position of Mars in your chart, conjunct Jupiter – he prefers to see in a man's chart, not a woman's. It speaks of a fiery nature, a leader in battle. He assumes although as youngest wife, you rise to top of zenana, Maharana's favorite, others are not liking."

"I would rather sink to the bottom of Meandering River!"

Devi stormed out of her father's house, ran down to the river to her favorite spot where willows overhang the lotus pool. She sat looking at the robust pink blossoms supported by thick green leaves, closed her eyes and prayed to Goddess Lakshmi for something to come between her and her appointed fate.

"Namaskar. What do you here?"

The girl looked up to see her childhood friend Jaswant, with his hunting bow slung across his shoulder. She tried to appear unmoved.

"Watching lotus blossoms."

"What are they doing?"

"You see how they float? Leaf pads keep them up, support them, so the huge, clean, beautiful flowers don't sink even though the water in this eddy is muddy and dark. They are protected."

Jaswant walked to the embankment, sat on his haunches. The girl's beauty, now as a seventeen year-old, made her not the girl he'd grown up with. Devi understood this. Her thin child body had changed. No matter how loose her clothes, they fell across her curves. Devi felt her presence lured him.

She knew he thought to pass her by, to avoid her, but in weeks she would be the Maharana's wife. This she thought might be her last time to sit with Jaswant. He would see her from afar, she in the jharokha and he standing guard down below as a member of the royal army from now on. She wished he would hold her, just once, smell the frangipani blossoms in her braid, feel her soft lashes brush his cheek like a bird's whisper. She snapped to attention and stood in front of him.

"Jaswant, you and I have long been friends."

"Yes," he said.

"Would you help me if you could?"

"I am at your service, always."

Devi grabbed his hand and placed it on her warm breast, pressed down by hers.

"Feel my heart's beat. It is only for you. It has only ever beaten for you. I cannot marry the Maharana when I... when I love you."

Devi felt a surge of warmth shoot through him, making the veins in his temples throb. He snapped his hand away, unable to speak.

"Jaswant, please help me! I know you could love me. Speak for me. Demand me!"

"I cannot. It would be my only wish in life, as you guessed. The price for what you ask , too dear to voice, prevents me."

"You? Afraid of losing your life for me?"

"No, Devi, afraid of losing yours."

"I have no life, sentenced to marry a man I do not love, to live in a palace compartment with women who hate me, to be kept like a caged bird only released for his pleasure, to produce children for him until he gives out, or I do. What life? I have the heart of a warrior. I shall languish and die: it will be upon your head! Remember that. You could have saved me!"

"How? Where are we to go?"

"We could travel with the gypsies to Afghanistan, or go to Persia, or south to the Deccan."

"We have no camels, horses or money. We would die before we crossed the desert, or the Maharana would hunt us down and shoot us like animals with his fine metal-tip arrows!"

"There is another way."

"What?"

"You could render me unfit for marriage." Devi wrapped her arms around his waist and felt a hard heat rise. "He would not want another man's woman."

Jaswant stepped back from her. "I could not have you and let you go! Because of my selfishness, I would condemn you, and your family, to certain death. No! I shall live my life as the guard below your window, content to spend my days protecting you."

"Content to see me taken by a man I do not love, wishing all the while you were he! No life for either of us. I choose death."

"Careful, Devi. Do not anger the gods. When you need me, send a message by pigeon. I keep the roost. In that way we can talk. I swear my loyalty to you. I will do whatever needed to protect you, with honor, on my life."

Devi jolted to the present when the guard grabbed her arm with force.

"Stay still, and quiet. The tigress nears." The man shifted his weight and craned his head to see past bushes in the forest shadows. "She waits. She follows. Stay next to me."

Devi followed him, feeling dazed. They picked their way along the mountain path and, round a huge rockslide, spotted a small pasture where the last of the fiery orange sun drowned on placid purple water like an ember giving up its last light. Devi watched deer drink unaware of their presence. White cranes picked insects from the rushes and stretched their long necks.

A loud shriek sent the deer running; cranes took flight. The monkey's warning, not soon enough for a doe to hurry her young one, alerted the tigress. She leapt from the bushes at a dead run, jumped the doe but missed. The doe careened off to the side in frantic terror, at the cub.

"Quick! We go now!"

Up the hill they scrambled, Devi stopped only to catch her breath, before they picked their way through the boulders to the dark forest. The guard stopped short when he heard a shrill bird call. He turned back to Devi, sword drawn. She looked up to see him hurtle towards her, a wild look in his eyes. She knew he intended to slay her. She screamed and veered off to the right, downhill. He called after her, she didn't stop.

Another shrill call pierced the sullen air. Soldiers rushed from hiding places in the trees. They seized the guard. Realizing him as one of their own, they ran after the fleeing woman. A rough hand seized Devi by the arm, swung her round, nearly crushing her into a tree. She tried to slug him. He stopped her.

"Lady! We came to escort you only. The Maharana sent us – his royal guard. Do not fear!"

Devi gasped for breath. She thought the young man familiar. Why? she wondered.

"Lady, come along. We are safe now," her guide said when he caught up to them. "These soldiers are here to escort us to the fortress."

Devi walked without a word amidst the men who lowered their eyes in her presence. No one looked at her, but they moved as a unit of armor around her. They made their way through the forest in the darkness until they reached a clearing. The purple-gray evening freed several silver stars. Others sparked yellow or red. Up above, on the hill, torches lit the way to the palace in a serpentine pattern that inched up the steep terrain. Devi spotted several women crowded into a jharokha, looking down at her.

A huge soldier approached with a long arched sword that dangled from his chest leathers and motioned for her to follow him. When they approached the palace gate, the guard pulled up the latch and swung the heavy wooden gate wide. He bowed in front of her. She couldn't see his face, but something about him seemed familiar.

They crossed to the far side of the garden where the soldier led her up a flight of stairs and left her standing at the door to the women's compartment, guarded by a eunuch. The eunuch knocked in a pattern. Devi heard whispers. When it opened, Devi found herself face to face with a petite woman with an impish smile and square teeth.

"Namaskar, Devi," she said and hugged her. "We have been waiting. You are most welcome. Come in."

Devi entered to see a room full of women who raised their hands palm to palm in blessed greeting: "Namaskar." She realized their shock when they studied her humble clothes. Theirs of fine silk reflected many candle-lit lamps in the room and made her feel more uncomfortable.

"Devi, I told you to wear the peacock blue sari. And you have come after such a long absence in the clothes of a peasant! Shame, shame. You must pay more attention."

"I came in what I had. Someone took the saris!"

"I shall get them back for you. Not to worry, you are here. All is well now. You must be wanting food after your long journey, and a bath. He will receive you this evening at dinner."

"He?"

"Our Maharana, of course, the reason you have traveled so far."

Looking round the apartment, Devi saw many familiar faces.

"Remember our names?" one woman called out.

"No, I am sorry, I don't, but I remember your faces."

"You have long been away. Names are difficult when you are fatigued. Your memory will dawn soon enough. I am

Mira, the Maharana's sister. These are his wives, just like you – although," she said with an edge to her voice, "they did not desert my brother. On this I shall hold silence until facts are known."

Mira embraced Devi and instructed the others to file by and do the same. "Ladies, our Devi is back with us again. For your husband's honor, embrace her, welcome her home."

Each one in turn walked forward to touch Devi's feet in blessing – except one, a small, beautiful woman with skin the color of young wheat, large doe eyes the color of loam earth, and full, crimson lips. She nodded and stepped aside.

Mira smiled and whispered in Devi's ear, "She has not forgiven you for what you said. Since your departure, she has enjoyed number one status. She is not happy you have returned."

"I don't feel happy myself."

"You will."

That evening a zenana eunuch came to the door to request the Maharana's sister, Mira, and his returned wife Devi to join him in his chamber for dinner. Mira wove pearls and teardrop rubies into Devi's hair to match her choker and advised her to wear the gold bracelets and anklets she had set out for her.

"You must look worthy. He doesn't want anyone to gossip."

When Mira led Devi into the open-air sitting room, the Maharana sat by the window admiring the pulsating stars tossed across the new moon night sky. She entered first to announce Devi's arrival. At both sides of the entrance robust men wearing accordion-pleated silk tunics, with peach colored cummerbunds cinched tightly over their scabbards, escorted Devi forward upon command. The large marble floor gleamed in amber candlelight. There in front of her, Devi realized, sat her husband, a man familiar and yet not so. Mira motioned for her to bow and kiss his feet in greeting. "Namaskar, husband," she said meekly after she touched his feet.

"Come closer. Are you so frightened you cannot approach? You should be. A wise woman would be. You caused me much sorrow, Devi, but all is forgiven. You are home, safe. That is all I desire."

His words played upon her like music, soft and uplifting. Afraid to move, she looked at him. In his ivory tunic detailed with gold thread embroidery, silk clinging to his muscular frame like shiny pale skin, he looked every bit a royal commander. A ruby cabochon encircled by Basra pearls adorned the golden turban that added inches to his medium height. His smile made her feel he undressed her. He approached to kiss her forehead.

"I have missed our nights together," he leaned in close to her ear and whispered.

Devi inhaled his scent and understood something familiar about this man. The arc of dark eyebrows, the light that surfaced in his impenetrable eyes, and yet... She pulled away from him and stared down at her adorned hands clasped tightly together.

"Do not be afraid. I have no intention of punishing you, Devi. I understand why, and how, you were deceived."

Devi felt relieved by his words, and confused. She said nothing.

The Maharana motioned for her to take a seat next to him while he finished discussing the recent hunt with his chief officer.

The more she watched him, the fonder she grew. His easy manner, the way he laughed as he tilted his head back, the wild gesticulations to make his point, his dark eyes that gleamed with passion, all this enchanted her. She wondered at ever having left this man... until a distant memory jolted her: Jaswant.

She saw him in the Maharana's face. It was Jaswant she desired. It was he she carried in her heart, not the regal man seated on the dais in front of her. She remembered now. The Maharana smothered her as she endured his passion to exhaustion, night after night. This, the man she had escaped only to find herself tonight again in front of him, admiring her like a rose-scented sweet, was not her love.

Mira leaned over to speak to Devi who sat on the Persian carpet to the side of her husband. "I missed you. Let us resume as sisters. I understand why you left. You thought it necessary, but you were tricked. My brother understands that now and will not reproach you," she said, looking down and twirling her bangle nonchalantly to divert attention.

"He searched the kingdom for you. Some believed you had drowned. Leaving made you appear involved in sabotaging my brother's efforts to negotiate the revolt with Prince Akbar against his father, Emperor Aurangzeb. A guard swore someone abducted you from the zenana. Of course, my brother, upon hearing you had ordered the stable boy to bring your saddled horse to the lake, thought you had stolen away with your lover.

"Devi, everyone knew of your affection for Captain Jaswant. You could see it in your eyes every time you and he looked at one another. I should not speak of these things. We must be very careful. Do not speak of this if my brother does not."

Devi saw Mira's admiration of her brother when she stopped to listen to him rehash the story of the recent shikar, how he brought down a wild boar with one arrow. Devi's mind drifted away. She heard her father's voice, the concern in his tone, the anguish in hers the day she declared to him:

"Father, please. I will not marry the Maharana!"

"Hush, child, someone may hear you! You do not know the thing you say. It brings ruin upon us, even the gods and goddesses will turn from us. You are a Rajput! Where is your honor? Your strength? Would you cast us down because of your stubborn nature? Would you see us exiled to the desert to suffer a terrible death? No! You will marry!"

"But I love another!"

"What? How could this be? Have you draped us in shame?"

"No, Father. I love the very one you had hoped for me, Jaswant."

Her father sprang from his haunches like a wild cat. "Does Jaswant know of this?"

"Yes. He swears his love, yet he says we cannot be together."

"Sensible boy, proud, too! Had the Maharana not requested you... Well, no need to discuss. We cannot live in dreams. You are promised to our ruler. We obey his command."

Devi burst into tears. "Father, I love only Jaswant! I will not allow the Maharana to touch me. He will tire of me... release me!"

"No, he will kill you. No one refuses. Do not talk so to your father, silly, disobedient girl. Leave me! I will not hear such words!"

Devi's father stormed out of the house to sit under the thin shade of the courtyard acacia tree.

"Let him alone, daughter," Devi's mother said, patting her shoulder. "The time has come for me to talk to you of a secret I have held all these years, one I thought would go to the pyre with me. Destiny, it seems, demands I reveal now to you, only to you, for your good. The gods and goddesses have mercy on me, seeing how long I have suffered my shame in silence."

"Mother, you make no sense! What shame?" Devi said sobbing into her long chunni.

"When I was young I was much like you, the color of desert sand, eyes like coal, lips full and soft. Many spoke of my beauty, almond eyes, skin like golden wheat... Too many things they said. Like you, my girl's body blossomed early and with such fullness that even in loose clothes, I did not go unnoticed. Unlike you, I had a father who considered me a debt. He worried about a dowry gotten from meager vegetable trade. He resented I was not a boy who could join with my two younger brothers and farm our small plot of land.

"One day while I was drawing water at the village well, soldiers of the old Maharana stopped to water their horses.

I covered my head and waited my turn on the side, but they did not leave. Instead they spoke to me. I stood horrified, not knowing what to do. One took his sword from the saddle scabbard and brushed the chunni back from my head, asked my name. Shaking, I told him. I was fifteen then. I never spoke of the incident, so ashamed was I, the way the soldiers stared at my body and face.

"One day, some weeks later, I picked sour berries down by the river. I saw horses and a palanquin approach. I hid as best I could in the thorny bush. When it stopped, I ran. A horseman galloped up alongside me, shouted for me to stop. I did as he ordered. He yanked me up on his horse with one sweep of his huge arm and placed me between his hardness and that of the saddle.

"When we returned to where the palanquin stood, he dismounted, leaving me perched high on that horse, and led the animal to a tree where he tied him. I begged to go home to my father.

"He spoke to someone within the closed drapes of the palanquin, took me down from the horse's back with a tight grip on my arm, carried me to the palanquin, and shoved me in. He yanked the curtains closed and rode off. I cried and begged the man inside to let me go home. He held me by the hair. He shamed me, not once but twice. He commanded me to silence, slapped my face. I thought I would die that day. I wished to. I bled, I cried, I hurt.

"He threw me out of the palanquin before the soldiers returned. I walked upriver to bathe in the lotus pool. Tears flowed like monsoon rain. He had sworn he would send for me to join the royal zenana, something that would have brought respect and wealth to my father. Within two weeks, my father announced he had the money for my dowry. I shook in terror. But he arranged my marriage to your father, not the Maharana, and chose the date, nine days hence, as foretold by the Brahmin, to bring good luck.

"I feared for my life on the wedding night. The truth would be known. There would be no virgin blood. I would be cast out into the desert to die. That very afternoon a gypsy woman came to our village. She knew a wedding was to take place. She announced the Maharana's court was sending a gift, a silver anklet, to every new bride of that month to celebrate bountiful harvest. She asked to see me. I didn't want to meet her. My father made me. She was a kind woman. Her silver hair draped across her shoulders like starlight. She decorated my hands and feet with henna, she said her gift to me.

"Mother left us and tended chores in the field. We were alone. The old gypsy told me she was a wise woman; she knew I was with child. I protested, but she silenced me. She said my child, a boy, would be a fine warrior, a sardar, but I could not raise him. At his birth, she would return to be my mid-wife. The child would appear stillborn. She would take him away to be raised by someone. In exchange, I would never speak of him and his father. Horrified, I agreed.

"When I confided the fear that my husband would discover I was not clean, she laughed and told me he would never guess. She gave me a bit of powder to put in rosewater to offer him that night as a sweet blessing for our union. She handed me a small leather pouch of chicken blood to put on the bed. I did exactly as she instructed me. Your father never knew my shame. I alone have, all these years," she said, breaking into tears.

"Mother, why do you tell me this? Now? You could have carried your shame to your death, the secret buried deep in your chest."

"I am trying," she sobbed, "to lighten your load of sadness, Devi. The boy-child presumed dead at birth, brought up by a wet nurse with her own son, lived near Lake Pichola. After seven years, her husband came to our village to sell his barley. His crop, abundant that year, caused him to travel to sell it. He and your father met and became friends. Some two years later when the rains failed in Lake Pichola district, that family moved near to ours. Here they remained. I had the blessing of watching my own son grow into a powerful young man, a very kind man. I came to love him very much."

Devi's face paled like the rising moon. "This boy," she said, her throat gripped the words like a vice, "this son of yours, tell me he is not Jaswant. Tell me, mother, Jaswant is not my own brother!"

"He is. That is why I have revealed my shame, to lighten your sad heart. You could not marry him anyway. He is your own blood!"

"The gods have cursed me! My only love is my mother's bastard child! Now I go to be the wife of the son of the Maharana who ravished my own mother."

"Let it end here, Devi. You will be well cared for. Our secret will remain asleep. Our family honor will increase, and in some small way I feel satisfied that the cruelty brought upon me by the old Maharana will be lessened by his son caring for you."

"But what of Jaswant?"

"He will find another. He is admired by many. He, too, will make a good match. I know the Maharana respects him. He will see to it that Jaswant receives well for his service. He knows they are brothers, but he will never acknowledge it."

"Mother, they are sons of the same father! Jaswant could be on the royal throne."

"I was never an official wife, not even an unofficial one. I was an afternoon's lust for the old man. And that Jaswant should never know – he a proud, strong warrior. We must see to it he remains that. I love him for the son he is, and you should love him as your brother only."

Mira's touch on Devi's arm reeled her back to the room where she looked at her husband, the Maharana. She felt him study her expression: knitted brows, narrowed eyes cocked to the side, faraway look. He pretended to listen to the reported sighting of the tigress and cub in the forest below, but she knew in his imagination he wrapped her in desire. She felt stifled, like wearing a silk sari in summer, sticky. He suffocated her with his heat from across the room. She knew he anticipated a torrid night; she, escape.

# CHAPTER 7 – ILL OMEN

Jaswant struggled to keep pace with Captain Sardar. Yellow dust made him blink. His brother's image wavered in front of him like an apparition, sometimes horse, sometimes man. He had spotted him on a side road but couldn't catch up with him. When Captain Sardar pulled his horse to a trot and jumped off, Captain Jaswant did the same.

"Brother, wait. I can't catch up. Forfeited your turban? Shall I go back for it?"

"I threw it down. I vowed to kill the man who claimed our Maharana a puppet of Emperor Aurangzeb. The liar boasted the Emperor will soon have the throne of the Mewars!"

"Never!"

"Come, Captain Jaswant, let us speak in private, away from hungry ears," Captain Sardar said, studying the stable boy's shuffling gait. "Who to trust?"

Captain Jaswant followed his brother, he supposed to the Maharana's durbar hall to counsel him. Instead they walked to a distant garden behind the palace. Jaswant kept up, with effort, listening to his brother's heavy breathing that sliced still air like a rapier. When they reached the back wall, out of view of the Maharana's guards, Captain Sardar slowed his pace, turned to face his brother.

"A braggart soldier at the bazaar, thinking no one was near, told his fellow officer the Emperor raises a massive army to fight the Marathas in the south."

"Sardar, such common knowledge! Even the Maharana, at dinner with his advisors, discussed the strategy as I stood guard."

"Do not interrupt me! You have but a piece of the information. Why do you think, Jaswant?"

"The Emperor's a fierce man. He wants to conquer all, to extend the empire, to subdue India, kingdom by kingdom, Mewar first?" Jaswant said.

"Exactly! He wants his subjugated people, in Mewar, born soldiers, to fight for him. And for what? What do we gain? We labor under his rule, his taxes, his dictates. We gain nothing. We lose everything!"

"Brother, the Maharana of Mewar retains power here. He and the Emperor agreed on this, a trade: relative autonomy for us, a passage route for the Emperor. His real battle remains to the south, with the Marathas. He will leave us alone up here."

"And if our best wage war for him, what then? How do you think our Maharana and our women and children will survive without us to protect them?"

"In exchange for our military service, the Emperor protects them, as promised, with his vast army. Even if all of us united, every Rajput in Rajasthan, every clan, we could not defeat him. With our Maharana avowed to the Emperor, we are obligated, honor-bound, to support his decision. I trust our Maharana, a clever diplomat, knows how to deal with the Emperor. At least here in Mewar, our women avoid forced marriage into the Mughal lineage that they have in the kingdom of Marwar."

"Honor-bound to the dishonorable, a fool's path to safety!" Sardar said and spat on the dry ground in disgust.

"You think Maharana a fool, Sardar?"

"Strong language, brother. What I think? Maharana's honor blinds his vision. He has milk in his eyes. The Emperor cannot be trusted, and yet I fear, neither can our Maharana."

Jaswant felt shocked by Sardar's words. It created a low rumble that rose in him and lodged in his throat. "Our Maharana, a noble Rajput! He shows himself trustworthy time and again."

"Jaswant, you trust with ease. Open your eyes, man."

"You suspect with ease. My eyes are open. What I see in you, brother, alarms me."

"Our Maharana showed himself weak," Captain Sardar said.

Jaswant watched Sardar chew on the sound 'weak', teeth moving under his bushy mustache as if he could rip it apart... like a jackal. "What proof have you?"

"None yet, but I believe Maharana orders his soldiers to the palace for a reason. I believe he intends to pledge troops for the Emperor's invasion of Maratha in an effort to strike a peace of sorts for Mewar, a hands-off agreement with Emperor Aurangzeb. The Emperor will not invade us if we contribute to his Maratha campaign with men – and with unfettered passage through our kingdom."

"Is that so bad?"

"Our fighting units would be spread very thin; Maharana's security, compromised. No, I do not trust the Emperor. His plan spells ruin. I believe he secretly wages war against us now, even as we speak!"

"What war?"

"Think, Jaswant, about the story of the ancient town of Mandore – how we defeated the Khiljis of Delhi."

"Every child knows that story: two thousand five hundred Rajput soldiers concealed in five hundred bullock carts of fodder entered the city of Mandore, massacred the Mughals, reclaimed their stolen land."

"Correct. Mughals have never forgotten that insult."

"Sardar, you suggest we attack the Emperor in his Delhi stronghold?"

"No! He employs a similar tactic against us Rajputs, especially us in Mewar. He enters with his motives covered, not by fodder, but by pretense as our protector. He subjugates us by sending us away, takes our land without a fight." Jaswant watched Sardar chew his lower lip until a thin split oozed blood.

"He has safe passage for his advancing troops even now. Let him take the south, what does it mean to us."

Captain Sardar countered: "And if he wants all of Rajputana? What easier way to obtain our lands than to send the Mewari soldiers to battle in the south and strike a concord with the Rathore clans of Marwar, our enemies. They annex our kingdom, in our absence, rule it for Emperor Aurangzeb as a vassal state. He could have a puppet government in his name and the women of the

Rathore clan to sire half-caste children, further binding the Rathores to his Mughal people. The Rathores would enjoy the Emperor's protection from retaliation by Mewaris – and would also benefit from the bounty of war."

"Brother, Maharana would never go along with such a disaster." Captain Jaswant felt weighed down to the earth, afraid to look up lest he see his brother could be right, a thought too terrible to entertain. He kicked up dust with his boot tip, shifted his weight side to side, shook his head in silent 'no.'

"I have informants watching. He meets with the Mughal Atmed, the Emperor's closest advisor, his vizier – as yet, I know not why. They speak in the palace garden, away from everyone."

"Well, station someone in the garden when the vizier next arrives. In a crawl space behind the terraced waterfall, one could hide unseen."

"What crawl space? To be found would mean immediate death," Captain Sardar said.

"True. Assign a trusted soldier – me. I know a secret passage. Devi and I used to meet there."

"Brother, use great care. We must understand his motive. Keep this between us only. I hope our Maharana is cleverer than he appears. I pray to the gods and goddesses he does not plot against his own people! I have no taste for bringing him down."

"Consider it done, brother. Notify me of the vizier's arrival."

"I meet with the Maharana in the durbar hall this afternoon."

The two captains walked together to the stable. Jaswant studied the palace verandah above where the zenana ladies lounged in the shaded recess of the jharokha. A long crimson scarf appeared from an opening in the marble screen, fluttered in the light breeze.

"You have not forgotten her. She has not forgotten you," Sardar said to his brother.

"How can I? My heart does not allow me. Had I acted swiftly, she would be mine. I should have taken her away. Now condemned to service a man she loathes, she longs for another she cannot have, a prisoner of luxury, not of love.

"She sends me messages. Often I cannot respond for fear my pigeon might be caught by another lady and our love revealed. She wrote she would fight the forces of nature to be with me, yet she feels I would not do the same.

"She misjudges me. I would endure any dishonor to have her – banishment, even death – but I would never endanger her."

"Take care. Your love revealed would mean her death, as well as yours."

"I understand. I shall not jeopardize her. I hoped our love would fade, in these years since her marriage, but I find it stronger with time. Her crimson scarf runs like blood in my veins. It sustains me."

"You should take a wife, have a family. That would change your heart. You must forget her!"

"I cannot!"

"Then suffer. Let village girls quench your thirst. With battle brewing, you may soon forsake this crimson scarf."

Captain Sardar saluted the guards at the palace and marched upstairs to the Maharana's durbar hall, empty except for the sweepers, and continued to the royal quarters. Soldiers at the door announced him.

He entered and bowed to the Maharana, who reclined on pillows, sucked on his hookah, made bubbling sounds. With a wave he swirled the hookah smoke around his head. "Come, Captain."

"Namaskar, Huzur." Captain Sardar bowed and touched the Maharana's feet in respect.

The Maharana twirled his long mustache and straightened the string of pearls at his chest. "Captain Sardar, report on my soldiers' readiness for battle."

"Fit and strong, Huzur, battle-ready. They speak nothing but praise for you and pride for our Mewar land."

"Do they desire combat, or do they grow indolent from women and food?"

"Huzur, I do not believe they desire combat. They are ever ready should you command them to protect our fair land. As to women and food, they have appetites, naturally. Do you desire combat, Huzur?"

"No, yet I may require it," the Maharana said looking down sideways at the pattern on the Persian carpet where shards of light played on the silk in the afternoon sunlight. A raven flew across the balcony, traced a shadow across the white marble floor.

The Maharana choked on his hookah. "Ill omen, to speak of war and see the raven's shadow." He rose to his feet, suddenly sobered. "What do you think, Captain?"

"I think the raven's nest hides in the marble screen near the door: she desires to see her children, Huzur, nothing more."

"Would the raven bring a falcon to protect her children?"

"Only if she knew she could protect her nest by cleverness. She would not leave her young to be devoured by a fierce bird like a falcon. She would dive and peck and lure him away, all the while making sure her young were protected by the strength of palace marble. That honorable path a wise raven would take. She would give her life to protect her children."

"And you, Captain Sardar?"

"Of course, I am a Rajput warrior, Huzur."

"What if that noble cause means much blood spilt... possibly with little gain?"

"A soldier fights for honor, Huzur, for his Maharana, his family, his land. These are noble virtues." Sardar watched the light fade on the verandah and from his leader's eyes. They appeared to grow dark, disturbed, like muddy water pounded by a lashing storm, whipped to sullen, defeated brown.

"Ah, yes, noble virtues. My dear father spoke of these. He, a great warrior, far greater than I. Time brings me a challenge greater: Aurangzeb's shadow falls across our land like the falcon's on the desert sand, moving swiftly, blocking the sun's light. Our land teeters on the edge of darkness."

"Huzur, the Emperor's interest lies in the land of the Afghans, far north. He hopes to subdue the wild tribes there." Sardar could see anguish creep into the Maharana:

he winced as if he looked ahead to distant vistas and recoiled from what he saw – battlegrounds and bloodshed. He turned to face his captain.

"Indeed, Captain Sardar, he does. He also desires to push the empire south, to the tip of India. He looks at the Marathas in the Deccan Plateau as the only impediment in his wide sweep to conquer all of India."

"Then he does not need to worry about our little kingdom."

"He wants our men to help in that effort. I am in no position to refuse him. And for what? For the Emperor to secure passage to the south? He will get passage, one way or another. His vizier soon arrives to discuss this matter. It grieves me."

The Maharana's eyes drifted to the large mural of Rama slaying the monkey god Hanuman. "I feel we may soon be at war."

"Huzur, consider well the request. If our troops go north to fight the Afghans, we will be vulnerable at home. If we go south, the same but worse. His troops move through our land. Offer men for the northern campaign only. Satisfy your obligation. Don't endanger our land."

"And if we refuse the Emperor troops for the southern campaign, will he unleash wrath upon us as he marches south? We are destined to fight, no doubt. Are we destined to prevail? That I wonder."

"Do not speak so, Huzur. We will find a way."

The Maharana receded into hookah smoke and motioned for Captain Sardar to leave. When he reached the door, the Maharana said in a barely audible voice:

"Be alert, my friend, I need all ears."

Captain Sardar nodded and exited the scalloped marble doorway. His sharp heels on the marble floor echoed down the corridor, faded on the grass lawn, followed by the sound of a creaking gate slamming behind him as he walked to his quarters. He spotted seven vultures circling a distant hill. He assumed the tigress had made a kill.

The Maharana commanded his servant to bring wife Devi to him. The servant ran to the women's quarters, roused the zenana eunuch as he dozed in the coolness of the stairwell and ordered him to get wife Devi. The eunuch knocked on the ladies' door. Women rushed to inquire who had been summoned: Devi.

Hearing her name, she approached for the message while the others grumbled and resumed their card games and pachisi. Devi walked through the Hall of Mirrors of the palace and saw her sadness reflected a thousand times in small discs of silver. Entering her husband's chamber, she bowed low.

"Namaskar, Huzur."

"Come in, I need entertainment. My mind is heavy with worry."

Devi joined her husband, sitting as far from him as possible on the carpet.

"You give me sadness, my prettiest of birds. You do not greet me with a smile. Longing rests in your eyes... but not for me."

Devi looked down and gathered her pale yellow silk chiffon chunni in her hands. "I am not sad, husband."

"I know something," he said moving closer to stroke her long hair.

"What, Huzur?"

"Your heart yearns for another," he said, watching her blank expression like a hawk moving in on its prey. "I feel it every time I embrace you, with every caress. You are not mine. Of all my wives, you are not mine, yet you remain my favorite. Why?" Devi's eyes widened to prevent tears from pooling. "I believe this very fact endears you to me. I have everything I desire, except one thing, you, and that one thing gives me purpose. Devi, my unfulfilled quest, my un-won battle. How can a man walk away from such a challenge?"

"Huzur, I have great respect for you. You are kind, and generous, and..."

"And your heart belongs to another. Devi, I hoped to win your affection with affection, but that has not worked. Now I shall win your affection with the truth: the truth about the one you love."

Devi felt the blood rise to her face; a thin bead of moisture blossomed above her dyed lips. "Huzur, I have no other love."

"Silence. Listen. My story may change the way you feel about me and about your affections. Before my dear father died, he requested me to care for you and your family, but especially for you, the girl child. He said our family owed yours a debt of honor. He swore to rectify a mistake."

Devi sighed. Her body slumped. With breath held, blood drained from her face and made her feel dizzy. She shivered with the reference to her mother's shame.

"I have done my duty, both to you and to the son your mother bore from disgrace. He is none the wiser. I have held silence, for your family's sake. My honorable father saw to it that your brother came to the palace and trained in the army – an enviable position for the son of a farmer. My father arranged the tug-of-war championship trials, knowing Sardar had broken all village records in the sport. As the winner, father granted him an army assignment. A good start in life.

"Not long after, when I took my dear father's position as ruler, I ordered Jaswant to join, not out of sympathy, but out of respect for his ability. I knew Sardar had secretly trained him. Now the brothers could provide for the family. In time I elevated Sardar to captain. In this way I could, in some small measure, make right the wrong inflicted upon you and your family. In time, Jaswant earned the honor. Both sons made captain of the royal guard – a rare privilege, especially for a peasant family. Our way of atoning for a dishonorable deed and appeasing Lord Shiva.

"So you see, you cannot be with your love, your mother's son, Captain Jaswant, because no sister lies with her own brother."

Devi buried her face in her chunni and sobbed, blocking her vision of the Maharana with her curtain of thick black hair. "I know the story. I did not know you knew. It is most painful to have my mother's shame spoken of. I know I cannot, and would not, be with my own brother. It is he who is unaware of our kinship. Please keep it from him."

"Wife, I am benefactor to you and to your brother. I treat him with great respect. In my heart I love him as my brother. He serves me well. I ask you to stop withholding your affection from me for a vision of love you will never have. I know you harbor feelings for him even if you deny the dream, an impossible one. I take no pleasure in your mother's shame."

Devi looked up, half-raising her eyes. "Huzur, I... I have known of this since... My mother told me the story as a way to encourage me to accept you in marriage, a way to force me to forget marriage to Jaswant."

With rage in her heart surging like daggers towards her husband, unspoken words cried out in her head: Do you think I can forgive the son of the man who raped my mother and ruined my happiness!

"Devi, if I could undo what was done, I would. I cannot. My father regretted this indiscretion. There is more to it, and less. I have long wondered what you knew about what happened. I felt you knew the story. I let it go at that. By your words today, I realize something. You have not known the truth.

"On my father's deathbed, he gave final decrees, including that your family be cared for. He told me the circumstances surrounding your mother's shame. Devi, my father didn't take your mother. His elder brother did.

"My uncle hated my father because their father favored the younger over the older. The older, heir to the throne, was known for foolishness and excess. My grandfather realized the kingdom would be gambled away if his elder son inherited the title. He sent his elder son away to lead a command against the Mughals. When he returned, crippled from battle, he ate opium to quell the pain.

"From that time on, he grew indolent and untrustworthy. It was my uncle who went to the river in the royal palanquin and spotted your mother. My uncle, not my father, defiled your mother. Jaswant, my cousin-brother, sired by the uncle I hated, for me is still a brother.

"My dear father would have insisted on the child being raised at the palace, had it not been so distasteful to reveal the degradation of a young peasant girl by a member of the royal family. My uncle intended to discredit my father in grandfather's eyes. But to have recounted the event would have only brought shame to the palace."

Devi shook violently. She cried into her chunni, not wanting to look into her husband's eyes. He touched her heart. When she looked up, for an instant she saw the same sweetness in his eyes as in Jaswant's. She felt true affection for him – but the horror of loving her mother's son rushed back and tightened her throat. She spoke with great effort as if cold metal fingers stuffed her words back down her throat.

"My mother, when she visits me here, it must be very difficult for her. We sit in the garden below the zenana. The women look on from the shadows of the jharokha. She speaks of the good fortune of having her daughter so well cared for. She makes some excuse for me to call for Captains Jaswant and Sardar. They greet her with great respect and affection.

"It seems if Jaswant, in his heart, knows – yet he could not. He is so kind to her. She asks him about his parents, their harvest. He asks about her welfare. Sardar looks on with little to say. When she leaves, you send an allotment of millet, lentils, cluster beans, and a pot of ghee for my family. She tells me, 'Devi, your husband is a generous man. Do not blame him for his father's lust. He has goodness in him.'

"Husband, I do not hate you. I am respectful of the honor you pay me. I am touched by your generosity..."

"And yet you do not love me. Is that it?"

Devi remained silent.

"Go to the ladies' quarters. I shall not call you tonight. I shall find pleasure in one of my other wives, wishing she were you. Tomorrow we have a visitor from the Emperor's court. It will be a night of entertainment and feasting. Several of the ladies will attend. If I send for you, wear the peacock blue sari with your pearl tikka and ruby necklace."

"I will do as you say, Huzur. Namaskar." Devi bowed her head. With her hands in front of her chest, palms pressed together, she left him with a prayer.

# CHAPTER 8 – VIZIER'S VISIT

The following morning, the sun rose dull orange through a dust-filled sky. Captain Sardar Singh studied the distant landscape with a seeing lens from his guard post below the Maharana's apartments.

"This wind brings an ill omen," he said, turning to his brother Captain Jaswant Singh.

"It brings no rain."

"It brings a desert rat hungering for food," Sardar said wiping the sweat from the edge of his turban. As he spoke, a yellow cloud took shape in the distance. He grabbed his lens and surveyed it. "Many ride in the vizier's party. The man comes with a troop, not a guard. A diplomatic mission has no need of so many."

"Mughals, they subjugate and show their might to the people of Mewar. Do not worry, brother, they aim at intimidation only."

"I think not, dressed for war, laden with swords and arrows. War elephants lumber along, kicking up dust. I watch them. They watch us. Jaswant, it's no diplomatic mission. I must speak to the Maharana immediately. Remain here, keep watch," Sardar said handing his brother the seeing lens.

Captain Sardar rushed up the steps towards the palace. As he reached the Maharana's door, the guards stepped aside, lowering their swords. He did not speak to them but knocked loudly on the bedchamber door.

"Huzur, I must speak with you."

The Maharana, slow to rise and bleary-eyed after a night with his ladies, opened the door.

"Yes, Captain. Speak."

"Huzur, the Mughal vizier rides with soldiers. Soon he will reach the fortress. Many men, fully armed, battle-ready, plus war elephants. They camp near the sandstone cliffs, I believe."

The Maharana rushed to the window. Without a distance lens he could only make out the dust cloud movement.

"Captain, I know of his visit. He arrives early, true, but desert travel demands the night."

"Why did he not send an advance rider to announce..."

Captain Sardar Singh heard shouting below. Captain Jaswant yelled, "Halt where you are!"

From the verandah the Maharana and Captain Sardar watched as Captain Jaswant drew his sword and approached the rider on horseback. Palace guards surrounded the man. Captain Jaswant ordered him to dismount, held him at sword point.

"There, Captain, you see, his messenger arrives."

"Huzur, I do not trust this Mughal."

"Captain, nor do I trust the Mughals. Nor am I such a fool as to forfeit my kingdom to the Emperor's wrath. A fine line to walk in the desert. I am aware of the danger. I must make concessions to preserve our kingdom. Do not doubt me, I know what I am doing! Do not think I will go unaware into agreement with a man who can dispense with his own brothers, imprison his father, ruthlessly disavow his children, all to secure his empire. No, Captain, I move gingerly, for the sake of us all!"

"But Huzur, there are many kinds of..."

"Remember your position! It is I, the Maharana of Mewar. I understand our situation. For this reason, I will try diplomacy to retain our freedom while the Mughals overrun the rest of India. I do not want to see my people whipped, beaten, killed, forced into servitude as people have been to the north. Do not forget, Captain Sardar, I have seen their handiwork, the earth soaked in blood."

"Huzur, I did not mean to offend you. I..."

A knock on the door ended the conversation.

"Go, Captain, receive the vizier. Escort him to the durbar hall and send for me."

Captain Sardar bowed and departed. After greeting the vizier's officer, he assembled the palace guards, strategically, to await the vizier's arrival. The vizier and three of his soldiers ascended the path to the palace, turned in their weapons and dismounted to follow a palace guard to the durbar hall.

Captain Sardar waved his brother over and whispered, "Hide in the recess of the garden fountain. Meet me in the stables later." He assumed the heat would drive the Maharana and the vizier to the coolness of the garden. After half an hour, the doors to the hall opened. The Maharana ordered tea served in the garden for his guest. The two men walked outside with their guards trailing behind them.

Seated in the verdant garden, water cascading over the marble fountain, the vizier said, "Yours is a most pleasing garden. The Emperor loves the sound of running water. Allah's Paradise, he says, but not filled with musicians. He has no love for earthly music."

"You must send his highness an invitation to join me for a shikar. We have tiger, wild boar, panther, sand grouse, rabbit, whatever his pleasure. My shikars are famous for our Mewari dishes like roasted rabbit in a roti, and my favorite, curried partridge... and a great many others."

"Yes, yes, the Emperor enjoys a good hunt, but at present he is much concerned with the empire, difficulty in Punjab with the Sikhs, an unruly lot, and the Afghans present even more opposition. They are wild up there in the north, savage. In fact, that is the reason I pay you a visit. The Emperor wants the aid of your Rajput warriors.

"The state of Marwar to the west provides soldiers for the northern front, yet you of Mewar have not contributed to the empire.

"The Emperor desires to push south to quell the Marathas in the Deccan, and for this he wants your aid. You will retain your kingdom's independent allegiance to the empire, naturally, in return for your help to extend the empire to the southern tip of India. Everyone profits."

"Does the Emperor require my men for weeks – or years?"

"Whatever time it takes. A quick defeat of the Marathas would mean a quick return for your soldiers. That would suit Emperor Aurangzeb very well!"

"Meanwhile, my kingdom would be vulnerable to attack!" the Maharana ended with a snort ruffling his mustache.

Captain Sardar witnessed the reaction and stiffened. He knew that quick jerk of the Maharana's head, a snort of stifled rage, and wished he were close enough to hear every word.

"You assume the Emperor would not secure your land? An attack on you is an attack on the Empire. You, a favored brother, would lead Mewar, and we, as family, with our Emperor father, would look to the good of us all. Do you not agree?"

"I agree I desire what is best for my people, and for me, as their Maharana. I sit on the throne of my ancestors chiseled from wars against other Rajput tribes and foreign invaders. My Sisodia clan has a long and proud history. I intend to hold my kingdom."

"But your kingdom needs our Emperor's support to thrive," the vizier argued. "On your border the Rathores of Marwar province wait and watch. Should you weaken, they will attack. That you know. With our Emperor to stabilize the area, no need to worry that an individual clan in Rajputana will overrun another, or for that matter, perish.

"It serves the Emperor's interest to have stability in the region. All clans understand this fact. No clan will overstep its boundary knowing the Emperor stands behind the regional Maharanas. The Emperor stands behind those who stand behind him."

"Unfortunately, with my best troops removed, I am vulnerable to attack. Help could not cross the desert in so short a time."

"Happily, the Emperor thought of that concern and appears quite willing for you, Maharana, to retain some of your best men, to which he will add a garrison of his own men while your other soldiers are away."

"That makes little sense. Does the Emperor not need his own men for the push south?"

"He bestows on you a great honor. He acknowledges Rajput warriors as fiercest of the Empire. We need the best men to push south. The Emperor's men he leaves with you are not the caliber of your men. They suit peace keeping – here."

"We should not underestimate the Rathore clan. Since their Maharana died leading the Emperor's troops in Peshawar, much has changed – especially when the Emperor isolated young Prince Ajit and his mother, keeping them in Delhi. Who knows what the Rathores will do to rescue the prince – and crown him."

"And does that resentment exist here also among your people? I believe the young prince's mother comes from your own Sisodia clan. Correct?"

"Yes, that's right. I will consider your proposal, sir," the Maharana said, confronting the vizier's stare with a cool look. "One thing exists that could soften my people's hearts in favor of the Emperor's request."

"What is that?"

"Repeal the jizya tax. It is very unpopular and stirs up resentment. Why should non-Muslim males pay such fines? It seems a punishment for being Hindu."

"Please, Huzur, that is not our Emperor's intention. Those excused from military duty because of their choice of religion, being non-converts, contribute to the protection of the empire from outside invaders. The Emperor has not called for forced conversion, has he? Nor will he. No, it's a simple matter of protection and procuring money for that. Your Hindus take it too personally."

"Let us put it this way: if the Emperor wants Hindu troops from Mewar to help him fight the Marathas, then the males of our state should be exempt from the tax."

"A point. I will pass that along to him. I am sure we can work out an amicable solution."

"The guest rooms are ready for you and your men," the Maharana said. For a split second it seemed to Captain Sardar the wings of a raven spread across the afternoon sky and darkened the Maharana's face. He looked to the sky but saw nothing.

"Thank you, but we cannot stay. I return to Ajmer. We ride in the cool of the night. I would like to leave with your answer, Huzur."

"So soon?"

"Do not underestimate its importance, Huzur."

The Maharana motioned for a servant to escort the vizier from the garden. Ladies of the zenana watched from behind the jharokha screen. Devi turned away and receded into the marble shadows.

"I will send my answer tonight before you break camp."


Captain Sardar approached to escort the Maharana back to his chamber. The Maharana kicked the strutting pigeons, forced them to leave bits of corn the servant had tossed on the grass. Without a word, he marched into his chamber and slammed the door shut before his guard could reach it.

Sardar strode briskly to meet his brother, waiting for him in the stables. He motioned for the stable boys to leave. "Jaswant, it is as we feared. The Emperor demands our best soldiers for the push south. In exchange he leaves a garrison here, for our protection."

"Did the Maharana agree?"

"No. He promised an answer before they break camp this evening. He appears neither a fool, nor strong enough to hold out against imperial forces, and possibly the Rathores as well."

Captain Sardar thought for a minute, his eyes cast up to the right, a tight knot in his sunburnt brow. "We must delay the vizier's parting to find out more about his troops. If we can stall him, we may have time to form alliances with the Rajput tribes and fight as a unified force. The Marathas' leader, Shivaji, died a week ago. The Emperor intends to expand to the south, thinking the Deccan weakened without him. We Rajput clans pose a threat to that expansion if we unite with the Marathas of the Deccan to resist the imperial forces. It is this only that worries him, not the northern front."

"But the vizier leaves this very night for Ajmer."

"Ha," Sardar snorted. "He wants to travel by night to go unseen, not back to the Emperor, but to our neighboring state of Marwar. He plans to foment war against us. We shall track the Emperor's dog and discover how he conspires against us!"

"Will the Maharana order this?" Captain Jaswant said, shaking his head 'no'.

"He will, brother, if presented rightly. I shall say I fear the envoy may be attacked by dacoits who have been raiding caravans, the very ones who slaughtered so many wild boar, spoiling the Maharana's shikars of late. I will offer to protect them without their knowing it, a face-saving gesture for the vizier."

"When do we depart, Sardar?"

"You remain here, in command. The vizier may yet pull some trickery, and as my most trusted warrior, Jaswant, I shall need you at the palace."

"Yes, captain. How many men do you need?"

"Ten only. It should look official to Huzur, but be small enough for us to ride fast, and undetected." A sound outside the stable hushed them. An errant water buffalo knocked over an earthen pot in search of food. "Meet me back here in an hour."

Captain Sardar entered the courtyard below the Maharana's chambers to witness a flurry of activity: servants washing marble floors, lighting incense burners, wiping dust from alabaster pedestals, and watering bougainvillea before the heat of the afternoon sun could wilt them. He knocked at the Maharana's door. A servant led him to the verandah where the Maharana was hunched over a map.

"Captain Sardar Singh," he said without looking up, "I am glad you have come. I was going to send for you. The Emperor's vizier intends to leave this eve and travel by night to Ajmer. Captain, I want you to follow him."

"Rear guard, Huzur?"

"No, unseen. Track him. I do not believe he intends what he says. Captain, the raven perched on my balcony yesterday. I tried to laugh it off, but now I see evil has come in the vizier's form. I believe he sets a trap for our kingdom. We teeter on the metal edge of a snare. Dangerous times. Confide in no one, except Captain Jaswant. I need my most trusted men. Follow the vizier. Send a message, where he goes, who he sees."

"Huzur, why has he come?" Captain Sardar said, assured that the Maharana was not aligned with the Emperor's wishes, but true to his people.

"Aurangzeb requests my best warriors for his push south. That would leave Mewar vulnerable. In exchange he would send a garrison of peace-keepers here, not his most able soldiers... for our protection."

The Maharana rose and paced the length of the verandah. "Does he think me a fool? Anyone can see the absurdity of the ploy. Either he intends to bring me down himself or to allow the Rathores of Marwar to overrun our border in exchange for imperial favors.

"Yet he underestimates the Rathores. True, we have our clan disputes, but they remain Rajputs. Since he imprisoned their heir to the throne, many of them distrust Emperor Aurangzeb. Blinded by his quest to subdue the Deccan Plateau and push to the tip of India, he fails to see how hated he is by the clans of Rajputana!"

"Or, Huzur, he intends to destroy us along with the Rathores, by pitting us against one another. He plays our clan rivalry like a board game. What could suit him better than having our best Rajput warriors, from both states, fighting the Marathas in the Deccan while he stirs boundary war here between us? We would be so weakened, he could do whatever he wants with our lands. It serves him both ways."

"True, he is a cobra waiting to strike. Let us strike first."

The Maharana, his face as hard as the marble wall, turned to his captain. "I may not be the legendary warrior my father was, but I love my people. We cannot fight the Emperor alone, Captain Sardar. He will destroy us, parade our heads on posts as he has done in Shahjahanabad. We must protect our women and children. I gladly throw my allegiance in with the Rathores rather than submit to the Mughal empire. We are, after all, noble clans of Rajputana. Let this be a time to forget our differences and unite! But if not possible, let us settle our disputes honorably – outside of the Emperor's view, between the clans only."

"Truly spoken, Huzur! Your command, Huzur?"

"You and three top officers stand guard at early dinner. I will arrange entertainment. A few ladies, music, dancing. We must detain him as long as possible. Meanwhile send a messenger to the Rathores advising them of what we suspect. I hope he has not yet sent word to them that we plan to attack and annex their lands, to set us against each other. They will greet our messenger with a sword, if we do not reach them first."

"Huzur, what if the vizier does not turn to the west but continues to Ajmer as he said?"

"He will not. The Emperor would not spare even a mediocre garrison of men at this time unless it served his purpose of expansion. The vizier will go to Marwar to secure Rathore support before reporting to the Emperor. Of this I am sure."

"And if he has already secured the Rathores' support, and they are waiting in the desert to assault us?"

"Be battle-ready. We have little time. Prepare your men. Leave Captain Jaswant in palace command in your stead. Send word when you determine the course the vizier takes."

"If to Marwar, what then?"

"Allow him. Our messenger would have contacted them first. They then can hear the plot from the plotter's mouth, thus confirming our message, not confounding it!"

"And?"

"Captain, the vizier must not reach the Emperor until we unify the clans."

"Slay him?"

"No, the Emperor will declare war upon us. Let the dacoits have their day. Notify them the Emperor's men carry gold. That will keep the vizier busy and give us time to organize the Rajput tribes. The Emperor will waste no time in sending men to subdue us. We must be ready."

When a knock came at the ladies' quarters, Mira, sister of the Maharana, walked quickly to open the door. The eunuch spoke quickly, tilting his head side to side like a riverweed bobbing in the current. He requested Mira and two wives to join the Maharana for early dinner, to entertain a special visitor from the Emperor's court.

When Mira closed the door, the room burst into lively chatter and widespread jealousy. The Maharana's first wife, mother of three sons, not invited. She sulked in the far corner, staring out the window. The other wives vied for their husband's affection, thrilled at the infrequent invitations to join him. His favorite wife, Devi, showed him cool affection, if not hostility, yet he always requested her. Yet he had not for this occasion.

During Devi's absence, Mira observed how things had changed. He sought the company of Neelu, a wife of two years, who had not yet provided him a son. She used her wits to secure her position by becoming Mira's closest friend during Devi's absence. Now with the mysterious return of the favored wife, she contented herself with being second favorite, discovering she genuinely liked Devi, and defended her against the insults first wife hurled in anger.

The Maharana showed Mira he held her in high esteem and honored her at every occasion. Mira had studied poetry in the language of love, Urdu, and could recite from memory for hours. In her youth, she had studied the elegant Bharatanatyam dance of South India and often performed for guests. Through perfected movement and rhythm, the dance, invoking the blessings of the deities, ushered the dancer and her audience into the heart of devotion. Her hand movements, fluid and graceful, told the story, yet she knew her eyes spoke of sorrow.

When her fiancée had died at war, Mira felt that her heart was not for loving. She chose not to marry thereafter, but to remain with her brother to manage the ladies' quarters. More than her brother's affectionate sister, she became his trusted advisor. So when Mira greeted Devi's return with joy, not condemnation, the others realized they, too, must pay her the same respect, or risk their husband's censure.

As the women readied themselves, Mira handed Devi the peacock blue sari saying, "It is his favorite. You owe him this on such an occasion. He told me he wants you to join him after the vizier departs."

"I know I owe your brother," Devi replied "always generous to me, and kind." She attached the gold tikka to her forehead, looking at her image in the mirror. "Many would give all they have to know him, to have him look their way..."

"I also owe my brother much. He treats me with every respect. Not all brothers, much less rulers, treat their sisters with kindness. Tonight I represent Mewar with him, an honor rarely bestowed. Show him affection, Devi, for both of your sakes. Make this a good night."

"Possibly he intends to make this visitor your husband, Mira – confirm Mewar's allegiance to the empire?"

"Never! A Sisodia with a Mughal, don't joke so. My brother would never!"

"Well, when did he last request you to dine with a representative of the Emperor?" Devi asked.

"Never. I see. This man must be of great importance. This is a rare occasion, but it is no betrothal. The ladies will be dismissed after the meal, so they may discuss matters of state. No time for eyes meeting.

"But you, no wonder your husband didn't invite you, as lovely as our legendary beauty, Queen Padmini. You would be the ruination of the dinner! If the Mughal decided he wanted you, would you have our brave men fight to their deaths, our loyal wives burn themselves rather than submit to the conqueror? It happened before, Devi, it could happen again. My brother is wise to leave you in the quarters."

"Mira, I am no legendary beauty, yet I am a Rajput warrior! I would take out my bow and arrows and fight to the death!"

"And that, my dear sister, is the reason my brother prizes you above all the rest. In you the glory of the Rajput warrior lives! If only you could give him a son. The other ladies gossip about you, out of jealousy, saying you cannot conceive because your heart belongs to another. Silly women! One conceives in the womb, not the heart. Many children would be unborn if that were the case."

"Yes, Mira, gossip, yet I cannot blame the ladies with precious little to do in the zenana but wait, pamper themselves, and gossip."

"Would you choose the village life, harsh sun on your back and little food in your stomach?"

"I would trade this luxury for freedom to pick berries, grind millet, hunt, bathe in the river, and be with my family."

Mira put her arm around Devi's shoulders. "A peasant in royal attire, not an easy role. Are you so unhappy here?"

"Not so unhappy, Mira, but I feel like a caged bird expected to sing when my throat is full of sand. This life is not mine. I am very fond of my husband; he has greatness. I would not dishonor him, but this life of luxury doesn't suit me. Had I been born of higher station..."

"Please, sister, have no regrets. Your children will be of noble birth. I never understood, until now, the source of your anguish."

Another wife drifted within hearing. Mira cut off. "Well, you will look very fine in this sari. Shall I have the servant weave jasmine blossoms in your hair?"

"Jasmine or acacia, all the same to me."

"Let us take the sweeter of the two," Mira said smiling at Devi. "I prefer blossoms to thorns."

Devi seized her chance to request the zenana eunuch to deliver a message to Captain Jaswant from the Maharana's sister – a note she wrote secretly, sealing it – and pressed it into the servant's hand. It was brief but she knew he would understand her meaning. She simply wrote: *The place.*

After checking the palace walls and seeing all was in order, Jaswant descended the stone steps to the courtyard to meet Devi behind the kitchen quarters that smelled of roasted onion and garlic, cumin, coriander, chili and turmeric, spices that made his mouth water. He skirted servants rocked back on their haunches patting rotis into rounds, placing them on charcoal fires. Cooks scurried from huge metal pot to pot, stirring vats of curried vegetables and meat. Old women ground roasted herbs and spices into aromatic powders and jabbered away. No one noticed him when he disappeared through the small door to the next courtyard.

Jaswant opened the heavy wooden door to the rear courtyard where milk buffalos grazed, tethered to wooden posts. Walking a narrow path past conical mounds of stacked hay, he slipped into a small corridor that led to cold storage rooms under the palace. In the dim light of the solitary candle at the entrance, burlap bags of grain looked like fat old men stacked one on another.

He picked his way along the sacks, stumbling at times on ones torn open by rats, millet popping beneath his boots, until he felt the uneven seam in the wall that led to the dank tunnel. Edging along sideways in the narrow cavity for many paces, his head cocked forward, almost scraping the wall, he came to the small chamber, their meeting place. Devi held a candle by the small altar of Ganesh in this, the only place she could escape the watchful eyes of the other women and the zenana eunuchs.

Devi greeted Jaswant with a silent caress of his forearm. He impulsively pulled her to his chest. She gently pushed him back. In the dim light he knew she saw his sadness. In the dim light he was blind to hers.

"Jaswant," she whispered, "I fear this night. The vizier, I feel he means to harm the Maharana, to harm us."

"I will protect him. Do not worry on that account. We have many guards stationed around the palace. All will be well. The Maharana knows the vizier is not to be trusted. Yet I am unsure if he has a plan as yet."

Jaswant felt his breathing become shallow. "No man shall harm you. On my life I promise you. I am pledged to you, in my heart and in my allegiance to your husband. You are as close to me as my own breath." His voice trailed off.

"I am pledged to you in my heart, Jaswant, as ever."

"Why did you risk calling me here tonight, Devi, of all nights?"

"To ask something of you."

Jaswant's heartbeat rocked in his ears like a frantic drum call. He raised his voice to speak over it. "What can I do for you?"

"Give me your dagger."

Without questioning, he unwrapped the blade hidden in his cummerbund and handed it to her.

"Do you remember how to use it?"

"I gutted enough rabbits. I remember," she replied, securing the dagger in the folds of her sari.

"A man is not a rabbit."

"That remains to be seen."

"Devi, no one will harm you. Take it if you want... but only for confidence."

"I fear not for me, but for others, Jaswant."

Jaswant moved closer. He smelled jasmine flower scent in her braid. He took her hand in his. The warmth brought him sad pleasure. He pulsated with longing. Devi averted her eyes, blinked away tears.

"Forgive me, Maharani, I forget who you are."

"Your dearest sister. You must think of me like that only."

"You know it's impossible for me to think of you like that. Since the famine drove my family to settle near the Meandering River when I was a boy, I have loved you. I remember the first day I saw you. You wore a bright orange sari and silver bangles that ran the length of your thin arms up to the elbow. Heavy silver anklets jingled when you walked. You had the thickest braid I'd ever seen, still do. Once you told me the weight of it gave you such headaches that you wanted to cut your hair and wear a turban like a man. I laughed and laughed, until you swatted me with a stick."

"You remember that?"

"Naturally. I believe that was the very day I fell in love with you."

"Please, Jaswant, do not speak of these things now."

"If not now, when? Do you expect me to go through my life with this burden weighing down my soul? Show me some kindness. Let me explain before I have to hold silence for a lifetime."

Devi nodded.

"You know our fathers bonded like brothers, mine ready to assist yours in planting or harvesting, yours ready to do the same. But as a child it was your mother, her tenderness, that impressed me most. She looked at me with such kindness, more even than my own mother who seemed to prefer Sardar over me. What love my mother had, my brother consumed like a fire, leaving only small embers for me. Yet something haunted me about your mother. I saw it at Diwali and when we visited at Holi to splash you with colors. She seemed to look directly into me and come out the other side, like I held a secret she wanted, or I stored something precious. One day she hugged me goodbye. I looked away, so she would not know I had seen her tears." Devi swallowed hard.

"I wondered at her sadness. One day while harvesting gavarfali, my hands racing to pluck the beans from the vine to fill my sack before Sardar could fill his, I declared to my father that I intended to marry you. I think I was twelve at the time. My father stopped. He dropped beans on the dry earth. He looked at me with a fierce expression. I felt like hiding. He declared I would marry whomever the Brahmin picked for me. I laughed nervously and said, 'Papa, I would never go against your wishes. I know the Brahmin will pick Devi for my wife. We are destined, that is all I meant.' He grumbled, picked up the beans, and began picking again with such fury that he left Sardar and me standing still in the row.

"Sardar laughed. He said, 'I am your elder brother. I came first. If I choose Devi, she will by rights be mine. What do you say to that?'

"I realized at that moment that he must have already spoken to Papa about you. 'Have you asked Papa?' I said. He laughed and said, 'No, do not worry, brother, I am destined to be a famous warrior one day. You can have your wife and your sack of cluster beans. The life of a farmer is not for me. I want to go to the palace and serve the Maharana. I grant you permission to marry Devi. Now do you feel better?' He cuffed me on the back and resumed working. Papa didn't speak to me the rest of the day.

"A week later when I was helping Mother make rotis, I told her about that day. She stopped and said, 'Jaswant, you are too young to speak of such things. Learn to farm and to hunt.' I told her I would, but that I knew Devi was my destiny. She shook me by the shoulders and shouted in a high voice, 'Only the gods and goddesses know what is in store, what joys, what sorrows!'

"As the years passed, I watched Sardar become a man, and I, too, left my boyish ways. He outdid me in hunting, tracking, slingshot. He outgrew me by three inches. People joked that he took all of mother's milk like a hungry calf and left little to me. I found I loved working the land with my hands. He had little use for it. When the old Maharana called for able young men to compete in games, to test who would make a good soldier, Sardar was the first to try. Remember? He beat everyone at tug-of-war, wrestling, running – even archery, although as farmers we only had clumsy handmade bows.

"Sometime later, the Maharana sent word for him to join the army. He moved to the palace grounds. I stayed at home, tended the crops so well that we increased our production threefold. I had a talent for it. Crops flourished at my touch. Do you recall the bullock carts of bricks we ordered for extending our house?"

"Yes."

"I saved for that, to build rooms for us, you and me. When I told my parents that I wanted them to ask your parents for you, they said I had to wait until the building was done, then only. I didn't want to wait, but I obeyed. I had no idea what obstacles would crush my dream."

"Don't think of these things now. It's too late."

"Two weeks later, when I came upon you at the river, you were gathering anise seeds."

"I remember."

"That night when I arrived home, I decided to tell Papa I would wait no longer. He wasn't home. He had taken a load of bajra to the next village to sell. On the very day he returned, Mother greeted me with news that spread like a dust storm in the village: the young Maharana had requested Devi – to join the zenana, as his wife. I tried to find you, to talk to you, to learn if this was true, but your family was nowhere to be seen. Villagers said your parents were sheltering you from curious eyes. Others said you had been taken to the palace at night, never to return. I passed fall and winter in torment. But one day in early spring, I came upon you at the river, by the lotus pool." "Please, Jaswant – stop."

"You were 'watching the lotus flowers', you said."

"That is what I said, not why I was there. I wanted to jump in, end my misery. I thought the lotus flower, even in muddy water, remains pure, so could I be if I drowned in them. Seeing you gave me the courage to beg for help. I would have run away with you, right then, but your sense of honor prevented you. Jaswant, you condemned me to be his wife. I've never forgiven you."

"Devi, not honor, but fear. I knew the Maharana would have you slain for the insult. I could not be the cause of your death. I wanted to steal you away, cross the desert with you, never to return. And yet, it seems you forgot me. You could have run away from your parents to see me, just see me, once, before you moved to the palace. You did not."

"I could not. They watched me day and night after I told them I wanted to run away with you. I refused to marry the Maharana. They tied me to my bed. The Maharana sent a guard to bring me to the palace, at their request. I lived as a prisoner until our marriage, confined to my chamber, watched by eunuch guards. They all feared I would end my life. They didn't realize it was already over."

Jaswant hugged Devi. "I gave up farming to be closer to you. When I first told Sardar I wanted to be a soldier like him, he laughed at me, but seeing my determination, he trained me in all he had learned. I competed in the trials. The Maharana chose me. He liked having brothers in his command. He said it meant we would think alike, show loyalty. Sardar had become the favorite of the young Maharana. I contented myself with guarding the palace, your home."

"My prison!"

"Seven years I have served the Maharana, your husband, the man I once hated, but now respect. I could not now go against him, and I would never stain your honor."

"Even I could not go against him. Much good is in that man, even if I do not love him like a husband. You and I will never be together as husband and wife. I know that. I must be a sister to you. You must protect Huzur from that man, the vizier."

"Sardar and I are aware of the vizier's treachery, as is the Maharana. Do not worry, the palace is safe, you are safe, but keep the dagger for your own comfort."

Devi took Jaswant's hands in hers. "We are as one."

"We are as one," Jaswant repeated, their childhood oath of allegiance, before Devi slipped away into the night.

When Jaswant later made his rounds and looked up, he saw Devi standing alone on the jharokha balcony, silhouetted against the night sky full of stars that spilled across the blackness like shimmering pinpoints of light fighting to conquer darkness. He heard the call of birds whose nighttime warble predicted war.

The vizier, a short, wiry man with a neatly trimmed beard and furtive eyes that flicked around the room like the tongue of a lizard, made no effort to turn when the servant ushered Mira and two ladies into the durbar hall. The ladies remained standing with downcast eyes, heads covered, until the Maharana nodded for them to sit, at a distance. They sat in silence, listening as the Maharana and the vizier exchanged tips on the best way to prepare partridge, the Maharana's favorite dish.

"At shikar I insist on cooking the partridge myself, quite the best in Rajputana."

"Of that I have no doubt, Huzur, since of all the princely states in Rajputana, yours is the best, the most reasonable, and, in the opinion of the Emperor and myself, the most dependable. The Emperor often says Mewar is the state he favors above all, and you, its ruler, of course."

The Maharana glanced over at his sister, turned back to the vizier, and continued, "Take the state of, say, neighboring Marwar – they do not know how to cook with delicacy. They are crude. If a leader cannot conduct shikar cooking with delicacy, how then is he to rule? A heavy-handed method with spices spoils the food – just as a heavy-handed method with the people spoils their spirit. We are warriors by nature, refined by valor and dedicated to the honorable path."

"Quite so," the vizier said stealing a glance at the ladies as he took a drag off the hookah. "Partridge has its place. But could a partridge compete with a falcon?"

"We don't hunt falcon. We keep them as treasures to hunt with."

"No, and why should you? A falcon with its keen sight looks over the land and spies even the smallest movement. It sees the partridge quivering in the reeds. The partridge sees only the reeds. Each is valuable, no doubt, but only one suited to rule, the other to allegiance, as nature intends."

A servant walked in with a tray of roasted wild boar and onion kebabs, sizzling hot on the ornate silver platter. The aroma flooded the room. He set it down in front of the vizier.

The vizier looked at his host through hookah smoke. "It is my belief, for the food to taste best, the first bite must be served by the hand of a beautiful woman. The Emperor insists on this. I think you know of the custom?"

"No, I did not know the Emperor cared for the refinements of a beautiful woman. But let it not be said I treated you ill in my palace," the Maharana said. Mira recognized his displeasure from restrained but obvious tightness in his husky voice.

He motioned one wife to step forward.

The vizier's beady eyes followed her slender hands and gold bracelets that jingled softly while she removed a kebab and handed it to him. He accepted it without looking up at her face. He took a bite. "Good to know the advantageous place to hunt, is it not? Otherwise one wastes time and effort."

"Yes," the Maharana said, his voice sounding tightly controlled.

"Hunting abounds far from here, to the north. I shall send a contingent of soldiers with you tonight to show you the best hunting grounds on your return."

"Do not trouble. I have no immediate need. No time for pleasure of the sort, unfortunately," he said, tracking the young wife's return to her cushion. "Someday I may return with the Emperor for shikar. I enjoy a good hunt, as does our Emperor."

"Yes, few things give greater satisfaction."

"War and women," the vizier said, through a blue smoke haze encircling him. "These noble conquests give great satisfaction."

"Conquer a woman?" the Maharana said, indignant at the vizier's implication. "Unwilling submission, a hollow victory at best."

"But if not willing submission, what then?"

"Walk away, the noble course of action."

"Walk away? What honor exists in that? Can an empty hand feed an empire? Can an empty bed warm the heart?" the vizier said, exhaling and slumping closer towards the pipe.

"Let us not talk of such things around the ladies. They tire of hunting stories... and threats."

The vizier's body tensed, thin muscles along his neck tightening like a bowstring.

The Maharana looked at Mira and requested her to sing a Persian poem. She stood and sang in a high, delicate voice. Notes dangled in the heady air of the hookah and fused with words that lost their meaning. Smoke rose to the ceiling, the vizier's anger drifted. He relaxed into the silk pillows on the Turkish carpet.

In a groggy voice he said, "Urdu, the language of love, a rare pleasure for me. Our Emperor is not fond of poetry and music, you know. He banned such entertainments, yet I have always enjoyed the..." Taking another long draft on the hookah he said, "Please, another. Your voice is the song of Paradise."

Servants brought platter after platter of savory dishes that drowned the room with spices that made the mouth water, but the vizier only picked at the food. Hookah and music filled him. He slumped back, head rolled to the side, mouth slightly open. By the time Mira started to dance, the vizier snored peacefully on the carpet, mustache buried in the cushion. The Maharana signaled the women to exit. Mira tipped her head to Captain Sardar standing outside the door, sword drawn.

Oblique rays of the setting sun pierced the marble filigree, casting long shadows across the floor. The vizier woke up, agitated. Smacking his bluish, dry lips, he turned to see the Maharana seated as before. "Why did you not awaken me?"

"It is our Mewari custom to make guests happy. Your happiness was sleep."

The vizier stumbled to his feet, tugged at his uniform. "You smoke a strong hookah."

"Only the finest for my honored guests."

"I must be away. The sun sets."

"My guards will escort you to the forest's edge. We have a pesky tiger with a love for human meat."

"Thank you, but no farther. I would not want to infringe on your hospitality."

"I would be honored to do so, but at present I am short of guards and require my men to be near."

"Short of guards?"

"Yes, a wedding party. Hindu weddings, they last for days."

"So I have heard. I shall pass along your invitation to the Emperor. We will return for a hunting party someday at his leisure, or you may host him when he passes this way going south to the Deccan."

"I await word of your arrival and will meet you at the border."

The vizier shot the Maharana a sour look and left the hall trying to look dignified, his wobbly gait comical in the Maharana's eyes. "Fool, nor can you walk, nor can you see."

He watched from above while the vizier and his men left the palace grounds, escorted by Captain Sardar and several soldiers. He spotted Captain Jaswant closing the gate. From the verandah the sound of horses' hooves striking the stone path beyond the lower garden faded with the afternoon light.

The Maharana shouted, "Bring Captain Jaswant!" Jaswant appeared within minutes at the door of the durbar hall in full battle gear. "Captain Jaswant Singh, you are commander in the absence of your brother. Position men at the gates. Post sentries along the wall, below and above. Notify me of any movement."

"Yes, Huzur. Do you anticipate an attack tonight?"

"No, but neither do I trust that viper. He incites the Rathores against us. Of that I am sure. They know, as does our clan, it is better to have a strong enemy than a weak friend. The Emperor is no friend to Rajputana, no matter the clan; his capture of young Prince Ajit proves that." Down below in the dark forest, the tigress growled, causing monkeys to screech in terror. "Good, she does not sleep. Captain, let us be as clever as the tigress protecting her cub, and as deadly!"

# CHAPTER 9 – KETTLE DRUM ALARM

Captain Sardar and his men rode unseen behind the vizier, grateful to move beyond the forest. He knew the vizier's party traversing the tigress' domain at night, her favorite time to hunt, had peaked the predator's interest. By the time Captain Sardar and his men entered the forest, she immediately started tracking them, irresistible sweet human flesh. She stalked from behind, leaping on rocky promontories to better watch their movement, her luminous gold eyes her only giveaway. Sardar studied her approach. Tightening her circle around the men on horseback, she roused a wild boar from its hiding place. The loud shrieks, grunts, and growls of the kill rent the night fabric and spooked the horses. Sardar relaxed knowing she would rest before hunting them further.

The soldiers rode out from under the forest canopy toward the distant hills. A half-moon hung like a beaten silver sickle in the sky, throwing mercurial highlights on the scrub grass that poked up here and there among the rolling sand dunes, but the captain knew this terrain. Like a hawk he surveyed it by day to navigate it by night. He had fought on this sand, watched his adversary's blood ooze red and disappear, as if the earth quickly sucked life from the fallen to remain untarnished.

He had assumed he would track the vizier's party through the night and catch them before they woke in pre-dawn blackness, but spotting torches at an encampment in the near distance surprised, and worried, him. He motioned for his men to slow down. They kept their distance, falling back to the west where the firelight disappeared below the sand cliff. He feared the Mughals might circle back toward the palace. With so small a force, what did they intend, he wondered.

He motioned for his men to hurry their pace. From the top of a dune they spotted a larger contingent of soldiers to the north, making for the sandstone cliffs. As they drew closer they saw a camp, secluded, protected by hills on three sides. Sardar whispered to a soldier who rode next to him, "They chose their cover well. No other formation could provide such apt cover for so many." Captain Sardar turned in his saddle to face his men, raised his hand to halt them. "The vizier has no honor. He means to take the palace – that is, after he lures our best soldiers away. They gather for a dawn attack, I am sure."

"Captain, we can defeat them. Let us ride back and gather our force."

"Do you think the vizier came all this way with only what you see? No. Only a portion of his army are here. The others... soon to join."

"We could mount an attack, leave them no time to send for help, slaughter them in camp as they sit planning," a soldier to the rear said.

"I do not think the vizier's reinforcements," the captain said, choosing his words carefully, knowing the weight of them could shock his men, "are in Ajmer. I believe he secured an ally closer, the Rathores. He means to ride to Jodhpur, gather a greater force there and storm Mewar. The imbecile nephew of their previous Maharana now rules the Rathores, the Emperor's puppet. They show proper allegiance to the Emperor, support the vizier's assault on our Mewar kingdom. The puppet claims our state as his, and the Emperor does what he likes with them, and with us."

"Rathores trust him?" a soldier asked, shaking his head in disbelief.

"It is not that they trust him but which plan serves them better. They are fools. Their Maharana did serve the Emperor. In return for service the Mughals stole the young heir, put him under house arrest. Fine payment. Going against us in Mewar provides an opportunity for the Rathores to appear conciliatory, so the Emperor will bring the prince back to his throne, or so they think. In return they assure him that the state of Mewar will not interfere with his push south to the Deccan, nor will our forces support his enemies there. We must have the Rathores of Marwar unite with us Sisodias of Mewar against our common enemy, Emperor Aurangzeb. We have to bury clan rivalry, work as brothers, as Rajputs only."

A soldier asked, straightening the reins in tense hands, "I fear we bring the wrath of the Empire down on our heads, Captain."

"Wrath is here. See the soldiers?" Captain Sardar said and dismounted to pace around his small band of men. "I want one man," he said and pointed. "You, Ummed Singh, come with me."

The soldier, called Scarface, stepped forward. Even in the dim moonlight the scar across his face, forehead to left earlobe and down his neck to the collar bone, remained visible, like a wide path that separated his face into two parts, one distorted, the other not. "I agree, Captain, but remember the Rathores for years did not see the Emperor as enemy. They grew fat on his bounty, married off their daughters into Mughal lineage. Why would they join us now?"

"Honor."

"Captain, they have no honor," snapped another soldier who spat in the sand.

Captain Sardar growled in disagreement. "They need proof – that is all. They must see."

"Sir," offered another soldier, "possibly the vizier travels heavily armed to join the Emperor's push south and came this way only to deliver the message."

"Do you not smell the scent of elephants on the desert breeze?"

"Yes."

"No need to overwork the animals and bring them this far out of the way for a polite visit. They haul cannons to bring our fortress down."

"And the Rathores, Captain, they, too, are camped with the vizier's troops?"

"No!" Captain Sardar said gritting his teeth, losing his patience. "The Rathores have not yet arrived; that is the crucial point. We must strike before they unite. Now, tonight."

The men protested, "We are so few, we will be slaughtered."

"Surprise is the greatest asset in battle! At times it is all you need."

Scarface saluted. "Captain, I go gladly."

"We go together to the north cliff. Scarface, you and Bijay come with me. If we do not return before dawn, the rest of you ride to alert the Maharana – to prepare for war."

The remaining soldiers nodded, stood at attention, and saluted their captain and his companions. The thud of horse hooves on hard-packed sand dissolved in the night. Star clusters looked like droplets of milk spilt across the sky.

Shadowy cliffs of moonlit domes separated by jagged, black crevices loomed large on the horizon. Hearing his horse so winded, Captain Sardar slowed and dismounted, motioned Scarface to follow. Bijay stayed with the horses, on the captain's command, ready to ride and sound the alarm if they did not return by morning's first light.

They scrambled over gullies, scaled boulders, picked their way along rocky ledges and ascended cliffs until they secured a good position from which to see the orange glow of campfires below. Captain Sardar realized a sentry must be stationed on the ridge where they crouched. He pulled a dagger from its sheath, placed it in his teeth, and climbed, motioning for Scarface to swing wide to the right.

Captain Sardar moved soundlessly over boulders, careful not to dislodge stones. He paused in a narrow crevice between two huge rocks. A hail of pebbles fell on his head from above. He sunk further into the crevice. A man jumped from above, landed on the ledge in front of him. Sardar sprang like a lion, brought him down, and ripped a dagger across his neck before the soldier could make a sound. He crouched over his victim, listening. He lifted the body to slide it down into the crevice.

He climbed to the ledge where the sentry had stood guard. Crouched down, he saw below in the firelight hundreds of men, horses, war elephants, cannons, and artillery littering the desert sand. No envoy's detail, this was a fighting unit, battle-ready, he thought.

Sardar knew he looked down on his future – no Rathores, only the vizier's troops. He took no time deciding how he wanted to live. He heard soldiers laugh and talk. The smell of the roasted antelope dangling from spits rose on the night air and made his mouth water.

He heard someone behind him call. No answer. He waited for him to draw closer. Captain Sardar jumped from his hiding place, tackled the soldier, threw him backwards, and slammed his head into the stone. A quick thrust of his dagger ended it. The body convulsed and fell quiet. Another soldier breeched the ridge above. His dark silhouette cut a black hole in the starry sky, briefly. He fell without a sound. Scarface stepped aside and gave the all clear to his captain.

Captain Sardar studied the closest tent, candlelight glowing inside. The shadow of a small man reclined with a hookah, Sardar recognized as the vizier. An armed guard sat out front eating a kebab.

Sardar motioned to Scarface to follow him down. He circled to the right where cliffs rose from the desert floor. The smell of animals grew strong. From the hiding place, they saw horses and elephants hobbled for the night and three sentries asleep by the saddles. They eased out into the darkness and swung wide.

Captain Sardar navigated with the stealth of a nocturnal cat, sensing the gentle rise and fall of the land's windblown mounds, as readable as the stars to him, and as silent. They stood in the darkness behind the vizier's tent, studied the pale orange glow.

Drowsy soldiers, full of meat, lay only fifteen yards from where he and Scarface stood in the blackness. Inside, the low, intermittent murmur of bubbling water could be heard; beyond that, muffled conversation around the fire. The tent guard rose to relieve himself. He walked around to the rear of the tent. Captain Sardar rushed him. With a quick thrust his blade silenced the man. Sardar caught the body before it hit the ground. Scarface grabbed the feet, Sardar the bloody head. They carried him to lower his body in the darkness beyond the firelight.

Stealing back, they listened for signs of movement in the tent. The vizier sighed with contentment and rolled on his side. His breathing slowed. His head shadow slipped off the cushion to the carpet. Captain Sardar slit a gaping hole in the back of the canvas tent with a lightning fast movement, no louder than a sigh. They climbed in, low to the ground. With one movement, Scarface smothered the vizier's mouth with his cotton sash. The captain drew a fatal line across his throat. Blood pulsed onto the carpet. Scarface sucked the hookah to fill the tent with bubbling noise while Captain Sardar carved through the neck, lifted the head, and wrapped it in his sash. They crawled silently from the tent and disappeared into the purple-black of near dawn.

When Captain Sardar and Scarface reached Bijay, they gasped from the hard run. Catching his breath, Captain Sardar commanded Bijay, "Ride to the palace. Inform the Maharana of the troops. Tell him the vizier is dead. I carry his head to the Rathores to secure their allegiance. Tell the Maharana no less than five hundred soldiers camp in the cliffs with horses, war elephants and arms. Prepare for war. I hope to come back with Rathore troops. Huzur must prepare for a siege!"

Captain Sardar and Scarface mounted their horses. The captain secured the bloody head of the vizier in his saddle bag. They rode west to the kingdom of Marwar. To the east the promise of a bloody sunrise grew in the gray of dawn.

They had ridden for two hours when early morning heat slowed them. Captain Sardar knew it was crucial for him to reach the trade route that led towards Mandore to send a message to enlist the aid of the Rathores. Finding the vizier dead would cause imperial troops to march upon the Emperor's command. That would give him a bit of time. The Emperor would divert some of his men from other fronts to take Mewar.

Captain Sardar knew Emperor Aurangzeb would be clever enough to realize the Rathores of Marwar might have assassinated his envoy to prompt the Emperor to attack the Sisodias of Mewar, thus starting clan war in Rajputana. The Rathores could then barter for their young Prince Ajit's freedom, in return for their support of the Emperor's offensive against Mewar.

He understood Emperor Aurangzeb remained intent on extending his empire to the southern tip of India, at any cost, and resented the drain on his resources that battle on the northern front in Afghanistan presented. Rajput clans hated him for banning the construction of Hindu temples, but he ruled as he saw fit. He outlawed the playing of music, a very innocent pastime Sardar thought. What celebration did not include music? Even gods and goddesses loved music. Every Hindu knew that.

The Rajput kingdom of Mewar had openly defied Aurangzeb's predecessor Emperor Akbar. Emperor Aurangzeb had no intention of allowing this to happen again to Mughal rule. Mewar's rebellious nature proved more reason to subjugate them, not less. The Hindu belief that Brahmin priests were superior to all other created beings repulsed him. No, the captain knew the Emperor would not succumb to Hindu defiance, on any front. Of this Captain Sardar felt sure.

Captain Sardar and Scarface dismounted their exhausted horses at a spring where the Mewari aonla bush, with its yellow flowers, existed no more. Here the rough thorn tree common to the Marwar desert flourished. Sardar kneeled, cupping his hands to drink, when the harsh sound of the kettledrum spooked the horses. He caught his animal's reins. A fainter drum answered from the distance.

He drew his sword and stood back to back with his companion to face the enemy. No one came. Again the drum sounded. Sardar swung up on his horse, sword raised, and galloped towards the sound. It stopped abruptly near a clump of babul trees.

Looking up he saw a young boy, drum in hand, clinging to a spindly branch.

"You there, boy, where are the others?"

"You can kill me. I will not say."

"It is true as you say, I can kill you, but if I let you live, if I tell you I am your friend, what then?"

"You are no friend. I do not know you. You ride from Mewar. I see the way you tie your turban. You are not to be trusted."

"You Rathores!" Captain Sardar said. "Go ahead, send your message, beat the drum, tell the troops you are in great danger!"

"I am not afraid to die. I am a warrior," the boy said, hugging the slender trunk as he inched to an upright position.

"And I am not afraid to kill you either, but it serves no purpose. I am here to help you, and your clan."

"How?"

"I have come to warn of Mughal invasion. The Emperor's troops in the desert advance to overrun us all. They camp not far from here on the border of Mewar. Send that with your drum."

"Why would the Emperor strike here?"

"Because his envoy is dead, murdered, his head chopped off, to show you Rathores."

"No one would do such a foolish thing. You lie," the boy said, shifting his weight on the branch, still clinging to the trunk.

The captain reached into his saddlebag and brought out the bloody head, hair matted in brown clumps. The boy involuntarily jumped, almost falling from his perch. He recovered his balance and beat a furious pattern of clangs on the metal drum. Soon he heard an equally grating answer from another drum.

"Good boy. You understand urgency."

"No matter where you run, my clan will hunt you and kill you like a wild boar," the boy boasted from his tree limb.

"And if I do not run? What then, boy?"

"You will die where you stand."

"Good boy, you have the warrior in you." The boy looked down, surprised. "I hope my men show bravery like you."

A harsh series of metallic clangs drew closer, growing louder, more urgent. The boy beat a reply.

"You are unlucky," the boy chided.

"Why?"

"Death runs at you from across the sand. You have no place to hide."

"I do not hide. I am pleased with your news, boy. How many soldiers come to slay me?"

"Many."

"Hundreds? I would not like to think I am worth less than one hundred men," Captain Sardar said, smiling at the boy.

"You will die happy. More than one hundred ride. Look there at the dust."

Captain Sardar and Scarface turned to see a billowing yellow cloud on the horizon.

"That is only the first. The message traveled down the line, even at Mehrangarh Fort they will hear."

"Excellent! I would not have it any other way. A great warrior such as myself must die a fitting death. An honorable one." He shrugged and continued, "Unfortunately, since

your Maharana's death in Peshawar, I know no Rathore
fit to slay me."

"I have heard stories of that great commander Nahur
Khan – 'tiger lord' the Emperor called him. You don't
deserve such a death." A smile lit the boy's dark face,
exposing pink gums pulled tight over milk-white teeth.

"My father will kick your turban in the dust," the boy
said, patting the colorful length of cloth piled lopsided
on his head.

"Not if you do it first. But you would have to come down
here from your perch where you sit like a bird waiting for
rain. Are you not brave enough?"

"I am! I am a Rathore! But I am no fool. You will take my
head off with your sword before I hit the ground."

"I am sure I would not. I never destroy the innocent,"
Captain Sardar said, leaning against the trunk of the tree,
"Boy, can you see the soldiers yet? When will they reach?"

"Soon. Worried?"

"No, in a hurry."

"To die?"

"If that is the case."

"What else?" the boy said.

"What else? Tell me where is your village."

"Not far, not near."

Captain Sardar smiled and walked toward Scarface to
whisper something. With his back turned he didn't see the
boy's foot catch on the edge of the drum as he repositioned
himself on the limb.

The boy tried to break his fall, but the branch he reached
for snapped. He fell with a smack to the ground, followed

by his kettledrum. Scarface lunged forward to grab him before he could run.

"Do not hurt the boy. I would not want the Rathores to say we men of Mewar are cruel to the innocent." On the ground the boy looked smaller and younger, and far less bold, with bloody scrapes along his thin legs and arms.

"Come here, boy. You must be thirsty." The boy swallowed hard. He edged toward the spring, with caution, eyeing the soldiers. "Drink. Drink so you can resume your beating. The soldiers should hurry."

The boy scooped the clear water into his hands and drank and drank. He splashed water on his turban. Hearing the thud of horse hooves, he jumped. "They are here! My father has come."

"Oh, your father is it? I shall tell him of his son's bravery. That is, if he lets me live long enough."

"My father, an honorable man, will give you a chance to speak."

"Will you see to it?"

"Yes."

"If you stand with me, your father will let me speak before he strikes. I have caused you no harm. Are you brave enough to stand beside a Mewari commander when the mighty Rathores storm the sands?"

"Yes, I am brave. I will show you."

"Excellent. Stand your ground. They approach."

The desert exploded with horses and men. The boy shook at the sight of them thundering straight at him. Captain Sardar tipped his head in a sign of respect.

The boy shouted, "Father, Father, wait."

The boy's father, his horse at a dead run, sword raised, swept down on them shouting, "Stand away from my son." He ripped his turban off and threw it at the captain's feet, narrowly missing his son when he yanked his horse around. The horse reared as if to echo the command. Soldiers surrounded the boy and his captors.

Captain Sardar and Scarface stood without flinching, without raising their swords.

"I challenge you to fight me, one on one, for the injustice you have done my son."

Before the captain could reply, the boy held up his arms. "Father, I am not held. I am free. This man asks to speak to you."

"Commander, as your brave son says, I wish to speak only. My companion and I are no match for your troops."

The commander motioned his son over. The boy bolted to his father's side. The Rathore soldiers made a human wall between him and the Mewari soldiers.

"I come for allegiance, Commander, between the kingdoms of Marwar and my own of Mewar. We must unite as Rajputs against our common enemy."

"What enemy?"

"The Mughal emperor. His men camp north of Udaipur, war ready with elephant and cannon, near the border between our kingdoms."

"You lie, there is no such encampment."

"I have proof," Captain Sardar said, moving toward his horse.

"Stop!" the Rathore commander shouted.

"Father, let him show you what he carries, the head."

"Whose head?"

"The head of the Emperor's vizier. I brought it as proof from the encampment where I slit him in the night." He pulled the bloody thing up for the soldiers to view, the characteristic Mughal beard clearly visible.

"This could be anyone, any Mughal."

"Yes. You must accompany me to the camp to see for yourself, south of here."

"Why would a Mughal army be at the door of Mewar kingdom?"

Captain Sardar realized that this commander, at least, did not appear privy to a plot against Mewar.

"Let us investigate. Come with me, so you can alert your superior."

"I am my superior. Commander Ram Singh, first in charge of the Maharana's troops, cousin of the late Rathore Maharana."

"I meant no offense," Captain Sardar said with surprise. "I am Captain Sardar Singh, first in charge of troops for the Maharana of Mewar."

"I will escort you, prisoner and murderer, if that is the vizier's head. I want no part of the hornet's nest you stir."

He motioned his soldiers to bind the men's hands. Captain Sardar and Scarface offered no resistance.

Turning to the boy, Captain Sardar said, "You see, young Rathore, we Mewaris can be agreeable. Greater honor lies in achieving one's purpose than in pride of appearance. I trust you will remember this."

Captain Sardar saw the boy squint, shield his eyes from the bright sun, while his father tied a lead rope to his horse. Sardar gave a sardonic smile when he heard a soldier mumble, "Mewaris aren't fierce."

Over the desert sand sounded the metallic cry of alarm. Sardar strained to listen. He could see ahead that the boy jumped involuntarily hearing the message. Soldiers lingering at the nearby spring bolted into action. One catapulted onto his horse and charged towards the approaching commanders. The boy grabbed his kettle drum and beat it with all his strength.

From the south a drummer relayed the alarm. Rathores drew their swords, shouting the Rathore war cry: "Ran banka Rathore!" We are Rathores, invincible in battle!

To Sardar it seemed from every grassy hillock to every mound of sand and beyond to sandstone cliffs, the desert reverberated with the call to war. The boy beat his drum again and again. The warning grew like a sandstorm overtaking the sun. Enemy troops in the desert.

Thundering hooves churned the morning air. Captain Sardar watched as the boy spotted his father, and beside him the Mewari captain, galloping straight back towards him. The Rathore commander shouted, "We fight the Mughals! We ride to protect the Maharana of Mewar for all Rajputana. Sound the war message for all to hear, son."

The soldiers exploded with "Ran banka Rathore!" and chased after their captains, leaving the boy with one escort to beat the message.

# CHAPTER 10 – FALSE PRETENSES

The Maharana sat with his secret guest in the privacy of his durbar, unattended by guards and servants.

"You took a great risk to reach me in this manner, Prince Akbar. Some three months ago you promised to return in a fortnight. And now you appear like the lake's mist, without notification. How can I spare you from my soldiers?"

"A soldier nearly beheaded me before I could present your stamped letter of passage," the man replied, pulling off the coarse weave tunic covering his fine silk one. "Peasants' clothes, so crude, yet so useful."

"So crude, yet so valuable. It saved you. Upon this coarse weave, an empire rests."

"Upon my father's savagery, his empire built!"

"And you would change that?" the Maharana said, fingering the fine Basrah pearls at his neck.

"Yes. I am a man different from my father. I desire benevolent rule. I will repeal taxes on farmers, allow Hindus their temple worship, even their music and gaiety, and rescind the jizya tax also. These are the ways to win support, not garner enemies.

"I am the namesake of Emperor Akbar, the finest ruler the Mughal Empire has known. I want to build on his foundation, to make the empire a place of peace, a center of learning. My father desires power for power's sake. I desire it for the good it can do."

"As Emperor?"

"Naturally."

"In that case, you should not be here. You should be challenging him at his door, not at mine. I can do you no good."

"I believe you can be of help, you and the kingdom of Mewar, along with that of Marwar," Prince Akbar said and reclined on the cushion as if he were visiting an old friend.

"I want you, both Rajput kingdoms of Mewar and Marwar, to join me to overthrow my father. I know with the support of Rajputana, my victory's assured."

"Your father has more enemies than you might guess. People may consider you as he. He has created a legacy of hatred, just south of here..."

"I know, his old enemy Shivaji. With his death, the Marathas appear subdued, but not for long. As we speak Shivaji's son takes up his father's cause. My father chided him, calling him 'the Mountain Rat,' but I knew he feared Shivaji. He feared him because the Marathas, clever, fierce opponents, stood between him and his push south to the Deccan and to the tip of India, his holy quest.

"He desires to be known as the emperor who expanded the empire to cover the length of India: Alamgir, World Conqueror.

"The older he gets, the more fixed on this goal. He thinks of little else. His desire for glory means my plan will work. I now have the support of Shambaji, Shivaji's son, who awaits our forces."

"And why do you think Rajput warriors will support you, the son of the man who slays Hindu protestors in the streets of Shahjahanabad with elephant stampedes?"

Prince Akbar sat up with a cold-rod spine but continued in a conciliatory tone: "I will ensure your sovereignty. You may rule your kingdom of Mewar as you wish, and the people of Marwar can bring their young prince out of hiding and install him as rightful heir. You may rule as you please, as long as you swear allegiance to the Empire. I will repeal the jizya tax that you non-Muslims bear. Your people can worship freely at their temples just as my Muslim people will go to their mosques.

"You may keep an army, but if I demand, they must fight for the empire. I will pay them handsomely for their service. No forced induction! We will be as brothers in one large house. Naturally, I will be the elder and as such, I shall protect you from invasion and intervene on your behalf when necessary. You will assist me against my enemies. Should you choose to lead forces to expand the empire under my direction, you will be entitled to a generous percentage of the spoils. Your kingdom will grow rich, your people prosperous. You will be well-respected by me, and by my administrators in Shahjahanabad. Our door will always be open to you!"

The Maharana studied Prince Akbar as he spoke, the younger man's eyes flashing with the glory of his empire, and for a brief minute he saw in the prince a glimmer of his predecessor Emperor Akbar, famed for his ability to compromise and inspire to achieve his ends.

Emperor Akbar's clever approach to the Rajput generals, bringing them to his court and making them heads of army units, secured their allegiance. It gave them a vested interest in Mughal success. They profited from the empire profiting. When Akbar allowed the Hindus religious freedom and married Marwari Rajput princesses into the Mughal ruling house, he further cemented the bond. Blood and money.

Yet the Maharana knew Mewar presented difficulty. The kingdom never willingly subjugated itself to imperial rule, as had neighboring Marwar. In fact, this became a splinter between the Rajput clans of Marwar and Mewar.

"In Mewar the siege of Fort Chittorgarh forever lives vividly in the minds of its people and colors the way we view Mughal rulers – adversaries not to be trusted. You know that."

"Yes, yes, Huzur. Let us put the past to rest."

The Maharana continued, "You may remember stories from your youth, told by the evening fire, of Mewari resistance that so enraged Emperor Akbar he laid siege to the fort, knowing Maharana Udai Singh and his son had earlier fled to preserve the royal lineage, yet he decimated the fort anyway."

"Yes, I have heard the story since I was little. Brutal fighting, the fort on the verge of falling, and the royal Rajput women chose valor over disgrace, ritually committing jauhur, burning in a communal fire, dressed in their wedding finery. Their husband soldiers donned saffron tunics, rode out to face the enemy, fought to the death as a true warrior should, not surrendering.

"I have to tell you, Huzur, the bravery stirred my soul... and continues to. I respect the Mewaris."

"Yet Emperor Akbar gratuitously murdered 20,000 Hindus for the insult. Is that how you reward a worthy adversary? Here, Mewari commanders exchange turbans, settle the dispute with honor," the Maharana said, his blood bolting through his veins like a wild horse. He stopped and caught his breath.

"Many Muslims, although they would never admit this openly, Huzur, admired the valor shown by the Mewaris. And yet, you don't always have polite turban exchanges. That I know."

"Continue with your proposition."

The Maharana studied Emperor Akbar's namesake, the young prince fomenting revolt, as he elaborated on the plan to depose his father, thinking of the irony that he, the Maharana of Mewar, upheld the custom of eating off leaves rather than silver platters, a ritual established by Maharana Udai Singh after the tragic fall of Fort Chittorgarh, to honor the lives lost. How, he wondered, does the young prince expect him to listen to this call to glory with anything but disdain?

Yet he listened with quiet resentment and peaked interest, wondering if this astute young man could know of his proposed alliance with the Marwari ruler to rise up against Emperor Aurangzeb.

"I need your support and the allegiance of Marwar," Prince Akbar was saying, smoothing his short beard. "Will you join me?"

"I cannot speak for Marwar. Times have changed. When their Maharana and the Emperor were friends, the Emperor elevated him to a high place of honor in his durbar. Since his death and with young Prince Ajit held hostage by your father, you have much Rathore hatred to contend with. That could work in your favor. Your father fears the Rathores' military power, or he would not have stormed Mehrangarh Fort. Many believe the reinstatement of the young Marwari prince would be a sure sign from the gods that the Emperor will soon be brought down. Have you considered facilitating this liberation as a means of winning support among the Marwaris?"

Prince Akbar's eyes lit up. "True, freeing the heir of Marwar would inflict a double blow to the Emperor: losing the heir and strengthening the Rathores. I could thereby gain their support for his overthrow!"

The Maharana, pleased Prince Akbar recognized value in his suggestion, thought of his cousin-sister, the Mewari princess, mother of young Prince Ajit, to whom he had promised aid. What better aid than securing the throne for her son, even if some minor concessions had to be made?

The Maharana watched as the prince revelled in the brilliance of the new plan he had stumbled upon. The prince smiled and licked his lips – his father's son alright – possibly less brutal, but that remained to be seen. The Maharana chose to use Prince Akbar as it suited him – and as it suited the welfare of the Sisodia and Rathore clans, Rajput cousins.

"And what guarantee do you give if I aid you in defeating your father?"

"My word. Sisodias of Mewar and Rathores of Marwar may live freely, rulers of your own lands. I would require only a nominal tithe for the empire. As I earlier said, should your able soldiers want to join my troops, I will compensate well, and protect you against all enemies."

"And you, what do you desire from such an allegiance, as emperor?"

"Stability in the region, stability in the empire. With peace comes prosperity. War drains resources. My father has ruined the treasury with his wars. I want to build. Let that be my legacy, grand structures fitting our fine Mughal tradition. I would foster the arts and literature and build monuments and gardens of lasting beauty for the glory of Allah, as Akbar did. These will be my contribution."

The Maharana, growing increasingly leery of his guest whose motives appeared as finely woven as the silk of his tunic, yet far less sturdy, said, "I must consider your plan and confer with the Rathores. Give me time."

"I have no time!" objected Prince Akbar. "My father and a small contingent of troops are camped in Ajmer as we speak!"

"Troops in Rajputana?"

"Yes, his vizier rides ahead. He intends to enlist your aid against the Marathas as a ploy, in truth a fact-finding mission to analyze your forces."

"How far behind are the rest of the Emperor's troops?"

"They leave Shahjahanabad soon, one or two days only. Time is crucial. My soldiers are northwest of here in the Aravalli Hills, halfway to Ajmer. We know the vizier's troops travel slowly to scout the terrain for the best march south for the Emperor, and the best attack route in Rajputana to suit his plan! Think well on this. Time to unite! You could sit beside me at my durbar – an honor not to be taken lightly!"

"Yes, Prince Akbar, not to be taken lightly."

A hard knock made the door rattle. Captain Jaswant Singh shouted: "Huzur, forgive the intrusion. I must speak with you!"

Alarm in his voice made the Maharana stiffen. Had this clandestine meeting been a clever ploy? He called in his captain before Prince Akbar could object, or cover his finery with the peasant robe. When Captain Jaswant saw the man, his eyes flickered, but he said nothing.

"I must speak to you in private, Huzur," Captain Jaswant said, ignoring the man so conspicuously uncomfortable in his presence.

The Maharana motioned for a guard to watch the door. He marched down the hall, whispering to his captain. A heavy teak door slammed, the loud thud reverberated down the marble corridor, growing louder as it slapped stone walls, muffling their conversation.

Captain Jaswant spoke in hushed, hurried tones. "A messenger came, the officer, Bijay. He had ridden with Sardar. Huzur, troops gather in the desert. The vizier travels with cannon and war elephants. Captain Sardar came upon them. The vizier, a spy, came to assess our fortifications and readiness for battle."

"I have no fear of the vizier – a snake, yet a small one."

"The snake came with war elephants, artillery, hundreds of men."

"I am aware."

"Huzur, Sardar killed the vizier, carried his head to the Rathores to prove the Emperor's treachery. As I speak they ride together, so the Rathores can see the troops gathered in the cliffs."

"Rash man! Your brother brings the Emperor's wrath down on us too soon!"

"Huzur, my brother – your Captain – did what he thought necessary. If the Rathores do not stand with us, all Rajputana will fall."

"Make ready all troops. Fortify the walls. Bring out the cannons. Prepare for siege. We stand and defend."

"Yes, Huzur. Immediately."

The Maharana spun hard on his heel and strode back to the durbar hall without further word. Entering he saw Prince Akbar, the lowly peasant, standing alone.

"Did you know of this? You came to distract me before the siege?"

"What?"

"The vizier's troops camp in the cliffs north of here! The vizier came yesterday to speak with me, and you today. I should slay you here, now," he said pulling the dagger from his cummerbund.

"Wait! I came separately, unaware of the vizier. Why should I risk my life when I could attack you with my father's troops?

"The vizier came for a different reason. The Emperor must have sent him to soften your defense, distract you, while his army marches from Shahjahanabad. I see his plan. He had not told me. He trusts his vizier only.

"Months earlier he intended to send me to subdue you, yet he did not. I wondered at this change. The vizier has long suspected me of plotting against my father, even when I did not. His accusations turned my father away from me, his own son. Together they planned this. If my father suspects me of treason, he also marches to destroy my forces here in the desert.

"I ride alone, as a peasant. My own men do not know where I go – safer for me and for them that way. One cannot say what one does not know.

"Huzur, I seek your allegiance to defeat the Emperor's troops here in Rajputana. With the Rathore and the Sisodia clans united with my troops, we will win. I have already forged an alliance with the Marathas. I have Shambaji's word. He will unite with me against my father. The sun sets on his rule. A new era of peace and prosperity awaits. We must defeat him before he reaches the Deccan Plateau."

"Prince Akbar, summon your troops!" shouted the Maharana. "Show me your loyalty. Attack the vizier's troops before they reach my fortress. When I receive word from my captain of this, I shall send my best men to aid you against the Emperor, then and only then. If no word comes, I shall hunt and defeat you, here in Rajputana."

"Huzur, I am not here to fight you but to defend you only. Let me prove this. I depart to destroy the vizier's troops. In return, do you pledge allegiance to me as the new emperor?"

The Maharana nodded in agreement, thinking it a broken promise already. "Go, an escort shall take you to the forest boundary. I prepare to defend my people against imperial troops, of any banner." The Maharana opened the door to see Captain Jaswant poised, hand on hilt, lion-ready to spring.

"Captain, send two men to the forest boundary with our guest. Report back to me."

Captain Jaswant nodded and walked the peasant down the corridor. From the verandah the Maharana watched his palace fortress come alive like a rain-soaked anthill, people scurrying back and forth carrying heavy bags of grain from the cellar granary to upper storehouses, elephants straining against leathers to haul cannons into place along the wall, kitchen servants carrying huge terra cotta vases of water on their backs from the lower courtyard to upper ones, eunuchs setting aside supplies for the women's siege quarters nestled in the heart of the fortress, soldiers cleaning their muskets, sharpening their swords and daggers.

The pounding beat of the naubat drum interrupted the metallic morchang, jaw harp, and haunting sarangi's strings to sound a call to war. Iron-spiked heavy gates slammed shut, huge metal beams locked them in place. Banners of Mewar fluttered along the hundred-foot ramparts. The Maharana's peregrine falcon sailed the wind, its shadow darkening the balcony, omen of impending war. Courtyards, usually a sunny place of enjoyment, groaned with the sound of armor being hoisted on man and beast.

The Maharana's chest collapsed with a heavy sigh, his peaceful world dissolving before him. From the main entrance on the north through Bari Pol Gate, throngs of worried villagers came seeking shelter within the walls, women carrying children, men carrying weapons, daggers, muskets and spears constructed from farm tools. With them came farm animals laden with bags of grain, legumes, spices, and family valuables. The Maharana knew his queens and children prepared for war, the dark prospect of his death unnerving them. The thought of their ritual self-immolation brought him greater sadness than his own death.

The Maharana glanced at the painting on the wall: Krishna and the Gopis. He admired the timeless joy of the blue-skinned god playing a flute for his ladies. He envied the serene garden, their happy smiles and simple pleasures.

Turning from the mural, he marched to the jharokha on the southern side of the fort. He saw servant women dip their jugs into the large wooden waterwheel pool and hurry to the zenana. The Maharana thought: Bathing at a time like this!

Servants crisscrossed the marble courtyard where he and his women celebrated Holi every spring, throwing colored powder on each other to symbolize forgetting previous enmities.

He recalled his first Holi with Devi, how the powders stained her, made her look like a fiery goddess with red tresses and a blue mane that reached to her knees. That suited her. She had never lost her wildness, an animal incapable of being subdued – the very trait that made her irresistible to him. She could only be admired.

In the interior of the fortress, thick walls protected from view a honeycomb of rooms – the queens' quarters in war. Tall, powerful eunuchs with swords at their sides would guard them to the end. For the guards, as for the entire fort, it was do or die to protect the women and children. In the Maharana's world, surrender didn't exist.

From the jharokha above, the Maharana heard the high-pitched birdcall he knew. Devi. Looking up, he saw her wave her chunni in the breeze. He motioned a eunuch to fetch her, surprised that she had not yet gone below.

"My favorite wife, you have come. I thought to secure a peaceful life for you here, a life of protection. Now I find the opposite."

"We prepare for war, against whom?"

"Mughal troops. The Rathores are on the move as well."

"Do they conspire against us, Huzur?"

"That question remains. I believe not. I await Captain Sardar's return. He only can advise me. The desert flows with rats! But trust a rat? That is my dilemma. Prince Akbar and his troops wait in the desert. He vowed to join us against his father's men."

"You spoke to him? The prince came here?"

"Yes, disguised as a peasant. He has come several times over the last few months. He asks Mewar to support insurrection against his father. He swears the Rathores of Marwar support the rebellion since he vows to restore young Prince Ajit to the throne."

"But Emperor Aurangzeb's troops number 180,000 or more."

"Yet the Emperor's force is spread thin, some on the northern front in Afghanistan, some in Punjab where the Sikhs give trouble, and some fight the Marathas in the south, while others search for the Rathore prince in Marwar, and a contingent hold Shahjahanabad.

"According to his own son, the Emperor approaches from Ajmer. Mughals everywhere, and now, at our door appear the vizier's men. Battle consumes the Emperor, yet he desires to rule the world. His vizier, whom you saw at lunch, lies dead – beheaded – in our desert, his men ready to attack our kingdom."

"The vizier, beheaded? Who managed to?"

"Captain Sardar. Not the best course of action, unleashing Mughal wrath on our heads."

"Why did he? Without your knowledge, Huzur, very unlike him."

"I do not know. He should have reported to me. I await his report."

The Maharana thought Devi had swayed into him, rested on his chest, like a woman would in times of fear, longing to be cared for, protected, and cherished by her husband.

She straightened up, looked down at the pebble in her sandal, kicked her foot, and stepped back. She tossed her hair behind her shoulders, and looked into her husband's eyes.

He saw a fierce narrowing of her almond eyes, dark and unfathomable like a deep well. The imagined softness, his wish, vanished in rock hard daylight, and with it, his understanding of her.

"Let me fight. I am the best archer and rider here. I beg you, Huzur, release me from the zenana. Let me guard the walls."

"I cannot. You may take up arms – for the zenana. Protect the ladies, if it comes to that. I pray it does not."

Devi paced, the vertical line between her brows now a crevice in her painted saffron bindi. "How far away are the imperial troops?"

"I do not know until a messenger returns. Several hours, a day at most. Fortress gates are secured. From the upper wall I saw only dust in the air, nothing more."

The Maharana took Devi's hands in his, placing them between his. He looked into her black eyes.

"Such spirit. My tigress, you must be strong for the zenana, particularly for the children. If the fortress falls, and I am slain..."

"Do not talk of it, husband. You will vanquish the enemy." The flood of warmth from Devi's hands soothed him and reminded him of their intimate moments.

"If the worst comes to pass, my queens will place their handprints on the fortress wall, and commit themselves to the funeral pyre. I cannot bear that."

"I know, but duty and honor dictate it. I honor you, my husband."

"I know, have long known, I do not own your heart. Your sense of duty dictates your actions only."

"Huzur, but I do love you."

"Not the love you feel for your brother Jaswant."

"You know, Huzur, I cannot, will not, act on that. We have affection, nothing more."

"Devi, I see your sadness. Your destiny is yours alone, but one thing I can do is something you must not oppose or lament."

"What, Huzur?"

"I denounce you as my Maharani. You are no longer my wife."

"Why, why are you doing this? I have not betrayed you. I have honored you. I have even come to love you. I never insulted your goodness, your generosity. I have honored you with my body and my loyalty. You dishonor me. Why?"

"To save you. You will not burn on the pyre. I cannot die with dignity knowing such beauty and joy for life is extinguished because of me. I took you from the people you loved, plucked you like a beautiful flower, and placed you here, in this palace that became your prison – your only joy the village boy you loved, standing guard below your chamber. Possibly it is weakness on my part, but it gives me consolation to know that my death is your freedom."

The Maharana knew what he proposed had never before happened. A dutiful Rajput wife committed sati upon her husband's funeral pyre, the only honorable thing to do, and gained great reward in the afterlife.

He knew Devi would do it, yet at the same time, he knew at age twenty-four she could start a new life, she so full of spirit and strength, far from Mewar. She could leave her past behind. That he desired. That gave him hope to face the Mughal invasion.

"Huzur, do not talk of such things! You will not die. Our fortress is strong, our men valiant. Do not worry yourself with ill thoughts. The Emperor has grander plans to expand his empire, and we do not stand in his path in Mewar."

"Not yet, but the time draws near when Mewar will attract his attention and wrath. He crushes those that oppose. I say again, I divorce you. You are no longer my wife. In front of a witness I shall repeat my promise and so it is done."

"You cast me out, in shame?"

"I cast you out!"

"I would starve, Huzur. I would have to live on the streets, condemned to servicing men's pleasures. No one would house me, the discarded wife of the Maharana. No one would feed me. If you care so little, let it be done here. Draw your dagger, slay me quickly!" Devi shouted at him, reaching for the dagger at his waist.

The Maharana grabbed Devi by the wrist to subdue her. "Devi, this is no punishment but my weakness only. I cannot see the only woman who brought me true joy destroyed – because of me."

"You will not see it. You will die first."

"If they breach the fortress wall, all my thoughts will be on you, your destiny. Let my death be noble. I could not face the gods with anything but shame, knowing you died in sati!" the Maharana said, looking into Devi's sorrowful black eyes, tears like points of light, a desert starry night.

For a few seconds Devi looked into his eyes. He sensed she looked through him. He felt her anguish and her love. She dropped to her knees, grasped both of his hands, and placed her forehead on his palms.

"Husband, let me do my duty to honor you if the time comes. Do not deny me."

"Devi, do you know why I have loved you even more than my first wife, mother of my son, heir to the throne of Mewar, more than all the mothers of my children? You who haven't provided a child?"

"No, Huzur, I do not although I have wondered why you chose to spend so much time with me when the other queens vied for your affection, and I... I shunned it."

"I have loved you, love you now, in a most special way for two reasons. One, your heart has never been mine. And two, you were condemned to this life by your beauty. You did not choose that, you did not choose me. For these reasons you have been more honest, more forthright, more exciting, and more vexing than any woman. I have loved you because you are free, like a wild horse running across the desert sand. You cannot be tamed.

"I was once like you, before I discovered the harness of leadership and tasted its metal bit. You remind me of what I have been. If you were to die, the best part of me would die as well, the part I want to live on beyond my body's death. If a man hasn't lived well, he cannot expect the gods to greet him with joy. By saving you, my spirit will be strong, my misdeeds forgiven, my future incarnation elevated."

Devi considered her husband's words. "I understand now," she said, rising to face him. "But denying me is my death sentence. No one will touch me. I will be an outcast. I have no skills, other than hunting – no way to clothe and feed myself, no place to live. I would rather join the flames than suffer for your love!"

The Maharana embraced Devi, wrapped his arms around her and pulled her close. "I shall assign my soldier to guard to you. I will give you enough gold and jewels to feed you for many lifetimes. I would not cast you out to suffer. Captain Jaswant will guide you from here. Follow the gypsy caravans, cross Marwar, travel on to Sindh, start a new life with the one you love."

"Huzur, your concern has turned to cruelty! You are my husband!"

"Yes, Devi, I am your husband, but I am not the one you love. Jaswant has that good fortune!"

"Do not speak so. My love for him is like sister for brother. I am and will always be faithful to you."

"This I know, and I could continue like that, but my love compels me otherwise. Desert sands shift beneath my feet. We have little time. You must leave. I set you free."

"I can never be free! My story follows – and would cause my death. No woman of value would ever leave her husband, especially a royal husband. People would stone me in the streets."

"Hear me and leave." The Maharana remembered the first time he saw Devi, how captivated he felt by her youthful beauty, how repelled he felt by her Vaishyas caste, farmers, so below him. Rajputs favor marrying up for women and since she would not be the first wife, or even second, he knew his father would consent, thinking the farmer girl a pretty addition to the zenana. He recalled his uncle's fierce rejection that day. He learned of her family tragedy, and now must explain it to her.

"Don't! I know what you want to say. I refuse to hear of it again."

The Maharana stroked Devi's hand to console her, feeling the chill against his flesh. "No, dearest wife, you must hear. I set you free."

"Please," she pleaded, wiping the tears from her eyes. "I know of my mother's tragedy."

"I cannot make wrong right. I cannot undo your mother's shame. I regret that. I can, however, and now must undo my shame. I have hidden something from you, something

I never thought would surface. You see, these seven years have been my happiest, watching you in the zenana. I looked to your youth for courage and strength."

"You, Huzur, why? You are not so much older than I."

"Your strength of body and mind, your quick movement, you, steeped in valor. The Rajput warrior shines in you, more than in me. I watched your coltish ways grow into steady power. I desired that strength and thought to have it by having you. But your heart remained with the one forbidden you, forever unobtainable, hidden. Correct?"

Devi looked down and whispered, "Yes. But I learned to love you."

"Listen now, hear me. I deceived you, I thought, to save you further disappointment. Devi, the child born to your mother from her seduction is not who you think. The boy child, villagers presumed stillborn to your mother, whisked away by the midwife, raised by another, is not Jaswant but Sardar. Sardar, your half-brother, son of my uncle.

"My father had the midwife place Sardar with a peasant woman to wet nurse, a long ride from the palace. The boys, her son and Sardar, grew up together. The family moved the year of the great drought. Many moved at that time. My father gave them a small parcel of land to farm, not far from your parents, near Meandering River. He did this so your mother could watch the son she could not acknowledge grow up. Yet she mistook the two and thought Jaswant hers."

"I am not Jaswant's sister?"

"No. Neither does Jaswant have royal blood. Captain Sardar carries the lineage of Mewar in his veins: your brother, my cousin. My own son, too sickly and too young to rule in my stead, will have Sardar as his advisor until the boy is fit to rule."

The Maharana watched Devi's face sink in, the softness of her cheeks collapsed into caverns. Her bright eyes filmed over. He felt her withdraw into herself, pull back her line of defence – her belief in her husband's goodness – to surround her heart with a barrier of stone as real as the palace walls. He realized he had lost the one thing she had given him, not love but respect. He saw her jaw tighten.

"Huzur. You will rule for a long time. We shall fight to preserve you."

"Devi, I lived for years unaware of your family. And on father's deathbed he asked if I knew of a bastard heir hidden away. I confessed my old nursemaid had spoken of it. I thought her mad.

"Father instructed me to show the child mercy and kindness. My life depended on it, he said. He recounted the story, how uncle had ridden that day in the royal palanquin, a weak man fond of hookah and women, and took a beautiful peasant girl.

"Some weeks later the royal astrologer pointed out an evil conjunction in the family sector of father's chart. He advised father to make pilgrimages, give alms to the poor, and consult the holy man at Eklingji Temple. The old priest told him to care for the son of his brother, yet my uncle had no son. Father relayed the priest's words to my uncle. He laughed through a veil of hookah smoke. Father smacked him. That's when he recounted the meeting.

"Father then arranged for a gypsy midwife to discover who in the neighboring villages carried child. She visited every expectant woman in the coming months but befriended only one, the peasant with sadness in her eyes, your mother.

The gypsy revealed the Maharana had commanded her to take the child. She assisted your mother at birthing time and whisked the baby away, declaring him stillborn, to be safely raised in secret. Father's last words to me were 'Care for the boy. Save yourself.' That boy is Sardar."

"At the death of my own beloved father, I learned the truth. On his deathbed he asked me to forgive him. He asked whether I had heard gossip of a peasant woman he forced whose bastard heir was hidden away? I confessed an old nursemaid had spoken of it. I remember I thought her mad and ran her out of the palace.

"He said he had not wanted to speak of the tragedy earlier to me. He explained my maternal uncle had forced your mother. He rode in the royal palanquin that day. My uncle, a weak man, overly fond of hookah and women, saw his chance with a beautiful girl and took it. My father, shamed, kept the secret buried. He arranged for a gypsy midwife to aid your mother. On his deathbed he told me to care for you and your family and atone for the shame, lest a curse befall our lineage.

"My cousin-brother, Sardar, will rule in my stead, if needed, until my son is able to assume the duties."

The Maharana sighed and felt an embankment deep in his chest cleave open, bringing him relief. "Devi, you finally know the full truth. No longer duty-bound to me, no need for jauhar upon my death. I command you to leave."

"But, Huzur, the shame. I am in your zenana, a wife. No one will believe this story, nor hear of it. I cannot, will not, reveal it. My mother suffered in silence. It would kill her, now, to make her shame public... and my father. I would never dishonor them so."

"Agreed, so you must leave in this time of mounting confusion. We prepare for war. You and Jaswant disappear. Any story can be told later of your deaths. Only your family will know the truth."

"How? Jaswant will not forsake you, Huzur. He would never leave with an enemy nearing. Neither would I!"

"He will when I command him. He cannot refuse me!"

"He would not refuse that order, Huzur. He would do anything for Sardar, and for you."

Devi looked at her husband. He knew she saw the sadness in his eyes, not knowing if it were for her, his kingdom, his son, or his brother. Her silence conveyed everything – and nothing.

"Please, see Mira before you leave. She loves you. Do not tell her of the plan."

"Yes, Huzur."

The Maharana watched the uneven rise and fall of her breath with deep, erratic exhales that made her shoulders twitch. He murmured, "The old Brahmin once told me only in losing love do you find it. Like a flower's scent, love retains its sweetness if left alone."

"Huzur?"

"All along I wanted to control you, to make you love me. I enjoyed your opposition – even, at times, your disdain. You, the untamed. I took great pleasure in trying to tame you to the ways of the zenana. In the process you became not a conquest, but something far greater – a treasure, one

I would be content to have, however short the time. And I have.

"But the old Brahmin also warned me of this day, saying there will be a tumultuous battle. I will suffer great loss but from an unexpected source will come help and from a woman will come victory. Devi, I believe you are that woman. My victory depends on your release.

"Huzur, I..."

"I make ready for battle, but first the scribe must note my decree."

The Maharana shouted at the closed door: "Guard, fetch the scribe."

"You are a good and generous man, one I honor. I..."

A knock at the door interrupted her. The scribe walked in, bowed to the Maharana and his Maharani.

"Take due note, scribe, of this declaration: I denounce Maharani Devi as wife and queen. I command she leave my palace immediately, unharmed, never to return without my request."

The Maharana watched the scribe's hand shake as he wrote the declaration in Hindi, black ink flowing across the page like the marks of a bird taking flight. He handed the stiff, cream-colored paper to the Maharana for signature and pressed the ruler's stamp into the ink to sanction it. His downcast eyes said everything. In one quick calligraphic moment, Devi had been stripped of honor in the eyes of the people. Royalty had never dismissed a queen. Such punishment surely meant a terrible injustice had taken place.

With her husband's blessing came his curse. He realized no decent person in Mewar would ever look upon her with favor again. She had been cast out. Her enemies in the zenana would assume her willfulness had finally proved too much for their husband. 'At last he saw the folly of making a peasant girl a queen!' he could hear them whisper. The Maharana knew Devi realized the one to miss her would be his sister Mira, the only one whose good opinion Devi cared about.

After the Maharana dismissed the scribe, she said, "Will you tell Mira the truth? I want one person to know I am not what I appear when the gossip spreads. She, at least, should know me for who I am."

"Yes, only she I shall tell, a wise and loving woman who, in her heart, will hold a candle for you, as I hold a torch."

"Thank you, Huzur."

"Go. Ready your bags. Travel light, on horseback. I shall meet with Captain Jaswant. A zenana eunuch will take you to him in the forest. Make sure no one follows. Ride hard to the west, skirt the Thar Desert, go north along the Indus. You will not encounter troops that way."

The Maharana kissed his wife. The taste of her salty tears lingered on his lips.

# CHAPTER 11 – THE BOAR HUNT

The zenana quaked with fear. Wives prepared to move into the underground chamber. Mothers with children had already left. Devi felt relieved she didn't have to look at the face of her nemesis, the Maharana's first wife, mother of the heir to the throne, a sickly boy with large doe eyes and a sweet but weak smile. Devi never wished her ill, yet she watched Devi's every movement.

Devi knew she did this not to monitor her activities but to try to understand why her husband chose a peasant girl to shower his affection upon, one so clearly below her own station, one so lacking in grace of movement rather than her...elegance. What pleasure could he have found in a girl of no breeding?

Devi had never produced an heir, something the Maharani had done within the first year of marriage, something she took every opportunity to remind Devi of. Devi had never shown proper respect. She would laugh, showing her teeth. She smelled of the stables, yet the Maharana indulged her love of horses.

For some mysterious reason the zenana could not fathom, she wore little or no jewelry unless he commanded her to, a sign of worse than peasant blood, a sign of disgrace, a willful attempt to lower her husband in the eyes of others. Surely a woman so ill-versed in the womanly arts of allurement would be repugnant to him, yet she was not, as all the zenana knew. Of all, it was she the Maharana prized most.

Devi suffered for his attention. First wife could never forgive her. She told Devi she was determined her son would not follow in his father's folly. He would have a proper queen, one who knew her place, one who paid particular attention to her royal mother-in-law, one who did as she was told, produced many healthy sons, and kept her husband from making the same error of judgment his father had made.

Devi felt no remorse in leaving the zenana. She gathered her rough weave tunics, the ones she used for riding, and jodhpurs. She stashed them in her leather saddlebag. She carefully wrapped the jewelry given her by the Maharana in a length of cotton, knowing it would feed her and Jaswant for a long time. Had he commanded her to leave it, she would have, but she felt grateful he had given it.

Devi realized a young wife was watching her, gathering her things at the same time. Devi assumed the girl thought if she were to die, she should look the part of a king's wife. She grabbed her gold bangles and anklets and put them on, fastened her ruby earrings and necklace, and admired herself one last time in the mirror.

She looked at Devi and smiled shyly, lowering her chin and tilting her head to the side. Devi acknowledged her with a compassionate smile... and silence.

Devi strapped on her leather boots and stored sandals in the saddlebag. She took her wooden hairpins but placed the jeweled ones on her bed, wanting to leave something of value behind to prove she had been an honored queen. When she saw the young woman admiring the emerald and diamond pins, she walked over to her.

"Sister," she said, holding out her hand, "these are my most beautiful hairpins. I want you to have them."

The young woman, Geeta, the Maharana's most recent wife, looked at her in wonder. She accepted the gift. She spoke, clearing her throat, forcing the words out.

"Thank you. I will treasure them and remember your kindness. You have never mistreated me like the others. I was scared. I did not want to leave my parents. I always felt close to you although I never approached. You see, like you, I come from a humble family. We are landowners and farmers, not nobles. The Maharana honored us by requesting me, yet I have been with my husband very few times in these two years. I fear he does not favor me. I have yet to produce children for him."

"Your time will come. You are young."

"Sister, I fear my time is over."

"Do not fear so. Your husband will protect you. An honorable warrior and king, he will defeat the enemy and take good care of his wives and children. I trust in him completely."

The girl looked down and her cheeks, once pale with fear, the color of sun-bleached bone, ripened to a healthy blush.

"You honor me, sister."

"Honor your husband."

"I will follow your example," she said, not lifting her eyes.

Devi put her hand on the girl's shoulder. "My example is not what it looks. In all things I do honor the Maharana. Remember that. I wish him every happiness."

"Of course, sister, we all do."

"Hurry down to the cellar. Have no fear. Our ruler will be triumphant. Soon you will reside here in the zenana."

Devi smiled and returned to her packing. Geeta threw her things in a bag and left with the eunuch escort for the underground chamber. Devi looked outside the door. All the eunuchs were helping stock the women's cellar with water, food, and personal possessions. The zenana door stood unguarded, but she knew her escort would soon arrive. She grabbed her saddlebag and descended the back stairs, down to the garden. A peacock paraded, his tail fanned out in brilliant turquoise feathers with indigo eyes. Devi smiled. The bird strutted with self-assurance, as if his world was as always an adjunct to his beauty. He didn't turn towards Devi. She slipped into a rock tunnel that led from the living quarters to the stables, a secret passage unknown to the other ladies, but one she had discovered early on – her place to cry. Later, her place to meet Jaswant for stolen minutes in private conversation. Now her place to meet, not her half-brother Jaswant but the Jaswant to whom she could express her love, without shame.

The coolness of the tunnel made her shiver, but she knew her action, leaving a life of luxury and protection for a life of hardship, travel, passion and disgrace chilled her more than the stone walls. She welcomed the challenge... but with some remorse. She found the tunnel more constricting the farther she went from the palace. Devi estimated where it wound past the Maharana's morning tea garden. She imagined him sitting there from days long past. She avoided jagged rocks in the rough ceiling, inched sideways, both hands gripping the uneven wall and followed the curve left towards the place where she could again stand upright.

In the confined darkness, she heard her uneven breath. She panted from fear, not exertion. She hadn't used this tunnel in many months and when she had, this narrow segment always made her uneasy. Confinement, she dreaded. She splayed out her left hand along the wall and touched damp rocks. She knew it couldn't be too far. Someone grabbed her. No one spoke. She felt a small hand squeeze hers.

"Sister, let me go with you," a shaky voice whispered in the darkness. "I fear to die on the pyre! I am eighteen only. I know you are escaping."

Devi growled, "You cannot, Geeta. You would shame your family and bring death upon yourself."

"I take the chance. My parents died last year in a terrible fire that swept our farm. I have no family to shame."

Devi's heart sank with Geeta's words. "You would dishonor your husband so?"

"Sister, you know love, the love of another while married to our king. You think the zenana hasn't gossiped about you? Ever since I arrived, I felt kinship to you, to your suffering. I admired you, tried to be like you. I tried to love our husband. He has no love for me. I was breeding stock, sturdy, healthy, like a Brahma cow only. Yet my womb did not agree. After a few months he tired of me. He has not called me to his bed in this last year. I live with women who ignore me, or worse. They order me around like a servant. Even my beauty fails me – my thick hair is brittle like dried millet stalks and my complexion is like overripe fruit with brown spots."

"You are a beauty, Geeta. I am sure the Maharana will return to your bed and give you a child. Stay with him. Honor him."

"Like you?"

"No! Your destiny is not mine."

"My destiny is not to die on the pyre of a man I fear and do not love."

"Where is the honor in you, Geeta?"

"I gave up that idea. I am a farmer's daughter. I can sew. I can make a living at labor. I can survive."

"In shame."

"Shame? An excuse, being too weak to try. I have no one to protect, no one to consult. People look upon me as they choose. I will wear shame like a new sari. Please sister, take me with you. Leave me at the first village. I ask that only."

"Can you ride?"

"Well enough."

Devi wanted to leave her, but she knew she could not since Geeta posed a liability to her own freedom. "If you fall, I will leave you there in the sand."

"Yes."

"We will meet my friend and travel together. I will call you 'sister.' Never use our proper names or say where we lived."

"Yes, sister."

"If you die, that is your fate. You are no concern of mine. Understand?"

"Yes, sister."

Devi worried over this twist in her plan, another knot in her escape rope. She hoped for no more. "Stay close, don't speak. Follow me," she said, inching forward. "Are you sure no one saw you enter the tunnel?"

"Yes. Everyone stockpiles the chamber for siege. I brushed my footprints from the dirt with a dry branch, something you had forgotten to do."

Devi looked at her with surprise. "You did not see the eunuchs?"

"I saw them, hauling sacks of grain from the granary. The weight pressed them over to the ground. They saw nothing other than their own feet."

The two women picked their way along the tunnel to an opening where a dim light outlined black statues. The rhythmic plink-plink of dripping water and the odor of sun-scorched grass mingled in the dank atmosphere.

"We wait here."

Devi slumped against the cave wall. Half an hour passed. She straightened. She heard someone approach. A man's silhouette pressed into the gray distance. He cooed like a pigeon. The sound seemed to float down the rocks and touch her face. Devi cooed in return. Jaswant walked forward but stopped abruptly, sliding on loose pebbles.

He sounded like an animal when he growled, "Who goes there?"

"Me, Devi." She heard him draw his dagger from its sheath. She continued to approach him, wondering if he had heard her. Geeta clung to the loose cotton at Devi's back.

"Halt."

"Jaswant, I had no choice," she said, coming to an abrupt stop. "Geeta, the newest wife, came also."

Jaswant, ordered them to step forward into the weak light. When they reached him, he stood poised, dagger in hand, sword drawn. Geeta trembled. Stifling tears, she bit her lip, inhaled in spurts, and said, "So sorry."

"Why have you come?"

"To escape death. Please, sir, let me travel with you to the first village only. Leave me there."

"Jaswant, we must. Yet two missing wives attracts notice even now."

Devi and Geeta hurried to follow Jaswant from the tunnel to where two horses stood tied under thin shade trees. Jaswant helped Devi mount. Geeta stood, unsure how to climb up behind Devi. Jaswant grimaced at Devi and interlocked his fingers.

"Hold on to the leathers, step on my hand with your left foot, throw your right over the horse's back." Jaswant's upward lift caused Geeta to overshoot the horse's back. She slipped but grabbed Devi's waist and righted herself. She leaned forward and pressed into Devi's back, clinging like a baby monkey to its mother.

"Loosen up. I can't breathe. You won't fall."

Jaswant untied his horse, mounted, and they bolted from a standstill to a canter before the girl could reply. Devi felt her ribs being crushed and wondered at the strength of the skinny girl. With time Geeta loosened her grip, seemed to find her balance. They rode at a fast canter until they reached the sparse woods that separated the western border of the palace grounds from the hills. Jaswant looked at Devi. She saw apprehension etched in the furrows of his brow. He reined his horse to walk.

"Let's let the horses breathe a bit. You two get down. Stay with the horses, Geeta. Devi, walk with me."

Once out of earshot, Devi said, "I will split my food with her. We'll leave her at the first opportunity."

"It isn't that, Devi. My brother, Sardar, I did not see him before I left. I fear for him. The land is alive with troops like a disturbed anthill, not only the vizier's, more Mughals as well, led by Prince Akbar. The Emperor means to crush Mewar kingdom into submission from east to west. My brother and my king need me."

Devi sat stunned at his words. "Jaswant, we are... Our chance, our dream of freedom."

"I know. But I am no coward – you know that."

"I do. No one would think that of you."

"Everyone would. Just look. Attack imminent, I disappear. What would you call that if not cowardice?"

"But you do it for me."

"Yes, for you. I will continue until you take refuge among the hill people, or in a village. Then I return to fight for Mewar. Whatever punishment comes to me, I will protect my brother, our Maharana, our way of life," Jaswant said and walked back to his horse.

Devi felt her world swirl in the tree shadows like a covey of ravens. This, she thought, is not my dream. Living free of the palace without Jaswant – a curse. She made no reply, only shook her head side to side and pursed her silent lips. She and Geeta climbed onto their horse. Jaswant turned, kicked his horse, and they rode west following him. The slowed pace of Devi's fatigued horse marked time with her sinking heart. The day's heat peaked and gave way to a chill dusk. Weary and barely able to grip the reins, Devi continued with Geeta slumped against her in a swaying sleep.

"She is exhausted. I also," she said to Jaswant. "Can we stop for the night?"

Jaswant looked at Devi. She knew he would understand her expression, even in dim light. She turned away. Had she given up her way of life for nothing? She knew he must turn back. What if he did not come for her? What then?

She knew by returning, he could cover his absence. What about her and Geeta? Even if they returned now, the wives would never accept them, even if Huzur did. They had deserted their husband while he prepared for war to defend them. So great the dishonor, they would be poisoned, maybe struck by a cobra placed in their beds. As good as dead now, she thought, yet Geeta rested like a warm, heavy blanket on her back.

"Devi, we have to move on, travel by moonlight. I want to take you as far as I can."

"Before you leave me."

"Yes, before I leave."

They rode slowly across the undulating hills until they reached a broad valley that spread out below them like a large dark hand reaching with fingers of vegetation that traced underground springs. "Not many hours until dawn. We must sleep a bit, let the horses rest."

They found a sheltered place near a rocky outcropping by a spring where they tethered the horses. Jaswant unstrapped a satchel from his saddle. The moon, a transparent wafer, glowed ivory on the hills across the valley. He handed bits of roasted meat and rotis to the women. The food revived them.

"From the palace kitchen? Clever, Jaswant," Devi said, sadness flowing in her voice like water over rocks, turning, twisting, disappearing into deep recesses. "You should sleep, leave by first light. You could reach the palace by evening. No one will question."

"Have you forgotten one thing? Your husband sent me on this mission to take you away. By returning, I fail his orders."

Devi turned to look at Geeta, whose eyes were wide with surprise.

"I am doomed either way to dishonor, but my heart tells me it is more noble to fight than to cower in the hills, hoping to be taken for a gypsy. In times of peace, Devi, I could endure the shame, but now with so much at stake, I cannot. I will return to the palace. But I will come back to find you, wherever you go."

"I will come with you."

"No! Nor will Geeta. There would be no way to save the Maharana from disgrace if we all three reappeared at the same time. It must look as if you two left on your own."

"So the dishonor is all ours? Is that what you want?"

"You are women, not warriors. Later, after the danger passes, you could return and ask for forgiveness, if you choose. You would be forgiven. Not me – a man, a soldier,

Huzur's Captain. No Rajput forgives cowardice, least of all Huzur."

"Leave before dawn, Jaswant. We will make our way west to the River Indus. I will not return, nor will the girl," Devi said, looking at Geeta's thin, rigid face illuminated by firelight, its pale yellow hardness like ancient stone. Geeta turned away from the light, nestled under the stiff horse blanket and fell into a deep sleep. Her gentle snoring made stars swell and contract in rhythm with her.

Jaswant wrapped Devi in his arms. They lay under the mirrorwork sky, each silver dot a reflection of their love and heat.

Devi stirred but did not rise when her horse whinnied to Jaswant's disappearing in the purple light of early dawn. She fell back to potent dreams. The brilliant, rising sun raced across the valley and touched Devi with a hot hand. She sat up, rubbed grit from her eyes. She felt her heart, heavy armor, render her immobile. She wondered whether she should have followed Jaswant, to serve her king, her husband, and died fighting beside her love – but the young woman asleep near her, too young and unskilled, would have perished.

She knew she must put Geeta's safety before all else, leave her in some village where she could survive. She looked over her shoulder at Geeta, who roused only to turn over on her stomach. Devi nudged her.

"Time to go. Soon the sun will scald the ground. We have little water and no food. Get up. I will saddle the horse."

Geeta said nothing. She ambled away to squat before returning to Devi, already mounted on the horse.

"How do I get up? No one to help me."

Devi took her foot out of the stirrup. "Put your foot in. Grab the leathers, here. Pull up. Swing your leg wide. Don't kick him in the flank."

Geeta tried several times but stumbled backwards, collapsing once in the sparse desert grass. Zenana life had weakened her peasant girl arms, something obvious to Devi. Geeta, a small woman, no match for a warrior's horse, with little physical skill, more a doe than a lioness, made Devi realize the futility of the approach. She dismounted and made a step of her interlaced hands to hoist the girl up. Geeta righted herself in the saddle.

"Now move back behind the saddle. Keep your weight centered on the horse's back."

Geeta inched back and over the ridge of leather to sit above the horse's flank. Devi went to the side of the horse, stretched her right foot up to the stirrup, pulled her left through a gap, and leaned forward over the horse's mane to wiggle her left leg over the horse's neck and settle into the saddle.

They rode at a slow pace for hours. Devi dozed, almost slipped off, but she woke up and grabbed the horse's withers to balance. Geeta began pinching Devi when she felt her list to one side or the other. Geeta's weight pressed Devi forward in the saddle when she dozed.

Devi studied the terrain. The horse picked his way over uneven ground that stretched out to the west where mirages danced on the dusty yellow-brown parched earth and broke into horizontal waves of pale blue sky.

Hours later Devi spotted a village. Its image flirted with them, rising, falling, disappearing, and rising again. A child ran out to greet them. Devi heard excited voices cry, "Gypsies! Gypsies!"

Kicking her leg over the horse's withers, Devi dismounted by the well but left Geeta on the horse. A man approached, dagger drawn.

"Namaste," Devi said. "We mean no harm. We need to water our horse and stay the night. We leave in the morning. Can you help us?"

"Where do you go?"

"To Sindh."

"You travel a long way. Why women alone? Your home?"

"A village near the Meandering River in Mewar kingdom. We traveled with gypsies, going north. The men would not leave my little sister alone. I feared for her safety. We set out on our own."

"Your family, your men?"

"Us two only, daughters of a poor farmer. Father died recently. We have no one to care for us. We go to find work. My sister, an expert tailor, and I – I work with leathers – horse leathers, and gear."

The old man patted the side of his turban in disbelief. "A woman doing such work? Where did you get such a fine horse?"

"I won him in a contest in Mewar."

"What kind of contest?"

"Hunting – boar hunting."

"I know the Mewaris are brave, but a woman bringing down a wild boar? You lie. Only royals hunt."

"I do not lie, Ji. The Maharana hosted a hunt. He permitted chosen peasants to attend the opening competitions. I won a spear throwing game, so I earned the right to hunt that day. If you or any other man of your village challenged me on a bet, I would accept. And no one will be the wiser, way out here. One who eats boar doesn't talk. Agreed?"

"What would be the bet?"

"Supplies, food for a week, lodging for this night."

"And you, what do you offer from your side?"

"My horse."

The old man's eyes gleamed. He studied the horse, checked his hooves, rubbed along the muscular neck and hindquarters. He sent a boy with word for the men to gather in the village center. He studied the women. They backed away from the water. The man ordered Geeta to dismount. Devi shook her head in refusal.

"Why does she not get down?" he said to Devi.

"She does what I say only. When we make public a declaration of our bet, she will."

Devi saw people seeping out of huts and gathering together in the small village center. When the old man arrived, walking beside the beautiful horse, he announced the terms of the proposed bet to the amused men, stunned women, and inquisitive children gathered there. They ambled closer to look at the women with the fine horse.

"Let the afternoon heat die," the man shouted. "Then we go to the grasslands. I pit my son, our best hunter, against you," the old man said with a craggy smile.

The young man, no older than twenty, stepped forward from the crowd to nod in agreement. He did not look directly at Devi. She pierced him with her gaze, analyzed his ability as a good runner and wondered how accurate his arrows would be. He stole quick glances at the woman still seated on the magnificent horse. Geeta's eyes remained glued to her sandaled feet, as Devi assumed they would.

"I accept this challenge."

The father said, "We must have proof this woman tells the truth. Soon we shall see what she can do in the hunt, but what about the sister? Can the tailor really sew?"

Hearing this, Geeta lifted her eyes. "Yes, sir, I can."

"Then give her cloth. Let her make a tunic for my son in exchange for a fine meal and a place for her sister and her to sleep tonight. When my son returns from the hunt dragging the boar, we all dance and feast, and the horse is mine."

Devi nodded to Geeta. "Yes, sir, I accept."

Devi added, "But when I return first from the hunt with the boar, I do not want your village to suffer. We feast just the same. The remaining roast meat I take with me."

The old man scowled at her vanity. His son smiled and said, "Agreed. Go to our house to rest until the day's heat passes."

The old man called him over. "Son, sharpen your weapons. No need to go home when you have work to do. I will take them."

"Yes, father."

Geeta dismounted, trying to look casual, and tripped on something in the path. She looked back briefly. The young man watched her. The interchange did not go unnoticed by Devi who felt it too, the admiration, and smiled. At that moment, she realized she had found the perfect place to abandon her sister.

She addressed the old man in a kind voice.

"Ji, yours is a fine village. The people are strong, that I can see. You show my sister and me great kindness by taking us to your home."

The old man's weathered face brightened with a wide, uneven smile. "The thing to do only, let you rest before you lose your horse."

"I imagine you fair in all things, especially in keeping a bargain."

"Yes. I come from a long line of honest Rajput farmers. We protect our women and our land. We honor our children. Is it so different for you?"

"No, Ji, it is also how our family raised us. Sadly, you do not find that everywhere, especially, I am afraid to say, with the Rathore clan."

"Do not judge them. My wife is Rathore and Bhil. I am Sisodia. The border of Marwar is not far from here. You find the two clans mix easily, only our rulers and nobles do not. We are all Rajputs!"

"Ji, I have a request. If I win the challenge – and I will – instead of supplies, I ask that my sister might stay with you, live in your village, for a week or two, while I travel to the pink city. She could earn her keep. It looks as if you have no tailor."

The old man harrumphed and smoothed his turban.

"Our tailor died some months back. His son takes no interest in the trade. Instead he became a weaver.

"Yes, we do need a tailor, but you should not leave the young woman alone."

"Can she not stay with you?"

"No. An old aunty, all alone, might take her in, as long as she does not have to feed her."

"My winnings will provide for her, and she will make her own way from sewing."

The old man squinted against the afternoon sun and studied Geeta. "How old is the girl?"

"Just eighteen years, and with no living parents."

"If she had a father, she would be married by now. Without a dowry who would take her?"

The girl hung her head. Devi said, "Father had, long ago, come from a wealthy farming family. She has a dowry. I have kept it for her."

"Is that so? With a dowry, and with no parents, you would make the arrangements? It is too late for you, sad to say. Your father should have at least provided an arrangement for you before his death. What are you, some twenty plus five years?"

"Very close. And indeed he did. I married at her age. I am now a widow. My husband died fighting the Mughals."

"You, then, should be honored, your husband a hero. I would be most happy to provide for the younger sister of a warrior's family, on my honor. The Emperor taxes us, the weight of an oxen cart on my head. And still he offers no protection from dacoits from across the border."

"You need protection?"

"You can never trust a Rathore, especially so close to the border, but I do not say this in front of my wife. Just yesterday we heard the cry of war drums off in the distance. Nothing came of it, but in these times we have to remain alert."

"Yes, these are dangerous times. I have heard imperial forces gather somewhere northeast of Mewar."

The old man whispered to Devi, "The Emperor's army camps in the Aravalli Hills, searching for the Marwari heir to the throne, I believe. The gypsies told us. They passed last week, tried to steal a camel from my neighbor. The entire village ran them off."

The old man turned to Geeta. "Look up, girl."

She raised her face but kept her eyes down. He studied her face. "She has strength and determination. I can see her Sisodia fire. What else can you do, girl?"

"Sewing best. I also sing and dance."

"Everyone dances. Sing."

Geeta started a Hindi love ballad, anklets jingling with her dance steps, eyes flickering side to side, her head synchronized with graceful hand gestures, while her fingers traced a lyrical design in the dry desert air. Her voice, a melodious breeze, soothed Devi's heart and uplifted her spirit. She knew she had found Geeta a home – and a husband. The old man grinned. "She must sing for us tonight."

Devi looked at Geeta's nod of consent and understood it to mean more than singing. Devi breathed a sigh of relief. "My sister is very special. No harm of any sort should come to her." Devi motioned for Geeta to walk ahead.

The old man took her meaning and threw his turban down in dismay. "You question my honor?"

"I do not insult you, Ji, only warn you. I saw the way your son looked at my sister. Is he married?"

"No. Please forgive him. I, too, saw. Her beauty... but he is a respectful boy. Nothing will happen to your sister. This I swear. Your sister remains safe with us."

"I think she would be safer married."

"Naturally, but since she is not, my wife and the old aunty will never leave her unattended. You have my word, on my honor as a Sisodia."

"Would you consider my sister for your son?"

"Without a dowry? I am sorry, we are not wealthy. We look to his wife's dowry to increase our holdings, not lessen them. A camel, a buffalo, at least would be needed."

Devi withdrew a gold necklace from the pocket of her tunic. "You could buy a camel, a buffalo, a horse, a plow, and three years' seed with this. I offer this, our family treasure, for my sister's dowry."

The old man reached for the necklace. He held it in the palm of his hand, studying the warm, gold metal. He tossed it up and down. He bit a link and made a small indentation. "Pure?"

"As pure as gold gets. Worth years of your crops. Think of it."

"Why sell her off? You want to be rid of your sister for some reason."

"No, Ji, I want her to be happier than I am. My time has passed. She nears the end of her prime marrying years. She deserves a chance in life. I see you are a good family, your village strong, your people kind. I think your son would make her happy. Plus, she endangers me on the road. She does not hunt or shoot. She cannot protect herself. I cannot protect us both."

The old man's brow wrinkled. The sun's glare seared his black eyes. He closed them while he considered Devi's words. "Let us go to the temple and pray, ask the sadhu to give his blessing."

They caught up to Geeta and steered her away from the houses to a small shrine of Goddess Lakshmi. An elderly sadhu in a dirty loincloth got up from where he squatted in the shade of the plastered dung-and-straw wall. The farmer put a paisa in his prayer bowl and mumbled a prayer. The sadhu smeared orange tikka paste on their foreheads and chanted a prayer.

Devi and Geeta didn't understand the villager when he spoke a local dialect to the sadhu, but they watched the holy man straighten the woven necklace across his bare chest. He regarded the women with a critical eye. He grumbled. Devi understood displeasure. He pointed at their sandaled feet and spoke rapidly.

The farmer turned to Devi. "Sadhu Ji wants to know why your feet are not calloused if you have been traveling."

"We have been on the road for a short while only. We worked in a village close to Udaipur after father's death, in a cloth shop."

He translated. The sadhu continued his dialogue with the farmer.

"He wants to know if you had religious training."

"Yes. We went to temple, observed holy days, offered pujas every morning. In fact, coming here is an answer to my prayer."

When the farmer translated, the sadhu smiled, his dry lips cracked and stained red from chewing betel nut pan. He said something more to the old man before again squatting in the shade of the mud-wattle shrine.

"He says he must cast her chart. Can you pay for it?"

"Yes," Devi said and produced a silver coin from the concealed pouch of her tunic.

Geeta's eyes grew wide with fear. Devi thought understandable, but she had no faith in the old sadhu as a true seer. He would not discover Geeta's secret. Geeta reached for Devi's arm to stop her, but Devi turned and asked, "When did mother say your birth time was? Oh, yes, I recall, three in the morning, seventh of Bhadra, 1661, in Mewar kingdom, village on the Meandering River, near Udaipur. Your chart was cast at your birth but burned in the fire. Remember?"

Geeta nodded, her relief evident, the information... false. Devi, Geeta and the farmer left the old sadhu, who instructed the farmer to return for a reading later, promising as a special favor he would put aside all other work. For this favor the farmer praised the old sadhu to the women on their walk back to his small house, calling him a 'most generous holy man'. Devi smiled knowing the silver coin bought the service, no favor needed.

When they reached the hut, the farmer's wife pulled out two charpoys for the women to lie on under the skimpy shade of the courtyard acacia tree. Eager to hear her husband's news, she dragged him into the hut after putting out a pitcher of water for the women.

"Devi, how could you lie to a sadhu?"

"Easy. He probably doesn't know how to cast charts. He is a simple villager. He liked the silver coin. He won't go against us. He will see you are not cursed, or at least he will say he sees, and that is all we need."

"But sister, what will my husband think on our wedding night? You know of what I speak."

"He will think what you tell him to think. A trusting boy, a good one. You had a bad accident, fell from a tree as a girl. You bled. Tell him before. He will believe you. In fact, even better, tell him as soon as your chart is cast. He sees your beauty only."

"He does like me. I can feel it. I have never felt that before. He looks at me with the wide eyes of someone looking at a goddess."

"Unfortunately for you, you came to the zenana so young and with so many before you. You had no time to see yourself for yourself. The farmer boy sees you – not just your outside – but you, inside. I sense that about him. You will be happy with him. Your life will be good."

"We must wait on the sadhu's chart. He could change everything, run us out of the village."

"Trust me. You will marry before I return."

"I want you here, my only family. My sister must attend to bless us, or the villagers will talk, even think I am cursed."

"When I leave, I make no promises, other than that you will have an ample dowry. I will try to return, but if I do not, enjoy your situation. You had no future at the zenana. Now you will have a life. And Geeta, hide the jewelry I saw you take from the zenana. Keep it safe. Say I gave it to you if your husband questions – your family legacy, for your daughter."

"Thank you."

Geeta threw her arms round Devi's neck like a child and kissed her cheek. "I pray the gods keep you safe, give you success in the hunt, and in love."

"No one is a better huntress. I know the boar is mine. I must rest, the light grows weak."

Devi turned on her side and fell asleep in seconds. Geeta remained awake, lost in daydreams about the farmer's son. When the farmer's wife roused them two hours later, a feeble breeze stirred a slight coolness. The farmer's wife rattled on about a coming storm, but Devi merely nodded in agreement to appease her. She asked Devi to go find her husband. Devi sat up, straightened her hair and tunic, and walked out to where the old sadhu, the farmer, and several men gathered by the well. Their excited voices fell silent when she approached.

Devi said, "You wanted me?"

Without looking at her, the sadhu seemed to study the space to the right and back of her, as if he expected something to lunge at him. He spoke in hushed tones to the farmer.

"Sadhu Ji completed the chart," the farmer said. Devi waited in strained silence. The others would not look at her. "Your sister, she has luck, four healthy sons. My son Kunal makes her a good match."

Relieved, Devi said, "Good. I want my sister to be happy."

"She has Bhil tribe in her. From her stars sadhu says you are different, her life easy, yours hard."

"He saw me in her chart?"

"Five times."

Devi's mind raced back to recall everything she had heard about her cousin-sister whose birth information she had given as Geeta's.

"Have you knowledge of your stars?" he wants to know.

"No."

"Your parents would have asked a Brahmin about you."

"Yes, they did, but the fire... With their deaths we lost everything. I only remembered my sister's by chance. Mother had talked of it before the fire."

"Sadhu Ji says he will cast your chart for a small fee."

"I have no need. My husband is dead. Thank him for the service, but it will do me no good."

"From what he says, from your chart, you face many enemies."

Devi felt exposed and uncomfortable. She remembered her cousin-sister. When she last saw her, they were not close. Devi had moved away. Yet in childhood they were like sisters, even lived together at times.

"Sadhu Ji, the person, how do you know it refers to me? Why would I show up in my sister's stars?"

The farmer translated for the old sadhu. "Your constellation, eldest, first-born female, stars show many things."

His words triggered a memory that surfaced from dark water in Devi's mind, a day when Devi had come into the courtyard where her mother and her aunty sat grinding corn into flour.

She watched her mother roll the stone, break kernels into yellow bits. She heard her say, "Such shame! Our poor family. You should have had first a son to guide her."

"What, Mother?"

Her mother looked up at her standing there barefoot, dark braids speared by bits of dry yellow grass. "Cousin-sister Pooja, she has gotten herself into trouble, stole a horse, ran away to Aravalli Hills with Rajput soldier." At this Devi's aunty burst into tears, stopped her grinding, and covered her face with a chunni.

"To marry?"

"No, to fight. Emperor's army came through their village last month to demand share of grain. Pooja watched her father give up more than half his harvest in taxes. He complained they had not left him enough for his family to live through the fallow season. A soldier dismounted, slapped his face. Pooja ran to help her father. Soldier slapped her also. Her father jumped at the soldier, shoved him away from his daughter. Soldier knocked him down, grabbed his turban, yanked it off. Soldier stepped on it, rubbed it in the dirt. Can you imagine? Such an insult. Struck down in front of his daughter, turban rubbed in dirt, by a Mughal. Shame, shame. Soldier pushed Pooja down on family grain, poured water from horse trough on her."

"I am happy they were not beaten, or worse," Devi said hugging her sobbing aunty.

"Devi," her mother said, "your cousin-sister ran away with a Rajput soldier to revenge her father. Pooja told her little sister to tell parents after she left only. She rides like a man with rebel soldiers in the hills."

"How? She owns no horse."

"Rebel soldier took her on his horse. Tracks from village, deep – one horse, two riders."

Devi had visualized the immortal Chetak, legendary Marwari warhorse of rebel Maharana Pratap Singh carrying her cousin-sister away, like he had carried his master to safety before he slumped down and died in the Maharana's arms. People swore the horse breathed fire from his nostrils.

Devi imagined he carried her cousin-sister across the grasslands, mane flowing, flames lighting the night in the Aravalli hills. To Devi, her cousin-sister became Goddess Kali, with fierce eyes, multiple hands slashing with every type of sword and dagger, seated behind her soldier-lover wearing a golden turban, his black hawk eyes just like Pratap Singh's, the warrior king, who rode without a saddle, his horse flying over uneven ground, hooves never touching the earth.

Devi recalled her cousin-sister when she returned a year later, her soldier-lover gone, her baby girl strapped to her back. For Devi the legend faded. Villagers called her cousin-sister dishonorable names, jeered at her. Only Pooja's parents believed she had fought the Mughals. Devi helped her cousin-sister with the baby until she, too, got swept away, against her will.

Devi looked at the sadhu, who searched her eyes, and said, "Only five times? We could not have been very close."

Her reply startled him. The sadhu spoke to the farmer. "Five times showing in another person's chart? Never saw before Mangala, god of war, join Brahaspati, god of leadership, equal distance from natal sign. Strong triangle. Much meaning."

Devi dispensed with the villagers' growing amazement by saying to the old farmer, "Well then, my sister will bring your son healthy boys, a good omen of harvests, and I will be on my way after the hunt. My destiny differs from hers."

The farmer translated the holy man's words. "No need for hunt. Family accepts girl."

Devi spoke up. "I do not accept so easily. I want you to know when you deal with my sister, you deal with me. Fair is fair. The hunt ensures my message. Also, I want roast meat to carry with me. I have a hard ride ahead."

The men nodded in agreement, uneasy at her intended meaning. Devi smiled, confident that her cousin's star legacy assured Geeta's safety, and wondered at the person who showed up so strongly in her cousin's fate. She meant to find out if she could. She wondered whether the soldier-lover had ever returned...

Devi walked away from the men to her horse, tethered under a tree, where he munched dried grass and a corncob, dried yellow kernels littering the ground. "My friend, they fed you well," she said rubbing the horse's shoulder. "I haven't done this in years, but I feel lucky. You are with me. I feel your strength. We will bring down a boar and leave at dawn."

She patted her horse and recited a poem learned as a child:

The horse is your home and the sword, your mate. You have only your hands and your heart to keep your life. And maybe a free moment now and then, to bake a bread – at the end of your spear!

"I have only a dagger, a dangerous disadvantage, no spear for this hunt," she whispered to her horse. "A boar's tusks at arm length could gore a person in seconds. Protect me."

Devi walked her horse to the mud-wattle stable. She saw no spear, only a long pole, a slender tree trunk, lay propped against the wall. She took it in hand to test its strength. The old farmer ambled in to speak with her. "Ji, I ask for a spear," she said turning to greet him. "I have none. It would be unfair for your son to have one and for me not to, not an honorable challenge. Can I have this pole?"

"My son has no spear. He uses dagger only."

"For boar?"

"We have no metal-tipped spears. Mughals took them, forbade us to forge new tips."

"Well then we shall both use sharpened wooden spears. I do not wish to be gored, nor do I want my sister's future husband hurt."

"I will sharpen two poles," he said and hurried away.

Devi bridled her horse, unknotted his mane and removed the burrs from his thick tail, pausing when the farmer's son walked up. She greeted him with a smile.

"Do not do this. I will care for your sister, with honor, not as prize of a hunt."

Devi liked this young man. She saw in him a kindness and strength she admired. "Thank you. But I want to."

The young man faltered. "I can provide supplies for your journey, no need to chase boar."

"Kunal, I want to. Do not worry for me." She watched the young man shrink before her, quite sure he had never met a female challenger, especially at a hunt. She continued with her horse in silence. The young man nodded and rushed out of the stable to ready for the chase.

The entire village came out in the soft light of dusk. When word spread that the competition involved wooden spears, much discussion among the elders broke out. Children clamored to pet the horses. Women passed around sweetened curdled milk balls rolled in pistachio pieces. Children squealed with delight, a festival. They pretended to hunt boar.

A small boy in a bright orange tunic, his face dwarfed by red and yellow paisley cloth piled in figure eights on his head to form a loose turban, played a homemade string instrument. He dragged a long bow over the hollow gourd opening strung with two strings to produce a moaning sound while he tapped a beat with his fingers on the gourd's round belly. Seeing the women dispense sweets, he dropped his instrument in the dirt and ran to get his share.

The farmer's son Kunal arrived in a fresh tunic, a silver earring dangling from his ear, his scarlet turban – the color of a fiery sunset – heaped high on his head, his broad mustache with upturned tips, perfectly shaped. To Devi's surprise, her sister Geeta arrived in a new outfit: a large circular skirt of red-orange panels over a full, white underskirt.

"You look festive," Devi said when Geeta joined her.

"When I told Kunal's mother I dance the gair ghoomar of the Bhil tribe, she told me to wear this and dance at the feast. She also has Bhil blood. She borrowed a clean suit for you, for after the hunt."

"I hope we kill a boar. This village needs to celebrate something!"

A loud drum roll drowned their words. The farmer stood to announce, "Gods blessed us. The traveler who challenges my son brought luck. When the Mughals took away our smith to forge their weapons in Shahjahanabad, not one metal-tipped spear remained here. In preparing wooden poles for the hunt, my neighbor and I discovered the smith's gift to our village. He had hidden many spear tips in earthen pots, buried them in his hut, along with more metal. My foot struck one just now."

A roar of jubilant shouts greeted his words. "Whoever brings down the boar is honored by the feast, but this stranger, Devi, the gods brought us, lives up to her goddess name, the giver of success and protector of our village. For her, the finest metal tip."

Devi blushed at the simplicity of their acceptance of her. The old man handed her the wooden pole with its metal tip point. She accepted the gift. When she reached for it, the heavy weight surprised her. She almost dropped it. She tried to conceal her dismay, but the farmer saw her tighten her grip to support it. He continued to address the crowd, but his words faded from her attention.

She focused on the spear's long wooden shaft and the broad metal tip securely fastened to it. The metal tip, a large triangular head that ended in a slightly rounded tip, like none she remembered seeing, gleamed like new. She felt the blade's edge, applying no pressure. She felt a sting, retracted her finger, surprised by a tiny line of blood across her finger.

She wiped it with her tunic. She stood the spear on end. The gray tip caught the late orange sun and smoldered.

Devi realized she had only seen metal like this once before, in a sword given to the Maharana by his grandfather, made from ukku ingots his grandfather had imported from the Andhra region in the south of India. The Maharana had proudly showed it to Devi one day explaining ukku in the Telegu language meant steel, a much finer metal than iron, highest quality.

He explained the art of forging it had all but vanished. In Aristotle's day, ukku had been known of, and exported, by way of Damascus, and from there throughout the major trading centers from Afghanistan to India. It had made the Deccan Kakatiyas famous swordsmen, according to him, as it was no ordinary metal. The Maharana had said, "With a sword of this ukku steel you could cut a man in two, even with his armor on. You could slice through him and his horse, that is, if you were so cruel as to hurt a horse, which, of course, I would never do! The swords never shatter, their edges never dull."

Devi turned to the old villager who watched his son's dark eyes gleam at Geeta, who looked down at her hands to avoid displaying her pleasure. The old man started to speak, but Devi interrupted. "Ji, thank you for your kindness. I want to offer something more for my sister's dowry." Geeta, hearing this, shot her a look of concern and apology. "I offer these as her wedding present."

The old man's eyes grew large when Devi withdrew earrings from her tunic pocket. The red glass mango shapes inset in white metal gleamed in the light. She placed the earrings on his palm. Geeta knew this surpassed the dowry of any woman in the village. The farmer, with more pride than greed said, "Do not pay for your misfortune. I see you and your sister come from a fine family, of higher means than me. I cannot accept such a gift on top of our bargain, only your sister can answer. I would be in your debt, with no way to repay."

Devi turned to see the crowd stare at the farmer in dismay. The son beamed at his father, at his dignity. Devi knew only Rajput women married up. Geeta had her chance with the Maharana, but she fit this farming village. She understood this life. Devi felt she owed the fatherless girl a chance at happiness. "Ji, you have not told me what you offer me in return for my sister. A token, at least, is customary. Then I could not allow you to refuse my gift."

The old man, caught off guard, said, "A thousand apologies. I have given it no thought, because... no time to think, not a plan to cheat. Offering a fatherless child a family, especially my son Kunal, seemed gift enough. I have one oxen for plowing. I offer..."

"Can I name my gift?"

The old man couldn't refuse, not the naming and not the named. All eyes were on him. "As you please."

Devi lifted the heavy spear and pointed to the urn. "If I had these tips I could make shafts for them, fashion leather sheaths, and sell them when I reach the Sindh. With that I could open a leather shop."

The old man smiled, exposing a gap where a tooth had broken. He touched the turret of cloth on his head. "You are most welcome to them all. The metal smith, my cousin, lived alone. I did not know he had these. To think he hid them like a treasure. His mind was not right in the end, the metal... too heavy. Let this be my family's gift to you, for your sister."

Devi smiled. "Settled. Let's begin the chase."

The old man presented the wooden spears, fitted with metal tips for the boar hunt, and blew the conch shell to announce the competition. Devi and Kunal mounted. He blew another long, haunting wail. They cantered off. Dust rose and hung like golden rain in the oblique rays.

Geeta accompanied the farmer's wife to the village center where women sat on their haunches making rotis for the feast. Geeta remembered how to make rotis. She had excelled at it in childhood, her mother saw to that. She knew when her mother taught her, she would have never thought her village daughter would marry a king, leave him, and live to return to a simple life. In a way Geeta felt glad her mother wasn't alive to see how life had turned out for her. She felt now she'd been given a chance to be the girl her mother had raised.

She studied the women. They mixed bajra, millet flour, with a little warm water and salt, kneaded it into a firm dough, pinched off enough for one roti, rolled it into a ball and shaped it with their palms until it stretched to a hand's length, and placed it on the heated griddle to roast.

Baskets of warm rotis littered the ground near the fires. The smell of dal curry mixed with flour, jiggery, and ghee, daal baati churma, a village staple, bubbled in heavy pots tended by women who chattered and stirred the yellow soup as it cooked. Children laughed and played near the glowing charcoal mounds where their mothers formed and roasted dal baatis, millet dumplings, that would be crushed and mixed with sugar and ghee for the celebration. Geeta saw men at their fire in the distance, she assumed, discussing the two women who had come into the village, the reason for the feast.

Geeta turned to Kunal's mother seated next to her. "Ji, what if they do not get a boar?"

"No matter. We feast. We found spear tips. We prepare for happiness of my son, his marriage, and to a Bhil girl, my own people. You come, a blessing to us." Geeta, surprised at the ease with which Kunal's parents and the villagers had accepted her, hoped she would not disappoint, and wondered if without a dowry would they be seated, preparing this feast? She thought not. The old woman looked her in the eyes and said, "Daughter, do not worry. Enough for feasting."

"I do not worry about the feast, Ji."

"You heard your fortune? Sadhu said many sons. Nothing to worry about."

"Tell me."

"First-born becomes famous warrior, saves our village from ruin. We celebrate him with this feast." Geeta grew pale and quiet. The old woman gave her an affectionate pinch. "I should not talk of these things. You must be fearing wedding night. I instruct you, not to worry. For tonight eat and drink to our future. Goddess Devi guided you and your sister here for a reason – Goddess Devi, protector of villages."

Geeta smiled. She hoped for Devi's success, as much for her own sake as for the poor villagers who attributed to her goddess powers, and she dreamed of a warrior son.

Devi, now at a slow walk in the forest, worried about the hunt, not for herself but for her young competitor. "Kunal, be very careful with these spears. The tips are the sharpest I have ever seen. Their weight makes them slice with little pressure. Take care you have a clean shot at the boar, away from you and from your horse's flank."

"I have my own spear, not a new tip although sharp. My tip belonged to my grandfather. My father had it hidden when the Mughals raided. He never took it out until today, not wanting to cause jealousy with the others who own no metal tips. Mine is better than yours. Its weight is balanced. Yours tips forward, wobbles. We had no time to attach two new tips to poles today. Father made yours only."

"I understand. I will do my best with what I have."

"Sister, do not worry. No need to kill a boar. My parents accept Geeta. I am most happy. We have food for a feast tonight without a kill."

"But I need to take meat with me."

Kunal turned toward something in the thicket far ahead. He kicked his horse and bolted away. Devi raced after him. The horses lathered from the exertion. Devi slowed to a stop behind Kunal. They watched and listened but heard only the hard blowing of the horses' nostrils.

"Not much time," Devi said looking at the afterglow where the sun had been.

"Boars sleep during the heat. Now they come out to feed on roots in the thicket, small eggs, rodents. Hunger makes them careless. Dusk, best time to hunt, if we find one soon."

Devi whispered, "Whoever spears first wins, no matter who brings him down."

"Sister, pigsticking is my favorite sport. As boys we pretended to hunt boar. I am sure I can do it. I will flush them out from the thicket. I know where they root."

"So, we should take two?"

"No. Let one live for another hunt. Our horses will have trouble enough pulling one."

"Agreed. Whoever sticks the boar wins," Devi stated again.

"Whoever brings it down."

Devi looked at Kunal and realized he would be a good mate for Geeta. His love of competition would serve him well in the marketplace. She glanced down. The grass and underbrush in the thicket reached their stirrups. Devi feared they could be on top of a boar before they saw it.

Kunal motioned Devi to swing left. He reined to the right. Devi saw tracks in damp mud where an underground spring bubbled to the surface. She could tell from the deep impressions the animal was large, possibly four hundred pounds. Unleashing the leathers supporting the spear, Devi balanced the weapon with her left arm, resting the tip on the metal bar of her stirrup. Her arm strained from the weight.

She heard a loud shriek. Twigs snapped. She tightened her grip and kicked her horse. Another loud shriek spooked birds in the overhanging trees and made her horse jump. She raced forward, spear out to the side, horizontal to the ground. Her horse leapt a low entanglement of thorny brush and came face to face with the charging boar.

Devi dug her heels into the horse's ribs. The boar lowered his head, his powerful tusks in line with the horse's chest. Devi yanked her horse abruptly to the right, stood in her stirrups and slammed the spear down with all her strength, narrowly missing a tusk to her foot. The blade struck the boar at the shoulder, cleaved him right down to the hoof. The ground shook when he collapsed. Devi's horse jumped and spun around out of control. She slid sideways in the saddle.

Kunal rounded the bushes on foot, spear raised. "You cut him in two!" he yelled, eyes wide with astonishment. "How?"

"On foot?" Devi gasped, reining in her nervous, stomping horse.

"The boar charged. I threw my spear. It struck his flank but fell out. My horse shied. I hit the ground. The boar veered away, towards you. What strength you have. Goddess Devi is in you. No woman, no man, could do that. You cleaved him in half with a spear."

Devi jumped down to inspect the boar, positive now the blade was ukku, the legendary metal smiths no longer knew how to forge, the secret having died in south India. But to find it in this small village? It made no sense. She knew the goddess looked upon her and enjoyed what she saw. "Help me prepare the litter. If we hurry, we can reach open fields before darkness falls."

Kunal took out his ax and cut sturdy branches for poles. Devi bound them with leather straps. They pushed and shoved branches under the animal to pivot its weight onto the litter. Kunal tied the boar to the poles, harnessed both their horses to the litter and slowly the horses, straining from the dead weight, walked towards the village. After an hour, with darkness wrapped around them, they spotted village fires. When they came into view, children squealed and jumped. Everyone ran to greet the successful hunters.

The old farmer limped at a brisk pace to his son. "Son, you have brought us a fine beast to celebrate your coming marriage. You must have fought hard. You cut the poor fellow in half."

The villagers laughed and smacked their lips in anticipation of roasted meat.

"Father, not me. I did not bring the boar down. Devi did."

The old man stood speechless for a moment and regarded the slender woman before him, the thrill of kill gleaming in her eyes. He stepped back, away from her, a quizzical look on his face and said no more.

At the celebration, Geeta led a group of women in bright orange and red skirts to swirl in a large circle. In the center, she performed the gair ghoomar. Men played drums and strummed homemade string instruments that created sounds like rising and falling rounds of laughter. Dancers stomped the beat with their huge silver anklets.

Children, especially the girls, re-enacted the hunt calling themselves Goddess Devi. By the time the pig was roasted and everyone had eaten their fill, the night was nearly spent.

Devi congratulated Kunal and Geeta and escorted her sister to the cot in the farmer's house, far from Kunal, who slept in the stable. She slipped silver coins under Geeta's pillow and kissed her goodnight.

Devi slept for an hour.

While the villagers snored, she saddled her horse. She tipped the heavy urn sideways to quietly fill her satchel. Beneath the metal tips lay a dagger, then another, wrapped in soiled cloth. She shoved them into her bag and struggled to secure the load to her saddle. Her horse stamped in annoyance at the additional weight, but Devi patted him and assured him it would not be there for long.

She carried with her only enough roasted boar and rotis for the journey, planning to reach the palace fortress before sunrise on the second day. She prayed Lord Shiva bless her horse and allow her to travel with the alert eyes of a tiger, the sure step of an elephant, and the strength and courage of a Rajput warrior.

# CHAPTER 12 – EKLINGJI TEMPLE

Captain Jaswant had ridden as far as his exhausted horse could take him in the heat of the day. He found a grassy hillock near a spring and decided to rest for a couple of hours before pushing on towards the palace. He grabbed the two remaining rotis, rolled in cloth, unsaddled his horse, watered him, tethered him to a rock, leaned back, and ate so fast he devoured the rotis without a pause. After a long drink of the sweet spring water, he leaned back and shut his eyes.

He knew nothing for hours until his horse stamped, twitched and snorted. He looked up. The horse's muzzle seemed gigantic, took up the sky. He nudged his rider. A blast of warm breath flowed over Jaswant's face, smelling of sweet grass. He reached up to rub the horse's muzzle and fought his way back from mind-numbing fatigue with a smile.

As he saddled him up, the animal let out a deafening whinny that made his entire body shake with the force of it. Jaswant came wide awake. A cloud of dust glowed yellow in the afternoon light. The captain tightened the girth and jumped into the saddle. He galloped to a rock formation to see what the dust cloud yielded: People on foot, bullock carts, a few horses, no army regiment. Captain Jaswant rode out to meet them. Seeing him, the travelers stopped and formed a circle with their carts to protect themselves. A horseman ran directly towards him.

"Halt! Halt!" the man shouted raising his sickle.

Jaswant realized they were Rajput peasants, not Mughal soldiers. "No harm," he shouted back. "I am a captain of the Maharana's guard."

The man dropped the sickle to his side when he saw the uniform and came to an abrupt halt in front of Jaswant's horse. He turned and signaled "all clear" to those behind him. The circle broke, travelers mounted their carts and horses and continued on at their slow pace.

"Where do you go?" Jaswant asked, surveying the ragged crew.

"Mughal army approaches. Emperor's forces invaded Rajputana. We seek shelter and protection for our wives and children at the palace fortress. We men have come to fight."

"You know this, imperial forces? You have seen them?"

"No. We live near the border of Marwar, just north of here. We heard battle drums. We fear the Rathores have joined with the Emperor and bear down on us."

"How many men?"

"Two thousand, at least, gypsies fleeing to the Sindh told us."

"Where are the troops now?"

"North of here, from last account, in the Aravalli hills. They head south towards Eklingji temple, it seems. We must reach the fortress before they do. Ride with us. Help protect our families."

Jaswant considered the man's words. "An evil turn of events, Rathores of Marwar joining forces with the Emperor against Sisodias of Mewar. We are cousin clans. I must have proof."

"Emperor scours the Aravalli Hills even now for young Prince Ajit. They say the Rathores struck a bargain – the prince's return to their throne in exchange for aiding imperial forces to take Mewar!"

"Helping the Emperor take Mewar in exchange for return of their heir, the son of a Sisodia princess whom we have pledged to protect? Never. Gossip only!" Jaswant bellowed.

"Why else?"

Jaswant's blood ran cold, as though Himalayan ice had crept into the desert, filled his veins, slowed them, numbed them. He felt impotent, shamed. He had disobeyed his king and deserted his brother at this most crucial time. For all his devoted service, he had now ended like this. He was a man without honor. He couldn't look his kinsman in the eye.

"Sir, will you help us?"

Jaswant snapped. He saw the fear and desperation in the man's eyes, the proud, scared man racing his loved ones to the fortress so he could fight for his king. As much as he wanted to protect these innocent people, he said, "I cannot. I am a scout for the Maharana. You have given me valuable information. I must ride and notify others. As we speak, the Emperor's men close in from the east as well. Make haste to the fortress, leave your slower animals behind."

"Gods be with us. Lord Shiva the Destroyer answer our prayers."

"I ride to Eklingji. Victory for Mewar," Captain Jaswant said, raising his sword.

"Blessing for our Sisodia warriors," the man answered. The approaching villagers joined in the cry raising their daggers, spears, sickles, and sticks to the sky.

"You are within a few hours of the fortress. You may reach there before nightfall," Jaswant said. He reined his horse to the northeast and spurred him. Jaswant planned to locate the enemy, estimate their force, decipher their route, and ride to the fortress with the information.

He knew this part of the Aravalli Hills better than anyone. As a boy he had collected dates, palm fruit, and figs for festivals; as a man he had hunted tiger, leopard, and panther. He had accompanied the Maharana on shikar for wild boar, sambhar, and spotted deer many times in these hills. He welcomed every chance to escort Huzur to Eklingji temple for prayers to Lord Shiva, Mewar's guardian, believing they had never been a vassal state to the Mughals because of reverence paid by the rulers of Mewar to their deity.

The hills grew higher, silhouettes uneven. Jagged quartzite crags hampered Jaswant's view ahead. The descending sun touched Guru Sikar peak, the highest mountain in the kingdom, and cast an orange tint along flat-bottomed, high puffy white clouds. To the right of the path, Jaswant spotted the waterfall, a thin orange ribbon that cascaded over dull gray granite to disappear into a thick stand of sheesham trees. In the distance, hills grew barren above the valley of the temple, Eklingji.

When Captain Jaswant approached the deep pool at the waterfall's base, a herd of spotted deer, camouflaged points of light in sun-filtered trees, bolted. He dismounted and walked his horse to the pool's edge. Nostrils pumping, the horse sucked in long, rhythmical draughts. Captain Jaswant splashed his face and neck with the cool water, cupping his hands to drink.

When his horse jerked its head up abruptly, Jaswant drew his sword. A flock of birds took flight. The captain saw movement and charged at it through the bushes at the pool's edge, towards a granite slab.

"Namaskar. Alone?" an old man said in a calm voice as Captain Jaswant rushed at him, sword drawn.

"No, my men follow close behind me," Jaswant said, scanning the rock crevices.

"Well, one is never alone in Lord Shiva's presence. I come often to this pool for cleansing ritual, water as sacred to me as Mother Ganges. I believe her to be one of Ganges children, surfaced after a long journey below ground. Do not raise your sword in this holy place."

"Pardon, Brahmin Ji. Enemies are in the hills."

"I know. I heard."

"You should return to your temple for safety, Ji."

"What? I have come all this way to be alone, to pray. Now you tell me soldiers come. How can I do my puja with you here to bother me?"

"What soldiers? You have seen them?"

"Yes, yes, no avoiding them."

"How many?"

"As many as knots on a wedding mandap canopy, it appears."

"Mughals?"

"No, no. Would I be doing cleansing ritual if Mughals were at Eklingji?"

Jaswant realized the stupidity of his question. "Then who?"

"Our valiant Rajputs!"

"Which clan?"

"Many clans. First time in long ages I see clansmen of Marwar, Mewar, and Sirohi, united, no anger between them. Answer to prayer. Lord Shiva told me two weeks back in a vision this would come. Early morning, three o'clock, when priests attend prayers, anointing the Lord, saying pujas, Lord Shiva took fiery form, the chamber glowed. Two priests fell to the ground, covered heads with hands. I remained on my knees, blinded by fire from four faces of Lord, seared my eyes. Then water clouded them. Blinking made them fill again like monsoons on the Ganges. Tears drenched my beard, dripped down my chest. I heard the gong sound three times, then long wail of conch. Lord Shiva, calling me home? My spirit flew from this body. I soared among clouds, laden with dewdrops of soul.

"I heard his words. Words not words, thunder. He instructed me, welcome soldiers to his temple. Brother to brother, they will stand. He warned of coming battle – ground shaking, blood flowing – do your duty, hold true." The elderly Brahmin rose, straightening his loincloth. Jaswant yearned for specifics of the battle. The old priest said nothing. He gathered his sandals and walked away, turned slightly and called back over his shoulder, "Come. Eat. Prepare for your destiny."

Jaswant tried to ask, but the words curdled in his chest. Fetching his horse, he dutifully followed the old man along a dirt path, downhill to the broad valley. He saw ahead a long wall that snaked around, encircling white marble temples, the raised circular knot canopy most visible.

In the courtyard soldiers relaxed in the shade the structures offered. Leaving his horse tethered there, he followed the Brahmin priest to the hall of carved pillars where Lord Shiva's bull Nandi reclined, cast in silver, horns and chest anointed with red paste, strings of marigold flowers around his humped neck. Jaswant paused to offer a prayer and anoint the bull. Someone called his name. He turned.

"Well, brother, I hope the Mughals do not find us as easily as you have!"

"Sardar!" Jaswant said, giving him an affectionate clap on the back.

Sardar Singh's face melted into despair. "Brother, I left you in command only. Why are you here, alone?"

Jaswant faltered, regained his composure, and chose his words. "I left the Maharana... to find you."

"Quicker than I expected, well you did, brother. I struck an agreement with the Rathores for our mutual protection. The vizier's men move from the east towards our fortress, the Emperor from Ajmer. From the northwest comes another: Prince Akbar, Aurangzeb's son. He rides less than two days behind us. Did you know of this?"

Jaswant shook his head with a tilt to the right. "Brother, come, I must speak in private."

Captain Sardar led Jaswant out of the great hall of carved pillars, stopping briefly to anoint Nandi in prayer, walked past the lounging soldiers, and took the narrow footpath up to the water tanks on the northern side of the complex. When sure they were alone, Sardar faced his brother. "What trouble speaks in your eyes?"

"Sardar, our king is not pleased. He fears you bring the Emperor down on our heads by beheading the vizier!"

Sardar snorted. "I sent a message: Leave Mewar alone! We will not be subjugated! I showed the Rathores his head to enlist their support and prove the threat real."

"The vizier and his troops were only making a presence, a show of force to persuade Huzur. They march south to the Deccan, the Emperor follows. The vizier conveyed the Emperor's request that our Maharana supply able Mewari warriors for the offensive against the Marathas in the south. He had not come to overrun us but to take some of our best men."

"Jaswant, can you see? They mean to weaken us. With our best away, overpowering Mewar would be feasible. The Emperor is on the move – to take Mewar and Marwar. He hunts for young Prince Ajit in the Aravalli Hills. He uses clan rivalry to keep us from uniting against him.

"If he were to strike some pact with the Rathores, say in exchange for their young prince, they repay, help him take Mewar. Then where will we be? Caught between imperial forces on our west in Marwar and imperial forces in the north, with our best men in the south. How long do you think we could last?"

"I believe, the Maharana believes, Sardar, that we could have had time to forge an alliance with Marwar, and with Shivaji's son in the Deccan, if you had not acted so rashly!"

"Think what you like! Fools wait. I saw a chance to act. I took it for the good of us all, for Rajputana."

"What chance?" Jaswant shouted.

"I showed the head of the vizier to the Rathores, to prove how imminent the danger. They joined us because of that only." Sardar paced, kicked small rocks out of his way. "You, go tell the Maharana that Captain Sardar stands ready to fight while his brother frets with his horse leathers, pines for the Maharana's wife, and is too afraid to act."

"I spit on your turban, brother. You insult me. I cannot tell Huzur. It is he who sent me away, assigned me a duty I could not do. I failed him only, not you."

"What?"

"He commanded me to take Devi from the palace for safety, take her for my wife. He disowned her, cast her out. He prepares for siege. He chose to spare her should he fall and his wives commit jauhar."

"Such dishonor, sending a wife away! And how would you fight to protect the palace if you are sheltering her somewhere away from here?"

"I would not. He dismissed me."

Sardar's eyes squeezed tight like shriveled black raisins. "Your lust for the woman became your shame."

"No! I acted at all times with honor, Sardar. The Maharana – he spoke to Devi, told her something, about you, about us."

"What?"

"Sardar, you are not my blood. The late Maharana's brother sired you. You are Huzur's cousin-brother. You have royal blood. Huzur's uncle violated Devi's mother. She thought it was the Maharana, Huzur's father, because the man arrived at the river in the royal palanquin. When she birthed you, you were declared dead, stillborn.

"The gypsy whisked you away, took you to a peasant woman, my mother, who had birthed me the same day. She wet nursed you. The village believed she had birthed twins. We grew up as such. We were born within hours of one another. You, son of Devi's mother, sired by the royal debaucher, Huzur's uncle. And me, the son of peasants. On his deathbed, Huzur's father told Huzur the story.

"When Huzur came to the throne, he thought it better to settle our family near the Meandering River. Only when Huzur requested Devi for his wife did her mother recount the story of her disgrace in order to explain why Devi could never marry me, as Devi and I wanted. Her mother believed me to be her blood."

"Jaswant, what evil befell us all! You are my brother, always. We grew to be men together, served together in Huzur's army. Nothing can change that. Such shame. Such disappointment for you and Devi. I am most sorry. How could the truth have been kept quiet?"

"Shame tightens lips. Jealousy opens them."

"Huzur called me to his service, yes – I thought because I won the tug-of-war contest, and then later he called you to serve under me, an honor to us both. Your ability with horses and archery made you a fitting choice. Now I understand. At times Huzur watched me at sports, sword practice, horse training. He seemed to seek me out above others. He would smile at me. I, of course, looked down out of respect."

"Devi never loved the Maharana, she loved me, from childhood. Yet the Maharana loved her, enough to force her to leave. He set her free, exiled her, to save her from jauhar should he fall. He commanded me to take her away to Sindh. Brother, at last I could be with her, yet I felt ashamed, running like a scared dog, just when our Maharana most needs his men. I disobeyed him. I couldn't run away. I took her as far as a village in the Aravallis, but no farther. I returned to defend Huzur and to serve at your side.

"Huzur told me he knows his own son is too young and sickly to rule at this time, cannot manage a kingdom. He commands you, his cousin-brother, to rule as guardian until his son comes of age. His scribe noted this for palace record."

Captain Sardar's weather-bronzed face appeared frozen. He stared through Jaswant. His angular jaw rippled with tension. "He prepares for a siege! Huzur, my cousin-brother, prepares for a siege!" A wild look came over him. "Jaswant, we must return, now."

"Sardar, the Emperor's son, Prince Akbar, came to the palace, clad as a peasant, seeking Huzur's allegiance in his bid to overthrow his father. The prince did not know of the vizier's visit. Huzur informed him. They do not work together. Many rats crawl the desert."

Sardar Singh straightened up. "The Rathores have joined us. Imperial forces must be nearing our gate. We ride within the hour, together, against our enemy. Notify the Brahmin to prepare to bless our journey. I shall inform the Marwari captain to make ready his men."

Marwari soldiers saddled their horses and gathered at the west gate, awaiting the Brahmin's blessing. Captain Jaswant looked at the Rathores, whom he distrusted, and wondered: What will it be like to fight alongside them?

The Brahmin anointed the black stone deity on all four faces, saluting Brahma to the west, Vishnu to the north, Maheshwar to the south, and Surya, the Sun, to the east. He beseeched the deity to bring Rajput victory. The soldiers, eyes closed in prayer, didn't see him swoon.

Sardar rushed to support him. The old priest suddenly straightened up and seemed large beside Captain Sardar, held his outstretched arms above his head and called out in a bellowing voice: Wait until dawn, resist movement until dawn, otherwise victory is in Mughal hands. He looked at the soldiers, seven hundred strong, spoke clearly and dropped to the ground unconscious.

"Brahmin Ji," Captain Sardar shouted in his face to rouse him. The old man opened his cloudy eyes. "Our palace-fortress, not three hours ride to the south, prepares for attack. You ask us to wait?"

The priest replied in a weak voice, barely audible even to Sardar and Jaswant, kneeling beside him. "Your fortress, already under siege. Lord Shiva commands, stay your troops until dawn."

"To give the Mughals certain victory? No, we ride now," Captain Sardar said.

"Then you ride without blessings. You ride to certain death. You do not understand workings of Lord Shiva. Obey."

Captain Jaswant grabbed Sardar's arm, "Brother, we obey the Brahmin only."

Hearing the dispute, the Rathore commander approached. "The army, mostly all Rathore, I command. We left our homes to fight for Rajputana." He raised a hand to hush the rumbling like shockwaves radiating out from the Brahmin. Palm turned to the sun, he shouted, "Brahmin Ji speaks for Lord Shiva. We Rathores stay at Eklingji temple tonight."

Horses stamped and snorted, soldiers mumbled to one another. Mewari soldiers, and farmers who had joined to fight, looked to Captain Sardar.

Captain Sardar shouted, "I ride now. Who will join me?" The horsemen of Marwar remained quiet; only Captain Jaswant and the Mewari villagers shouted their support. "It is as Lord Shiva decrees. Rathores remain. We ride ahead to send news of what we find."

The Rathore commander Ram Singh shouted, "I ride with you to see with my own eyes the danger. Only then will my men join you in battle."

Captain Sardar nodded in agreement. The soldiers dispersed to unsaddle their war horses and await word of battle. Captain Sardar raised his sword and pledged, "Word will return to you this night." He cantered out the gate, followed by Captain Jaswant, the Rathore commander, and twenty Mewari villagers on horseback, armed with bow and arrows. Their trail of dust billowed down the valley and disappeared behind jagged hills.

Captains Sardar and Ram Singh led the soldiers. Captain Jaswant followed as rear guard. The horses picked their way around granite boulders, down shallow ravines, and up rocky crags, trotting when the uneven terrain allowed, even galloping in grassy stretches, but mostly trudging slowly over the terrain with little but the waxing moon to light their way.

They reached the river where Captain Sardar signaled halt. Jaswant knew the place well from his youth, a wide channel with a weak current. He watched until everyone joined Captain Sardar on the opposite side before he crossed over. Hidden in the trees, they waited for orders from Captain Sardar.

"The fortress lies a few miles ahead. We keep to the trees and remain unseen, but near Lake Pichola from the palace we may be spotted in dawn light."

Captain Sardar's words drowned in a volley of cannon fire. The horses neighed and stamped, sidestepping into one another.

Captain Sardar, his face as rigid as his armor, shouted, "They attack the palace! I know every tree of the forest, every rock of the shore, I go ahead to check the Mughal position and return as soon as possible to report to you. Stay in the cover of trees."

Before his brother could say anything, Sardar looked at him. "You, Commander Jaswant, are in charge here. If I do not return within two hours, swing wide to the northeast, climb the bluff for a better look at the battlefield. Send word to Eklingji. Take what action you and Captain Ram Singh find necessary."

Ram Singh said, "I come with you. I must see the enemy's position for myself."

Captain Sardar tilted his head in reluctant agreement. Jaswant knew his brother's fear.

If Ram Singh died, his Rathore troops would see it as a trap, a way to pull them into battle, to fight on Mewari soil for Mewaris. Jaswant nodded a tacit acknowledgment to his brother.

The captains galloped off towards the fortress. The remaining soldiers followed Captain Jaswant to a thick stand of trees where the river swung wide round a low cliff. Hiding in the shadows, they heard musket fire and loud cannon bursts that rumbled through the remaining heat of the day.

Captain Jaswant felt relieved knowing Devi had been spared, but feared for his people. The palace with its fortress iron gates had repelled many attacks, yet he knew the men of Udaipur, some 30,000, would face a formidable enemy if the Emperor marched with his 180,000 troops.

Udaipur would fight, as Rajputs do, but he feared its historical legacy would be as bloody as that of Fort Chittorgarh: suicide by self-immolation for the women, death by battle for the men. He winced at the thought of it, tried to shake the image from his mind.

Jaswant dismounted to join the men solemnly checking and re-checking their muskets, swords, and spears. Several villagers had only spears – no shields, no daggers.

A young boy, no more than fifteen, had borrowed a horse to join – against his mother's pleas – and stood battle-ready in tattered tunic, stained cotton pants, and his new turban, a wealth of green cloth lying coiled on his head like a sleeping snake, downy mustache and beard not fully hiding his nutmeg skin.

Captain Jaswant spoke to the boy. He loosened his second shield, the one he wore on his back, and handed it to him. "Here, strap this to your chest."

"Thank you, Captain Ji, but you should wear both."

"How can I lead such a fine warrior as yourself into battle knowing you have no metal cover? People will call me names – your mother will spit at my feet."

The boy gasped, "No, Captain Ji, my mother is a simple woman, she is not stupid."

"You call it stupidity for a mother to love her son?"

"Ji, I meant she would not fault you for fighting our enemy. She would not fault me. I fight for her only."

"And that is why you must wear this shield, so you can return to tell your mother how valiantly we fought and how quickly we sent the Mughals flying!"

"Yes, Huzur." The boy dipped his head in acknowledgement of the gift and strapped the heavy shield across his chest.

"Show me your spear." The boy handed his iron-tipped spear to the captain. Jaswant felt its weight and followed the edge of the blade with his finger. "This is very dull. It will ram, not slice." He handed him a sharpening stone from his saddlebag. "Bring the edge to a sharp angle. Then I will let you go with me."

The boy sat on the ground and began sharpening. Captain Jaswant wanted to leave him like that, carefully working on the metal... without ever using it. Had he a choice, he would have refused the boy, but even one additional soldier was an advantage he could not negate, even a spear-carrying boy.

War thunder grew louder. The men became more agitated, their horses danced with every explosion. To wait proved worse than facing the enemy. Jaswant worried – Sardar should have returned by now. A breeze from the river teased the trees. Oblique sunlight striped the forest floor where his horse paced.

Hearing a loud splash, the men jumped to attention. Suddenly a rider charged from the lake edge to the thicket, his sword catching sunlight, a white-hot streak that disappeared in dense tree foliage. Jaswant leapt onto his horse, raised his sword and galloped full on at the rider. The rider crouched low over his horse's neck, spurred him into a dusty frenzy of flying hooves. The other men spread out on all sides. One soldier raised his musket, missed a clean shot. Another soldier reached the rider, came alongside to strike with his spear. The rider lurched to the side narrowly missing the spear's tip. Captain Jaswant charged, sword drawn.

The rider screamed, "Jaswant!"

He dropped his sword mid-air. Devi slipped sideways on her saddle, trying to right herself, grabbed the leathers and pulled herself erect. She reined in her frantic horse. The animal, lathered white at the mouth, reared whinneying, then stamped in place, trembling, eye whites wide from fear, nostrils blood red and blowing. "The cannon, are we under siege?" she said gasping for breath.

"Yes. You... why?" Captain Jaswant leaned over to grab her shoulder to steady her.

"To help the Maharana."

Catching her breath, she shot at him: "And why do you hide in this thicket with cannon fire in the distance?"

"Captain Sardar's orders. We await his return. He and the Rathore commander, Ram Singh, rode ahead to scout. Too long ago. I ride now to the bluff to see. I will find Sardar and join him and the others. More men, Rathores, wait at Eklingji to join us. They await their commander's word."

"How long have we been under siege?"

"I am not sure, many hours, a day."

"How many Mughals?"

"I don't know. The vizier's troops, several hundred. The Emperor, 180,000."

"Where?"

"We don't know. One report put imperial troops at the Alwar Hills north of Jaipur. Another, as far south as Ajmer. He must be amassing troops from Shahjahanabad."

"I met a gypsy this morning. He had traveled to Ajmer to sell his goods. He said there was talk of several thousand Mughals along the river near Bijai Nagar."

"They could be close behind us by now. We must send word to the men at Eklingji. It's a trap. Devi, ride, warn them. You know the terrain better than these men. Here, take my horse. The Brahmin at the temple will hide you."

"I did not ride so hard to hide. I go home to fight." The fire in her eyes made the captain hiss disapproval. The soldiers looked at them in dismay. "You send one of these men. I know the aqueduct. I can sneak into the palace, unnoticed."

Captain Jaswant spun around to face the village boy. "You, son, can you find your way back to the temple?"

"Yes, sir. I remember the way."

"Go then, as fast as you can. Warn the Rathores that the Mughals are upon them. Udaipur is under siege. We fight for our lives. Get more troops. Tell them, I am certain the Emperor looks for young Prince Ajit... to kill him. He plans to overrun our kingdoms on his march south. Bring soldiers here," he shouted as the boy rode away.

"Men, remain hidden. I ride to the bluff to survey the enemy's numbers and report back here, to you. We wait for reinforcements. Devi, you ride ahead. Take no chances. If you cannot get a clear passage to the aqueduct, turn around and join the men back here. If you make it through, tell the Maharana we gather our forces to attack. With Lord Shiva's grace, we will prevail."

"Jaswant," Devi said, opening her saddlebag, "take this dagger."

"I have mine."

"No, take this one." Jaswant reached out, took it from her, surprised by its weight. "I have one like it. I believe they are blessed!" Jaswant saluted and reined his horse towards the bluff above Udaipur.

Devi watched Jaswant grow smaller, until he disappeared. She weaved her way through the forest's long shadows, black fingers gripping the earth, until she saw the shore of Lake Pichola peeking out from the dusty yellow-orange afternoon haze.

From her vantage point everything looked peaceful, yet the sound of pounding cannons dispelled her false hope. She could see Mughal troops had not yet surrounded the lake. They remained at the far end, near the palace fortress.

She heard dull thwacks – the slamming of the north gate wall by war elephants, answered by musket fire from the ramparts. The fighting sounded less fierce than she had imagined, at least for now. She knew the Maharana would be conserving his supplies. He would not waste gunpowder, arrows, and spears without clear targets.

Devi knew the Emperor's large army could camp around the fortress, build wooden ramps to reach the highest walls, have war elephants drag cannons to the upper levels and batter the fortress day and night until a wall gave way... or the Maharana's supplies ran out.

It could be months, but inevitably the men of the fortress would ride out in a desperate final offensive. After donning wedding finery to see their men off, admonishing them not to return with marks on their backs but to fight to the death, the women would mount a funeral pyre and burn rather than submit to the enemy.

Devi knew to be on the outside of the palace and watch her husband face the enemy would crush her. She chose to fight alongside Huzur and Jaswant.

Devi loosened the girth on her horse and hid the saddle in the rushes. Taking his head in her hands, she removed the horse's bridle, said a prayer, and then shooed him away, hoping a villager would care for him. She hoisted the heavy satchel of metal tips onto her back, keeping the dagger in hand, and walked to where the passage to the aqueduct lay hidden.

She stumbled through tall reeds, stopping to rest often, the weight of her load half of her own. She yanked a piece of roasted boar and a dried roti from her bag and ate so fast she hardly chewed. The nourishment and a drink of lake water renewed her.

Stumbling along like an old woman carrying a load of bricks to the kiln, she realized she couldn't make good time with so heavy a load. She found a double tree trunk. With the butt of her spear, she dug a shallow grave for her treasure. Devi continued on, holding her spear but bracing the triple-head dagger in the sash of her tunic.

No life stirred on this side of the lake, no one bathed, no woman washed her saris, no child frolicked in the blue water, not even a deer or jackal stirred. All nature stands silent before the wrath of this Mughal storm, she thought. An eerie feeling of impending loss grew black in her heart. She thought how frightened her zenana sisters, and all the women would be, how the children would howl and cry. She thought of the old man who sold fragrant oils at the palace, how he boasted to her that no one used such fine sandalwood or such potent rose water or such intoxicating frangipani as he did. He had told her he desired to lift the soul to the heavens with purifying scents, for the gods favored them, and in return would favor him. She wondered whether the old man would now be smelling the scent of death and destruction, the acrid smoke of cannon fire?

Devi roused herself from dismal thoughts. The sun had fallen behind the hills, light grew dim. She must find the opening to the aqueduct. She followed the lake bed, weaving low through tall rushes until she heard a horse snort. She fell flat, the scent of dried grass rose into the air. Two horses ran past her so close she felt the ground shake. After what seemed to her a long time, she lifted up, looked around, but saw no one. Devi walked on as fast as she could, keeping low to the ground.

Near a small escarpment filled with haphazardly stacked boulders – evidence of a violent flood – she knelt down, dug into the caked mud until her fingers bled. Water seeped into the pit. She moved downhill and began again, the earth softer here. She clawed with her dagger, going deeper and deeper, removing the soil. She felt she had found the place, but she couldn't remember it. Losing her resolve, she collapsed on the mound of displaced dirt and cried. She had forgotten the tunnel's entrance.

She thought back to a day Jaswant was to meet her at their hiding place. She was late. When she arrived, he was nowhere to be seen. She remembered the joy she felt when a bird's whistle caught her attention. She turned to see him high in a tree, beyond the river bank. Devi looked up. She saw that tree again, uphill from where she was digging, just as she remembered it. She knew she was in the right place.

With renewed determination, she climbed into the pit again. Her arm quaked when the dagger struck the marble surface below, the low tone reverberating throughout her body. She cleared the spot and saw the dirty, rusted grate. She lifted an edge with her blade, freed the grate from the dirt, wedged the dagger under the lip of the grate, and shoved with all her strength. It inched to the side causing a small landslide of pebbles and dirt to fall onto the barrier below, a solid marble disk.

She rotated it on its track, enough to slip into the passageway sideways. Grabbing dried riverweeds and brush, she covered her tracks and the opening and then crawled all the way in, pulling the marble disk shut over her head, whispering a prayer.

She stumbled down the dank, dark tunnel with her spear raised in front of her chest to gage the height of the ceiling. Devi realized she had never traveled the tunnel's length and had no idea where it surfaced in the fortress.

The air grew cooler, yet lifeless, as she continued trudging. The uneven ground caused her to trip and careen into the walls. She followed the closest wall with her hand, at times feeling rough clusters of faceted crystal deposits, striated bands of rock, and smooth segments like the plaster and inlaid glass designs in the palace.

She came to a smooth floor, marble she guessed, that made walking easier until she tripped on something. She lurched forward, caught herself on a root creeping from a fissure in the rock wall. She felt along the length of the obstacle, a curved pole attached to a flat piece. She jumped back, slamming into the wall. It was the rib of a skeleton. Devi wiped her hands furiously on her tunic, stabbed the darkness with her dagger. Nothing moved, no sound carried – only her shallow, uneven breathing. No foul odor. The person had died long ago.

She kicked the skeleton aside. With one hand holding her spear, she felt along the wall with the other. Sweat poured from her forehead, stinging her eyes, in the clammy, cool dead air. She felt her stomach roll and lurch. She tried to calm herself, to think of something, anything but bones reaching out to grab her.

She recalled the day she and Jaswant first found the secret entrance. They had been swimming while the other villagers slept in the noonday heat. They stumbled into the tunnel's entrance and into each other's arms. She was fourteen. Jaswant pressed his lips on hers, warm lips, full and alive. She had never felt anything like that. At first she had backed away but then she moved closer to feel that warmth again. His body came close to hers. They touched. He stroked her hair and kissed her again. She giggled with excitement.

Devi shook her head and the memory loose. Her father had sentenced her to death by marriage, her mother to death by shame. She stepped up her pace, a running walk, no longer afraid of dead bodies strewn in her path. She was one herself.

# CHAPTER 13 – THE SIEGE

Evening settled in the forest, devoid of the usual cries of wolf and jackal, the tigress's nocturnal hunt, disrupted by booming sounds of war. Three men approached at a dead run out of dim gray light. They appeared like phantoms under the pale rising moon. Recognizing his brother, Captain Sardar shouted at his men, "Lower your muskets." Captain Jaswant, Commander Ram Singh, and a guard jumped down from their horses, tried to catch their breath.

"We scouted the west shore. Mughals ram elephant gate, Hathi Pol, from the north and move into position at moon gate, Chand Pol, from the west. Cannon and musket fire are filling the valley with noise. The air stinks of it. For now the ramparts hold. Maharana answers volleys, musket to musket, cannon to cannon," Captain Jaswant blurted out. "The siege is raging."

The villagers who had run up to listen to the men puffed up with pride. "Long live the Rajputs! Lord Shiva protects those who stand steadfast to fight the enemy. The sun never sets on our City of Dawn."

"How many enemies?" a voice asked from the crowd.

"Difficult to say – less than one thousand – it seems, led by the vizier," Commander Ram Singh interjected.

"Not so many," another villager said in defiance.

"Sardar, the Emperor himself has not yet arrived with his troops," Captain Jaswant said turning to face his brother. "Thirty thousand within the fortress walls. Food and water for people and animals... The siege cannot last too long. The granary before harvest stands half-full only. We have enough food for a few months, five, maybe six."

"We defeat them in less time, one week or two," a villager said, shaking his pitchfork in the air.

Captain Sardar snorted. "This, the first wave only. If the Emperor comes from Shahjahanabad with 180,000 men, the siege could go on for twelve months. He calculates his opponent's battle ability. He means to starve us out, so he can save his soldiers for the southern front in the Deccan."

Captain Jaswant stepped forward, leaned into Sardar and said, "From the bluff I saw no additional troops. If he travels south from Bijai Nagar, as we were told, the road from there back to Shahjahanabad must be thick with Mughal soldiers." Turning to Commander Ram Singh, he raised his voice. "Your city, Jaipur, will be sacked – possibly it has been already."

"I heard no such news. If his troops are as close as Bijai Nagar then he passed Jaipur, Ajmer also. Kettledrums sounded no such alarm. I think he travels a different route, possibly from the east, through the land of Kota, if he rode from Shahjahanabad to Agra."

Captain Sardar shook his head. "Whatever way he approaches, we must fight. We return now to Eklingji to gather our men."

Slowly they traversed the wide valley spread out before them like black water. A blood red-orange haze hung low along the horizon. By the time they reached the temple, its white marble domes had merged into the night. Within the grounds, soldiers talked around small fires. Hearing the sentry's whistled alarm, they jumped up and grabbed muskets swords. The tense pause caught some off guard. A thrice repeated shrill whistle sounded an all clear.

Captain Sardar yelled as he galloped in, "Your captains arrive."

Commander Ram Singh dismounted from his trotting horse and ran to his soldiers. "Troops from Marwar must come. The siege has begun. We are too few to aid the Maharana now. We serve better by amassing more soldiers for the assault."

Captain Jaswant didn't like the Rathore's words. He doubted Mewar could count on the Rathore clan to come to his ruler's aid rather than protect their own forts. He knew they could inflict damage to hamper the siege, if they acted swiftly. They could drive the enemy back long enough to take the road into the palace and join the Maharana's army within.

He looked at Captain Sardar for assurance. "I say we press on, surprise the Mughals, bite their flanks like jackals. What do you say, Captain Sardar?"

"Yes, force them to break rank before more troops arrive. Catch them by surprise."

"I will not commit my men to a siege in Mewar, leaving my own land unprotected," Ram Singh said sternly in anger. "If the Emperor overruns Ajmer, he would take Mehrangarh Fort on his march through Jodhpur. Marwar would fall."

"Open your eyes, man. The desert crawls with enemies. Your prince hides in the Aravalli Hills, not far from here. I know where he stays. How long do you think it will be before the enemy finds him? Before they kill him? Your hope lies with Mewar. We defeat the Mughals, now, here. Bring the boy to our fortress for safety. Either we defeat the Emperor here and now, or lose everything. Your kingdom's alliance with the Emperor, finished! He's your enemy – and ours. Together we fight. Together we win."

Captain Sardar glared at Ram Singh. Jaswant saw his brother's evident disgust, lips pulled taut, jaw muscles quivering, face a deep red-brown. He wondered, if he were Ram Singh would he align with a man displaying such barely controlled aggression.

"You Sisodias, you only see the tiger when it's in front of you! You react only, not plan. With time, troops and strategy, we defeat the Mughals. Look beyond the siege of your fortress to the siege of all Rajputana. We must use the best approach, in total, not just for today in Mewar only."

"Friends, brothers," Captain Jaswant said, "don't waste yourselves before battle. We must band together to survive. If more Mughal troops approach from the north, from Bijai Nagar, we must see their strength first. As much as I do not want to, I would wait to attack if that means keeping our clans united."

The men grumbled among themselves, Mewaris gathered together on one side of the courtyard, Marwaris on the other. Captain Sardar paced up and down between the two, spitting out his words like water hitting flame.

"I wait only to see what we face, no more. You, Ram Singh, send a messenger to Jodhpur, gather news. As for me and my men, we strike out at dawn, scout east and south, to see what imperial soldiers lurk in the desert. If Marwar refuses to join, better we know sooner than later."

"Agreed," Commander Ram Singh growled. "I take my men north. You," he said, pointing at his officer, "ride for Jodhpur tonight. Tell the council all you have heard."

Captain Sardar stormed from the temple courtyard. The Mewari village-soldiers saluted him then drifted away from the Rathores to make their bedding for the night far from them on the opposite courtyard within the compound wall.

Captain Jaswant walked the grounds in search of the village messenger boy but couldn't find him. When he asked, no one had seen the boy since morning. Jaswant walked back to check his horse, tethered in the makeshift stable by the well. He found his brother.

Sardar leaned against the wall, his body rigid like a post askew trying to support a heavy lintel, his shoulders sloping to the ground. Jaswant understood that inside Sardar a cobra was ready to strike.

"Look here, Sardar, look at what Devi gave me," Jaswant said, handing his brother the ukku steel triple-blade dagger.

"How heavy it is, this metal. Where did she get it?"

"There are more," Jaswant said.

"Such fine work," Captain Sardar said with disbelief. "Look at the engraving on this dagger, feel the weight, the exact balance, the sharpness. This is... I have seen this workmanship before – in the Maharana's personal armory.

I believe this is ukku, a legendary metal from the south. Only royalty owned it. Did Devi steal these?"

"No. A villager, to the west, gave them as a gift."

"When? To the Maharana?"

"Not long ago, I believe."

Captain Jaswant didn't want to tell Sardar he had seen Devi – and let her travel alone to the besieged palace. Yet he knew soon someone would mention her having been in the forest. "She rode through the forest this afternoon as we waited for you and Commander Ram Singh to return."

Sardar looked at him with a quizzical expression, his massive black eyebrows reaching to touch his tightly wound golden turban. "Where is she now? I haven't seen her."

"She rode for the... palace, to be with the Maharana."

"After all that, she leaves you! And you let her go into the enemy's hands? Have you gone mad? What kind of man are you? She must be dead by now."

Jaswant sighed. A thousand fears spilled out, weighing down his chest like boulders. "She would not listen. She would not stop. She handed me the satchel of ukku and said she would enter the palace by the old aqueduct."

"What old aqueduct? Where?"

"When she... when we were young, we used to meet there. We discovered it by accident as children, on the west shore. Afterwards, it became our secret place. It must have been built and abandoned, even before the palace was finished. We never traveled its length. The tunnel is lined with marble, large enough for a man to walk, even two abreast in places. I do not know if it reaches within the rampart walls of the palace. She rode to find out."

"I know nothing of this."

"Huzur may not know either."

Captain Sardar appeared lost in thought for a moment. "I'll rest here tonight, food and sleep, necessary before battle, call to me. I will ride to the west shore before dawn. I must find where Devi entered, follow the passage, warn the Maharana. He can determine how I may best serve him – inside the fortress or out here."

"Should we take the Mewari men?"

"No. We risk being spotted. Come with me. Bring a soldier to return our horses here to the temple. The villagers serve better by protecting the old priest."

Captain Jaswant looked at his brother and smiled. "A lifetime of brotherhood ends not with the revelation of an old gypsy's trick, stealing an infant. Sardar, you are my brother as sure as I breathe. We remain forever bound."

"Yes, and if destined to rule in Maharana's stead for his heir, I appoint you commander of the army, if you do not flee across the Rann of Kutch, or tie a lazy, bright turban and declare yourself a gypsy of Sindh."

"I cannot flee my home."

"And Devi?"

"I cannot leave her. She cannot flee him."

Sardar tugged at his beard as if he could straighten out their lives.

"People's memories are long, Jaswant. Gossip must have spread. Her parents – my mother – will be publicly shamed. I know Devi. She will do anything to spare her mother. Brother, I fear you have few options that offer you peace – and the title of captain."

Jaswant inhaled deeply, his chest rising like armor. "Brother, first things first. I cannot weave a tomorrow on the scant threads of today. More than gossip threatens our world. Rest. We ride hard before the light." Jaswant walked to his horse and settled down on a sweat-stained saddle blanket.

"I will make my rounds and join you. Rathores keep watch tonight."

"Sardar, I worry about the village boy. He must have lost his way, or else he would have returned by now. Tiger and panther traverse those hills."

"He missed his mother's curry only. I cannot fault him. He had never taken up arms – knew only the plow. Just as well he left. She will need him."

Captain Jaswant's horse nuzzled him. The warm breath smelling of dried sweetgrass comforted him. He slept. In a dream he heard soldiers. A shrill whistle. He grabbed his sword and ran out into the night. He heard a horseman approaching at a run. Muskets exploded bright rings of light in the darkness. A horse neighed and crashed through a gap in the gate, splintering the wooden post. Jaswant bolted awake.

A dislodged rider stumbled forward, shouting, "Stop! I am Mewari." The boy collapsed.

Captain Sardar roared, "All halt!" He rushed to the fallen boy and bent over him. "Are you shot?"

"No, sir," he mumbled, too fatigued to elaborate.

"Bring water."

After the boy drank and cleared his throat of dust, Captain Sardar stood him up. "I am sorry, sir, I got lost.

Captain Jaswant sent me back from the forest for Eklingji, but I lost my way. I traveled north towards Raj Samund, by the River Banas. Sir, an old camel driver told me Mughals gather there, thousands! From the hills I watched their camp. Fires spread all along the river. A city of tents up river as far as I could see. I turned back and rode hard to warn you."

Captain Ram Singh said, "I believe the Emperor means to crush Rajputana! With so many in the hills, they will find the Rathore prince."

"Send word to the prince's family," Captain Sardar said, looking at the boy. "What a fine young soldier you are," he said and straightened the boy's turban. "I should like a brave man like you in my army."

Commander Ram Singh broke in: "Captain, I would if I were able. The prince's whereabouts are not known, even to us commanders."

"Captain Ram Singh, I can send word. We have tracked him, for his safety. What do you think now?"

"I return to Marwar to gather an army. We shall join the battle at your fortress within two weeks. The Maharana of Udaipur will not fall in so short a time, not even with thousands at his door. Your fortress and soldiers stand strong. With 30,000 troops I shall march against the Mughals."

Captain Jaswant knew the Rathore commander was correct, yet the thought of so many Mughal troops approaching made him wild with anger and impatience. "Captain Sardar, what now?"

"We leave before dawn," Captain Sardar replied quietly. "We'll follow the secret tunnel into the fortress on foot. We protect the Maharana. The Mughal army, if they march from Raj Samund, will not leave before morning light. We have no time to waste."

The young boy rocked on unsteady feet. "I will come, sir. I can report all I have seen."

"Captain Ram Singh, we await your men," Sardar said with urgency in his voice.

"Captain Sardar, I send a man with you to take your war horses to safety far from here. I fear Eklingji soon will be destroyed."

Captain Jaswant raised his sword. His brother and all the men joined their weapon tips together and shouted, "Victory to the mighty Rajputs! Long live our clans! Long live Rajputana!"

Captain Sardar walked away to speak in privacy with the Rathore commander while Jaswant walked up to the boy.

"You are a fine soldier, son. No easy matter to ride those jagged hills in the dark."

"The horse, sir, he decided the way. I thought I knew the way to Eklingji. He pulled the other way. He convinced me. He wanted to see what trouble fouled the air. He discovered Mughals. Only then did he guide me here through the darkness."

"Yes, he's a fine horse. We trained him. He understands what it means to be a war horse. A horse such as this, worth a fortune, will always protect his rider."

"Yes, sir," the boy said stroking the horse's forelock. The animal nuzzled the boy's shoulder, gummed his tunic in his mouth.

"I gift him to you, son."

"Sir?"

"He chose you. Consider him a gift from the Maharana for brave service."

The peasant boy's eyes lit up. "Such a fine animal, he's too good for the plow, yet that is all I know. I cannot accept such a gift. I thank you for the offer, sir."

"True. Too fine for the plow, but for the Royal Army? With your commission, your family can live comfortably."

The boy looked at Captain Jaswant. He removed his turban, bowed, and placed it at the captain's feet.

"Your name, son?"

"Rawal Singh, sir."

"Well, Rawal Singh," Captain Jaswant said, removing his own turban and placing it in the boy's hands. "We exchange turbans now as brothers."

The boy's huge smile crinkled his eyes to raisins. "I swear to protect you and serve you with honor, sir."

"And I you," Captain Jaswant said with a smile. "Now, get some rest. We ride before dawn."

Captain Sardar and Captain Jaswant slept fitfully, startled awake throughout the night at sounds from the darkness. But it was only boar grunts and jackal yips. When the priests rose at three o'clock to prepare for morning puja, they roused the soldiers.

When the captains approached, the old man smiled at them as if he already knew and blessed them. "Lord Shiva protect you and bring you victory! Great storm clouds subside and reveal greater light."

"Old priest, you should leave. The Mughals will sack Eklingji," Sardar replied.

"No, they lay siege at our Maharana's palace. We priests remain safe here at our temple, after your soldiers depart."

"Mughals spare no one. Rathore soldiers will escort you to safety in Marwar," Captain Jaswant said, exasperated.

"We remain. Our duty lies here only, with our Lord," the old Brahmin replied and mumbled a prayer, rubbing his sandalwood prayer beads.

Captain Sardar clasped his hands in blessing and said, "When able, I will send troops for your protection."

"And I beseech Lord Shiva, our greatest protector, to grant you success in your destiny." The old priest turned away from the soldiers to light his incense.

In the darkness of a gray world before first light streaked the sky, the men saddled their horses, ate the warm rotis the priests had prepared for them, and packed their weapons. After prayers, the Rathores marched west, the Mewaris south, led by Captain Sardar, slowly, over jagged hills, leaving the valley of temples behind.

Jaswant rode ahead to scout. When the rocky granite terrain grew brighter, the soldiers increased their pace. Some three hours later Captain Jaswant spied Lake Pichola in the distance, its white marble palace a dull amber illuminated by a dusty morning sun. He rode back to speak to Sardar.

He approached the soldiers. Sardar lowered his sword, recognizing him, even at a full canter. "Captain Sardar, I know the aqueduct, not easy to find, less so to describe, with your permission, I request to ride ahead. With so many horses stirring dust, we could be spotted. Please, remain in place until I signal. Keep to the trees for the next mile. Tether your horses, uphill, in the thicket. Go on foot through the reeds after you see my all clear."

"Understood. Down there, where the trees curve away from the lake, I shall dismount," Captain Sardar said, pointing. "If you do not signal or return, the men will retreat deeper into forest cover. I shall come alone on foot to find the opening. Describe it again."

"Thick grasses and reeds mark the area; blue hyacinth flowers choke the lake in the small inlet nearby. You should see granite rocks, hewn into squares, part-buried in mud near the lake's shore. Look uphill from that spot for a dirt embankment. It hides the opening. I do not know its appearance after so many years, but when Devi and I discovered it, rocks flanked the embankment, grasses grew in front of the marble slab that partially topped the opening. Squeeze sideways through the narrow opening. It widens out into a tunnel."

Jaswant kept to the trees, his form blending with the foliage. But shafts of morning light cut through the branches and fell across him, he knew, making him appear and reappear. He wished it were later in the day. He craned his head side to side to listen, relieved to hear only the heavy breathing of his horse. He dismounted and tethered his horse, rubbed his forelock. The horse nudged up and down his arm and gave a hard shake to shoo the flies away. The saddle leathers flapped. It sounded like thunder to Jaswant in the stillness of the trees.

He continued on foot to the tall reeds that bordered the shore. Crouching low, his vision impaired by the broad spiny leaves as he moved them aside, he made his way toward the piles of squared rocks strewn by the shore, remnants of a structure destroyed by flood waters. He stopped. Ahead he sighted a lone Mughal by the water's edge, his horse taking long gulps. The soldier looked in Jaswant's direction at swaying reeds in the windless morning.

Jaswant charged him, dagger drawn. The Mughal reached for his musket secured in saddle leathers, but turned to face the on-comer with his sword. He stepped away from his horse and lunged when Jaswant attacked. He sliced but missed. Jaswant jumped back. From the side he sprang on the Mughal. They wrestled to the ground. Jaswant's dagger ripped into the man's chest. With little pressure it continued to his groin. Jaswant jumped up, backed away, stunned by what he saw – the man's chest flayed wide open. He grabbed the man's sword and dagger and tossed them into the reeds. The horse shied away from him and trotted into the trees.

He spotted Sardar grabbing the horse's reins and tying him in the shade of the trees. Jaswant motioned him to join him.

"Ukku, sliced clear through him," Sardar whispered. "Legendary metal."

Captain Sardar followed his brother through lake grasses along the water's edge to the inlet choked by blue hyacinth. They searched uphill for the embankment. Grass and limbs from many floods had modified the earth. They spread out to study the terrain. When Jaswant spotted disturbed soil, uphill, he pointed.

Sardar approached where Jaswant kneeled, digging with a dagger. Metal screeched on stone. He cleared a small area, pushed crusted dirt off gray marble, and used grasses to wipe away his and Sardar's footprints.

"This is the entrance, filled with years of flood debris, but from here the tunnel rises up away from the lake to the palace. Your orders, brother?"

"Wait here, we go together. Let me fetch the men and send the horses back with the escort," Captain Sardar said.

By the time the last man slipped into the hidden channel, morning heat beat down. But inside, the tunnel remained cool – and stale. Sardar tore his cotton turban into shreds and balled it around his sword tip. He poured ghee the priest had given him for his bread and struck stones to ignite the mass.

The first half-mile, easy to follow, became constricted farther on, too narrow for two men to walk upright, abreast. Smooth marble walls gave way in segments to jagged rock that oozed water from tiny fissures. Uneven ground with protruding sharp angles made it difficult to walk. A foul smell filled the channel.

Sardar halted the party and made his way back to Jaswant, who brought up the rear. Quietly he asked, "Not a trap, a false tunnel, meant for intruders? Did you ever come this far?"

"Never."

They pushed on, eyes watering from the stench and smoke of the cotton torch. A village-soldier spoke. "Captain Sardar Ji, I am noticing one thing not here."

"What?"

"Rats. The tunnel has no rats. You know where there are no rats..."

"Shh, silence."

As if on cue, the men stopped in place to listen. They heard loud scratching noises ahead in the blackness.

"Rats?" someone asked.

"No, a deliberate pattern," Jaswant said. "Sardar, we go first."

Captain Jaswant squeezed past the others to reach his brother's back. They pulled their daggers. Sardar handed off the torch, and they continued forward. After several minutes the scratching stopped. Stooping low in the narrowing space, they walked until Sardar hit something and pitched forward toward the ground. He landed on a spiky mound. He jumped up.

"A body."

Jaswant pushed his brother aside. "A man!" he said, retracting his fingers from a crusty beard. "Not her." He side-stepped over the body, fearing what – or who – the next few steps might bring. He tapped the dimly lit ground with his sword. No obstructions. He called for the others to follow. For an hour they inched along hunched over, cramped and fatigued. They squatted periodically to rest.

"This seems too long, brother. I fear this leads us to the field behind the palace," Captain Sardar said.

A village-soldier spoke up. "Sir, this tunnel weaves side to side but goes uphill only, sometimes more, sometimes less. I think, unless it drops soon, we must be high in the fortress grounds, part of the aqueduct system. I work as a gardener in the palace when my uncle cannot. We may come out behind the palace where the spring flows from a field."

Another man added, "Captain, I also farm. On my land the spring bubbles low. I lift water up to higher crops with persian wheel, pulled by my buffalo. I have heard the palace has running water on every level, terraces with trees and shrubs. How possible? Water runs downhill, unless lifted by persian wheels."

"I do not know where this tunnel opens, yet I thought I knew the palace-fortress well," Captain Sardar said. "We may find ourselves above the fortress, out in the open, but I do not believe the Mughals could be there, yet. Or we could exit in the palace itself. No time to waste. Follow me."

From a distance, the sound of scratching resumed, louder now, with more force. They marched along, hunched in the darkness since the turban lamp had gone out. A dull clattering echoed along the walls. A faint glimmer of light appeared ahead in a small opening. It disappeared. A landslide filled it in, extinguishing the light.

A loud rumble echoed down the tunnel. The soldiers retreated as fast as they could in the darkness. A large boulder slammed into the wall ahead of them and became lodged between the walls. A hail of small stones pelted them. They crouched in place, their own stifled breaths filling the space.

With daggers, spears, hands and swords they chipped away at the stones to create a narrow gap between the boulder and the wall. Captain Jaswant squeezed through the rubble first and saw light shining ahead, through an opening above. They enlarged the gap, slipped past the boulder one by one. They scrambled to an enlarged area where they could stand at full height in a cavern dripping with water, populated by strange rock arms hanging down and growing up from the uneven floor.

Jaswant spotted a simple pole ladder resting against the cave wall below the opening in the ceiling. He climbed out into daylight and stood in a place he had never seen before: the zenana.

The women's quarters were deserted. Only the fragrance of rose and sandalwood lingered around the large silver metal bath. Captain Jaswant rushed from the quarters to the open balcony. Emerging from the zenana, covered in dirt and carrying a sword, Jaswant saw a soldier on the rampart take aim and fire at him. He dove behind the heavy wooden door.

Captain Sardar ran up from behind him and yelled: "Hold your fire. Captain Sardar Singh here and Captain Jaswant Singh!"

The soldier, recognizing his captain's voice, dropped his musket, and shouted, "Hold fire!" down the line. Astonished soldiers turned, looked up from their stations, and saluted. Men rushed down from the upper parapet to cover the captains and the soldiers as they crossed to the rampart.

Captain Jaswant spotted a Mughal war elephant deposit a huge cannon in front of the spiked gate. He yelled, "Take cover!" just before the cannon fired.

The palace shook. Masonry cracked and fell away leaving ugly holes in the white marble. A soldier on the parapet shot the Mughal before he could load another cannon ball. The Mughals fired back with a cascade of arrows, striking the soldier's metal breastplate, bouncing off his helmet, chipping the marble floor. He stumbled from the impact and fell forward, almost falling from the wall. Musket fire exploded on the Mughals. Captain Jaswant ran for his brother.

"Sardar, I go to find Huzur, to tell him about Devi and let him know we have joined."

"Yes, we stay and hold the rampart."

Captain Jaswant bolted across the zenana courtyard hidden by its marble filigree screen where soldiers treated many wounded, staunching their bleeding with wads of cotton and aromatic herbs, before transporting them down to the cellar. Their numbers horrified and worried him. Had the battles been so savage in so short a time? He ran past hundreds who lay moaning on makeshift hay bedding, women tending their wounds.

Captain Jaswant ran up the steps towards the durbar hall, past soldiers who saluted him, when a volley of arrows, like deadly silver birds dropping from the sky, whined in the air. He shielded his head with a shard of marble. Soldiers flashed past him to the west wall where a cannon ball had struck. The air reeked of bitter smoke that burned his mouth and nose. Gray haze blotted the late morning sun, casting a dull pallor over the scene. Soldiers slumped against the cool interior courtyard wall for a moment of rest while others pummeled the Mughals with musket fire and arrows.

From the entrance to the durbar hall, Jaswant saw a soldier in the lower courtyard yank a team of stomping, fidgeting horses into position, straining on their leathers, to position a cannon inside the west gate courtyard. They unhooked the exhausted animals and led them to safety before two men hoisted the lead ball, shoved it down the channel, and lit the fuse. Everyone jumped back.

The cannon fired, rocked backwards, and started a quake that rumbled along the fortress floor and echoed off palace walls. Screams and shouts followed. Below, a Mughal cannon and war elephant slipped down the incline. The elephant broke his restraints and ran in panic, crushing soldiers below the cannon's path. The hole in the Mughal advance filled quickly with new soldiers firing at the palace ramparts.

Captain Jaswant burst into the durbar hall. The guard jumped aside to admit him. He rushed to the Maharana, hunched over a parchment map of the palace, making large black marks in charcoal for the heaviest fighting, and saluted.

The Maharana looked at him and winced.

"Huzur, here to report. Mughals march from the north, from Raj Samund, north of Eklingji! Only hours from here, thousands strong."

"Vizier's men have been at us day and night. East gate suffered damage but holds, the west wall, crumbling in spots. Sardar? Your men?"

"On the west wall, fighting."

"How many march from the north?"

"Huzur, I have no first-hand knowledge. Estimates, as many as 180,000 men led by the Emperor."

"So, he comes. Let him. We fight to the last man. Come with me to the tower, witness the scourge bearing down on us."

"Huzur, please accept this dagger." The Maharana studied it and studied his captain.

"Ukku, very fine, a welcome gift."

The Maharana grabbed his leather-clad seeing lens. Holding the jeweled hilt of his musket, he marched out of the durbar hall. They climbed covered stairs that opened onto the highest point of the fortress from where they could see for miles in all directions. Jaswant didn't need to look far. Approaching along the lake, horsemen, behind them, bullocks pulling huge cannons. The Maharana steadied his lens.

After a moment, he spoke. "180,000 men? Less than a thousand. An advance to soften us, no doubt. That lying jackal leads."

"Emperor Aurangzeb?"

"No, his son, Prince Akbar. He rode here to enlist my support. He plans to overthrow his father, rule in his stead, as a friend to Rajputs – and with temperance, he says. Not to be trusted, this son, a sly fox. He called me Rajput brother. Now he rides against me, brings the Emperor's forces down on me.

"The vizier warned me about the Emperor's errant son, but I trusted the vizier less than a snake, his words – poison. The son, I liked – for a Mughal. By murdering the vizier, Captain Sardar revealed and unleashed the coming storm. The imperial force must stretch from our door to Shahjahanabad. Well, let Aurangzeb come. We fight for the glory of Mewar. I pray Shiva the Destroyer guides us in battle. Mewar has never been subjugated. My eyes will not see it. May the gods give us victory!"

The Maharana handed the seeing lens to Captain Jaswant. He spotted Prince Akbar sitting atop a fine gray horse in full battle gear. Turning he said, "Huzur, Rathores gather forces to come to our aid."

"Rathores? If they number less than 30,000, they will be of little use. They may impede the assault by biting the Emperor's flanks, but the teeth of jackal Prince Akbar rip from the other end, a battle no man wants."

"Huzur, I failed you."

"Failed Devi, you mean. She's injured. Do not fail me. I charge you with guarding the heir to the throne if the battle goes against me. Take him to Sardar, for safety. Captain Sardar will serve as guardian until he comes of age. If Sardar falls, you serve. The court scribe recorded my command. Do as I say."

"Yes, Huzur. I will do as you say."

After a moment of silence, Jaswant said, "May I ask how is Devi?"

"Devi returned, not very long before my men spotted you. She dug her way back through the tunnel. The women tend her now."

"Dying?"

"Not Devi! But you found the body? A Mughal followed her into the tunnel. They fought. He sliced her shoulder. She slayed him. Devi rests in the infirmary."

"Huzur, we found a decomposed body, not a fresh one."

"She must have dragged him out of the way, into a side chamber."

A loud explosion rocked the palace. "Excuse me, Huzur. I must see."

Captain Jaswant flew down four levels of stairs to the cellar for women and children. He surprised the eunuchs guarding the door. They lunged forward, crossed their swords over the entrance. Recognizing him, they eased their grips and stepped aside.

"Too slow! I could have broken through!"

One of the eunuchs, incensed by Captain Jaswant's words, straightened his tunic and flicked his sword in the air. He and the other eunuch assumed their iron-like stances, swords crossed over their chests, feet planted below their shoulders, at the ready.

Women gasped when Captain Jaswant flashed into the infirmary. Mira ran up to him.

"Namaste, Captain, we know you ran a brave mission for our king. Thank you. My brother has much need of you. You saved Devi. She is recovering well."

Mira led him to Devi's private compartment where she reclined on a mat. As soon as Devi saw Jaswant, she pushed herself to a sitting position with one arm, stifling a moan and tears. "I take my leave, for now," Mira said and closed the door behind her.

"You are safe, Jaswant. I prayed you would be. The others? Sardar?"

"Safe, for now. Here. Rathores returned to Marwar to gather forces. Village-soldiers, some thirty, joined the battle. What happened, Devi?"

"A lone soldier followed me into the tunnel. We fought. He died. He sliced my shoulder. I had no time to turn. I stabbed backwards with my dagger. He died so quickly he fell on top of me," she said wincing. "I had to wiggle out from under his bloody body. My dagger, like the one I gave to you, slices with little force. I almost cleaved him in two. Horrible."

"I carry one as does the Maharana. I gave him one just now. Those villagers gifted you a great prize."

"I gifted them a great prize also. I left Geeta there, to marry. Promise, Jaswant, keep this secret. She chose her fate."

"I must go up top. I wanted to see you, to convince my heart. To see you safe gives me strength for the battle."

Devi's dark lashes squeezed back tears. "Jaswant, whatever this day holds, remember in your heart I have always loved you."

"I know, Devi. Had our destinies been different..." Jaswant said and kissed her forehead.

"Forever," Devi said.

Mira walked in, carrying yellow dahl and rice for her patient. From the hallway came fitful cries of anxious children.

"Namaste," Captain Jaswant said and rushed out of the cellar to the hall and took the stairs in great leaps until a cannonball hit the fortress, throwing him up against the wall.

A huge cloud of blue smoke rose to the second balcony. He ran to the rampart wall, looked below, and shook his head in disbelief to see the imperial forces under Prince Akbar's banner approach. Bullocks straining to pull cannons uphill led the way.

Captain Jaswant watched riders halt, position the cannons, and fire. The fortress shuddered from the explosion. Men collapsed on the rough ground outside the palace wall.

Jaswant craned his neck to the left to see the fallen soldiers and recognized them: vizier's soldiers.

To the right, below, he spotted Prince Akbar in imperial military uniform, firing on the vizier's troops who lay siege to the fortress. The captain caught his breath. A Mughul, true to his promise! he thought in dismay. He bolted. Reaching the Maharana's compartment at a dead run, he nearly knocked down Captain Sardar. Another round of blasts rocked the air. The brothers rushed into the durbar hall.

They found the Maharana on the balcony studying the battle below and witnessed the prince's men open fire and charge the vizier's men, breaking their formation and sending them in all directions. Muskets fired, swords clashed, arrows flew. Men on both sides dropped.

The vizier's men hurried to reposition their cannons to fire on the assaulting troops, not the palace. A round of cannonballs hurtled into the vizier's troops before they could aim, sending horses and riders to the ground.

Prince Akbar cleared a swath with cannon fire before his mounted soldiers charged, swords drawn. A few musket shots sounded, but the battle progressed so fast the vizier's men had no time to close ranks. Hand-to-hand combat raged while the Mewaris watched the Mughals slay one another.

"What you see, Captains," the Maharana said, "is son against father. Prince Akbar wages war to depose his father, crown prince versus emperor, as he proposed to me when requesting our support. Yet battle came without my reply."

"And where is the Emperor?" Captain Sardar said.

"Not close enough to stop this slaughter. The prince may not like his father, but he is born of him, as we see. He will, now or soon, die at his father's hand unless we aid him in his effort. The prince declared his father's troops will obey him; well, that remains to be seen.

"Captain Sardar, give the hold-fire signal to our men. Let the Mughals have their day, pitted one against another while we conserve our resources."

When Captain Sardar and Captain Jaswant reached the wall and waved cease fire, the Mewari soldiers stopped firing and watched the battle below. The vizier's remaining men broke rank and ran. Prince Akbar's soldiers cut them down as they fled.

Musket fire and cannon volleys ceased. Anguished cries and the clang of metal to metal pierced the dissipating blue cannon smoke. The remaining vizier's soldiers ran toward the forest. The prince pursued. From the fortress walls, the sound of random musket fire, even the roar of a tiger, wafted in murky air.

"I hope she escapes," the Maharana said. "The Mughals will suffer if my prize tigress is hurt. Captains, fortify the walls. Call every man we have into position. Stand ready. Prince Akbar may yet turn on me. Let's see if he keeps his word."

"Huzur?" Captain Sardar said.

The Maharana faced his captain. "He promised this, what you witnessed. He was not to let the vizier's men attack. In that he failed. He may have a motive beyond the obvious. He has met me in secret for months to form an alliance with Mewar against the Emperor. The vizier, on the other hand, came to seek my support for the Emperor's push into the Deccan, assurance of safe passage, loan of my ablest soldiers.

"The vizier's was no attack force, or so I thought. Captain Sardar, when you slit the vizier's throat, his men assumed it was on my order and attacked the fortress. You acted rashly, Captain, but in destiny's hand it seems you may have acted for the best. Now the Emperor will focus his brutal reprisal on his insurgent son. That gives us time to fortify, to strike, if the Rathores will join us.

"The Emperor intends to subdue Shivaji's son, Shambaji, in the Deccan, now that Shambaji continues his father's battle against the emperor. For that the Emperor sought the help of Mewar. Do not assume the old man had no idea his son planned to overthrow him. He is not so simple. He himself did the same to his father. We must move with care. If the Emperor thinks we are aligned with his son, he will unleash his full force upon us as punishment.

"We must appear to support the Emperor until the final hour when we launch a united attack with the forces of Mewar, Marwar, and Prince Akbar. If Prince Akbar succeeds in his bid for the empire, he swears he will rule in the way of his namesake Emperor Akbar – glory words at best – yet I know he does not have the prowess in battle. He would make an easier enemy for Mewar to defeat."

"What good to exchange one Mughal emperor for another? I am sure Prince Akbar would wear the Koh-i-Noor diamond just as boldly as any other Mughal ruler," Captain Sardar said. "Yet Prince Akbar is not his father.

"I believe he desires a legacy of advancement, in the arts, the elegant arts, not the art of war as his father chooses.

We must be practical. Can we trust a man who turns on his father? It takes no fool to see a male in the Emperor's family is not safe, not son, nor father. We must watch this prince with an eagle's eye. Should he prove successful, I will negotiate for peace and autonomy for Mewar – on my terms. No subjugation."

"Huzur, the prince's troops," Captain Jaswant said, "how many swear him allegiance? Emperor Aurangzeb has 180,000 men to our north."

"Your account is mistaken. The Emperor's troops spread along the northern front of Afghanistan, throughout Punjab, and south to the Deccan. A special contingent holds Shahjahanabad only. In total 180,000 but spread wide.

"The movement of troops you heard about are the prince's men. He has been amassing forces in the north between Mewar and Marwar for some time, the numbers far fewer than gossip implies. He plans to attack his father's troops in Ajmer, with the help of Mewar and Marwar, cut them off, thus defeating the Deccan offensive. That is when we rout the Mughals from our lands and secure an alliance with Shambaji's forces. Mewar will not be a vassal state!"

The Maharana walked to the balcony and looked out over the battlefield strewn with dead and wounded soldiers. "We will see what comes of this. Should he turn on us now, we remain battle-ready. Await my signal, Captains."

"Huzur, may I speak to you on a private matter?" Captain Jaswant said.

The Maharana, fingering the pearls on his turban, averted his eyes from his captain. "No, you may not. Take word to your men to keep the cannons positioned. And tell my former wife Devi to come to me."

"Yes, Huzur," Captain Jaswant said.

Jaswant knew neither he nor Devi could live with the shame of abandoning their king, especially in such perilous times. Every time he looked at her, he would see his own failure. She would resent the man she loved for luring her from the life of honor she had known, her way to atone for her mother's shame.

He wished Devi had never learned they were not related by blood. At least her rejection of him as her blood brother made it possible for him to serve his king and her. He made up his mind as he walked to the women's quarters: he would request a posting in the prince's company should Akbar turn out to be true. He could serve Huzur from a distance, show his loyalty. He could keep his king apprised of the prince's movements and aspirations.

The eunuch stepped aside and saluted the captain. Mira met Captain Jaswant at the entrance.

"How goes the battle? It seems the firing is farther away."

"Yes, Mughals are now fighting each other. Prince Akbar's men have routed the vizier's troops into the forest."

A smile spread across Mira's small face, revealing her square, even teeth. She said no more.

"Your brother wishes Queen Devi to join him in his quarters."

"I will bring her as soon as she dresses."

Captain Jaswant gave her a quick nod of retreat and left. Soldiers along the rampart walls stood casually, talked among themselves and watched the dust in the distance. From one tower to another the "all clear" call livened their spirits. Captain Jaswant stood at the uppermost tower, surveying the battlefield. His brother approached.

"I will send out a detachment soon to survey the walls and grounds below the palace, Jaswant. Would you like to join?"

"Yes, Captain."

"Just us two, then – my brother and me. We lead together."

"You consider me as such?"

"Jaswant, we grew up together – twins! That creates kinship. You remain my brother, as ever."

"Does anyone know about you, Sardar?"

"Yes, I believe Mira does. Huzur told her since I am her cousin-brother too."

"Does that change things for you?"

"No. Well, yes... in a way. How could it not? I will never speak of this unless he chooses to make it known. But I feel a greater fondness for Lady Mira and Huzur, a recognition of sorts, not there before. No longer captain of the guard in his service only, I am captain and brother."

"Sardar, what of the divorce decree? Does he speak of it?" "No, not directly, but when he came to visit Devi, I burst in on them to report the west gate had cracked. I heard him say 'I destroyed the paper, an act of anger... at the moment.'"

# CHAPTER 14 –
## DAYS OF SPECULATION

Days passed. Devi felt herself in a dream, a memory barely retrieved from an abyss of war, love, and loss, all tangled together yet without distinct form. She wondered if the herbal concoction to ease her shoulder pain caused her confusion.

The world outside the fortress wall grew quiet: no cannon fired, no musket cracked the still air, no movement stirred, other than villagers plying their paths to market. Peace settled on the palace like a welcome fog flowing down from large puffy thunderheads gathered in the distance, portending rain. The air became sticky with expectancy.

The women returned to the zenana and enjoyed life as before, fanned by eunuchs while they played pachisi, exchanged battle stories, mostly fabricated, and relaxed in flower-scented baths, hoping for a request from the Maharana. One topic on everyone's lips, discussed in hushed tones, remained the disappearance of Huzur's youngest wife, Geeta. No one had seen her go. Many feared the worst – she was of nervous disposition and in youthful folly might have fled in a vain attempt to reach her village one last time to see her parents. Others accused her of fearing sati and chanced death by Mughal over death by flame. Her terrible insult to their husband justified whatever she suffered. She, a woman not fit to carry their night soil, had now disappeared in combat, abandoned her duty.

Devi heard the talk. She offered, "Geeta, very young, a child only – naturally she was afraid. Our zenana is at fault if she came to harm." At this statement the women grumbled and returned to their games, unwilling to challenge Devi to the point of angering her. Her injury horrified them, no explanation accompanied it and Mira instructed no questions either.

Devi had changed. Her sullenness had shifted to strength. She, more than ever, their husband's favorite, now was adored for her valor in war. "For what?" the women questioned among themselves, just close enough for Devi to hear, knowing for a Rajput ruler nothing could be more attractive, or enduring.

They acquiesced to her in every way, and kept their distance, which suited her well. Only Mira spoke to her. On the rare occasion when Huzur called one of his queens to his chamber, she made every effort to subtly criticize the youngest for desertion and Devi for they knew not what. Yet he would not reply. The wives perceived the profound insults they had inflicted, to the point of silencing him, and felt they had somehow wounded him, so they themselves ceased to comment – in his presence.

They assumed Geeta was dead. Huzur sent no troops to look for her. He did not speak of her. He seemed not to lament her going. This, more than anything, alarmed them and increased their desire to seek favor in whatever way possible. Devi knew they thought: Could they, too, be so easily lost? Fear fueled private battles to please. The Maharana's love of betel nut became a focal point. Each wife sought to serve him the freshest betel nut leaf smeared with the most pungent spices, sometimes ground while walking to his chamber to ensure the strongest aromatic appeal. Cardamom and clove drifted down the marble corridors like sunlight on the lake. Each wife put a pinch of khimam in the rolled leaf to increase personal pleasure.

Each wife proclaimed herself the favorite, knowing he spoke only of Devi, yet he rarely called for her and when he did, she remained for a very few minutes, never a night.

She, whom he had treasured above all, now healed from her wound, spent much time alone. His first wife, mother of his heir, studied Devi with a stare that implied her husband had finally seen the limitations of a village girl in courtly matters. Devi, nearing twenty-and-five years without producing a child, more useless than an old plow horse, and she couldn't dance, she overheard her say.

When she passed Devi on the balcony she whispered to her, "Clearly the gods and goddesses have closed your womb." Devi smiled and said, "I lament, the gods did not close your mouth. Take care how you address me," and pointed to the scar on her shoulder.

Devi sat alone in the zenana jharokha and watched life below through the marble screen. Masons repaired the damage done by Mughal cannons, metal workers forged new and greater spikes for the heavy gates, villagers arrived with bullock carts filled with supplies: bags of kumtia, the desert bean she so loved; saunth, dried ginger root; lentils;

stacks of paper-thin papadams, lentil wafers, spiced with black pepper and chili; small wheels of dark brown raw sugar; chickpeas; chickpea flour; wheat and rice; dried gavarfali, cluster beans, and the dried desert bean, sangri. She recognized the vendors and their carts, many of whom she had grown up with in her peasant life. She longed for their freedom.

The storehouse bulged with supplies. Earthen pots full of ghee lined the walls. When the spice vendors came, the scent of tej patta, bay leaves, asafetida, anise, fenugreek, chili powder, coriander, nutmeg, turmeric, cinnamon, black poppy seeds, and dried mango filled the courtyards with sweet and pungent aromas, enough to make anyone salivate with expectancy.

For Devi, it triggered home, her parents, her life at the market. Only Devi, of all the women, watched, listened and understood from her perch what lay beneath the pleasure of the aromas: Maharana stockpiling supplies for a long siege. Yet no news of war disturbed their days, at least not in the zenana.

She longed to speak to Jaswant, but since the siege he had not contacted her. She longed to speak to her husband; but he too avoided calling her.

One day she spotted a small hunting party leave the palace grounds, not a shikar for pleasure hunting with festive tents and noble guests, but a group of hunters outfitted to bring back on carts a large kill of wild boar, deer, rabbit, partridge – any meat that could be cured and stored. Upon their return, as Devi had correctly assumed, no lavish dinners, no important guests, no merriment enlivened palace life.

From a eunuch guard she learned the Maharana often took his evening meal alone, served by a wife but not enjoyed in her presence. In the Maharana Udai Singh tradition, she would lay out the huge leaf plate, denoting humility, and place on top the symbolic gold plate of rulership. He would then dismiss her and eat alone, in private.

From the zenana balcony Devi watched heavy, gray monsoon clouds gather. The rainy season approached. Hunting parties ceased in breeding season. Enough meat had been cured. Bags of grain and spices continued to come on camel, horse, and bullock, but at a slower pace.

Devi overheard two village farmers in the courtyard below discussing the Maharana's order to keep a portion for their family for the coming year and to store starter seed in earthen jars for the planting season. They gossiped that Brahmins had foretold of drought, famine, and war.

Fear ran high among the people. Devi knew that in the bazaar, alive with rumor, stories circulated about the Mughal prince. Prince Akbar's successful battles in the south would mean he would return to overrun Mewar, with the help of Shambaji.

Others feared the Rathores were gathering forces to annex Mewar to Marwar and subjugate their noble Sisodia clan.

Life seemed to pulse like a wildly beating heart – for everyone except Devi. She felt a chill in her veins, an emptiness in her heart. Her wound had healed, leaving only a scar, but the damage to her spirit she could not undo. She was bereft of Jaswant, for the duration of the war. And afterwards, if they survived – what then?

She longed to see her aging parents again, to smell the damp earth of the Meandering River, to wade among the large round leaves of pink lotuses in the inlet where as a child she pretended to reign as water diva. She begged the Maharana to invite her parents to the palace. Word came back to her, delivered by a eunuch, that he had complied with her request only to learn her mother was too ill to travel.

Devi considered her life at the palace. She knew she had to leave, whatever the cost. She swore to say goodbye to her parents before disappearing into the vast region of Sindh to the west. She had nothing to lose, except her life, which at this point she felt not worth preserving. To go on living as a caged bird meant to die a daily death.

Her only friend, Mira, was as lost to her now as if Devi had already run away – she never saw her any more. The Maharana had assigned her to design an upper apartment for housing historic paintings and relics of their lineage. Mira conferred with her brother by night and directed the artisans by day.

Halls decorated with colored glass mosaics, inlaid mirror work, and marble filigree screens to separate the display chambers required many workers and close supervision. Devi understood that her husband wanted to leave finery as his legacy – not war – so his people would remember him as a connoisseur of art, a thought that alarmed Devi for its finality even more than stockpiling supplies.

She watched painters from Udaipur row across the lake, bringing with them the miniature paintings the Maharana had commissioned – everything from partridges to people. Mira arranged for Devi to have a zenana eunuch escort her to the entrance to the new Hall of Paintings, where Devi saw a very fine miniature portrait of Mira. The Maharana liked it so well he commissioned the artist to duplicate it in a mural in his favorite suite – Mira leaning against a tree smiling at the viewer, her small even square teeth framed by a wide, mischievous smile. The painter captured a gleam of satisfaction in Mira's eyes, no doubt derived from directing so grand a project.

When Devi saw the mural, she couldn't hide her envy – not of Mira, whom she loved like a real sister, but of her opportunity to do something meaningful. Zenana women gossiped that the smile in the portrait came from Mira enjoying the painter himself, a talented yet common man.

Devi observed the first queen's happiness also, based, she assumed, on the crown prince's improving health. With the aid of Ayurvedic medicine, the boy had grown beyond childhood weakness and would most certainly be the future Maharana and keep his mother in devoted luxury. Her husband, with renewed interest, conferred often about the boy's progress.

Devi remained isolated in her thoughts, in her situation, and in her silent love for Jaswant.

Monsoon winds rolled over the Aravalli Hills with a fierceness not seen in years. In the distance, angry black clouds stabbed jagged white lightning daggers into the ground and made the earth shake and the zenana women jump. The smell of rain and fire mingled in the air. Parrots flew out of control trying to reach the safety of trees. Adventuresome ravens sought shelter in the marble eaves of the palace, some battered against the eaves dropped dead on the verandah. Cows tethered in the courtyard shelter stamped and wedged closer together. May-ur, may-ur, peacocks called to the impending rain, their cries filling the atmosphere like the lonely cry of love in Devi's heart.

At the lake, peasants gathered their washed clothes from the rocks to run for shelter. Devi watched large drops of rain splatter on the white marble city, turning it transparent gray. Vendors rushed to cover their wares and find a dry place to wait out the first storm of the monsoon season. Village children danced and played stick games in the cool rain, until their mothers called them in. Guards positioned along the fortress wall laughed and joked, retreated to shelter, sitting on their haunches to watch the sheets of rain stain the white marble walkways. In the distance Devi heard the tigress growl. Baboons shrieked. She realized that for everyone but her, joy replaced sorrow. Gods and goddesses had routed the Mughals and brought rain to Mewar. What greater sign did the people need that all was well?

Devi felt a shadow cross her heart. She looked up to see her husband. The Maharana studied long-fingered lightning on the horizon that slit a pregnant cloud and poured black rain on the hills. He jumped back from the verandah's edge, eyes wide. The raven's black shadow grew long across his body before the last ray of light beneath the distant cloud went out. Devi knew that boded no good. She saw fear in his face before he disappeared into his chamber.

The Maharana's summons reached Captain Jaswant in the field where he trained a three-year-old stallion for battle. The captain ran the animal straight at a wooden opponent over and over again, only allowing him to veer off to the side at the last second. The young horse bolted prematurely every time, until exhausted he did as his rider urged him. He ran straight at the target, allowing the captain to stab the dummy soldier with his sword. The captain dismounted and rubbed the horse down.

"He will make a fine battle horse with his sire's boldness and his dam's temper," Captain Jaswant said, handing the reins to the servant.

"Yes, Captain Ji, very fine. Last week he kicked down the stall door to attack a gelding that had come close to his grain! I would not want to meet this young horse in battle."

Then another servant arrived and saluted. "Captain Ji, the Maharana requests you in the durbar hall."

"Cool the horse down, then light food only today," the captain said to the stable boy. "He must be hungry for training. It increases his desire to please."

"Yes, sir, little grain," the stable boy said, walking the horse towards the stables.

Captain Jaswant didn't go to his chamber to change his soiled clothes before hurrying to the durbar hall. He felt agitated that Huzur would interrupt the training of a warhorse. When Captain Jaswant approached the entrance to the hall, the Maharana greeted him at the entrance. He appeared to be waiting for him there.

"Good, you have come," he said, ushering Captain Jaswant in and slamming the heavy door behind him.

"Huzur?"

"Captain, you have seen Prince Akbar up close. I know you could recognize him again, and he will recognize you. I need you to find him and deliver this message. I have received word from the Rathores. It is time to unite our troops with theirs to help the prince overthrow his father. We cannot wait. The Emperor's troops at Ajmer broke camp. At present his force, relatively small, numbers some thirty thousand. Soon, he means to march south.

"If Mewar is not his ally, we are his enemy, and he will overrun our lands. His wrath will flow like blood. If the prince means to strike, now is the time for a fatal blow. Ride to his camp in the hills, tell him we, Mewar and Marwar, stand ready. We must strike within three days, before the waxing moon reaches full."

"Before the full moon, Huzur?"

"Sardar reported to me Brahmin Ji said Lord Shiva spoke to him saying before the moon peaks, truth will be tested, troops will move. Alliances will become clear. Prepare for battle. The Rathore spies inform me the prince's men hide in the hills near Bilara. Find him. Report back to me. Our men stand ready."

"Yes, Huzur. Captain Sardar…"

"Say nothing of your mission, not even to Sardar. Should the prince lay a trap for us on his father's command, I would not want my men to know how close I came to gambling our freedom. Should he be true, we will know soon enough. If Sardar makes a move, his men will know. I need secrecy."

Captain Jaswant wasted no time. He collected his gear and rode out, unnoticed, into the forest. He kept off the main trails and traveled north before stopping for the night in a small canyon. Arising at dawn he rode on. The day had not yet grown warm when he stopped at a spring to water his horse. He crouched to wash his face and drink the sweet water. His horse side-stepped nervously beside him. He sensed someone approach.

Captain Jaswant jumped back on his horse and hid in the grasses behind the babul tree to watch. A rider galloped up, yanked his winded horse to a halt, and jumped down to drink. Captain Jaswant knew from his tunic he was a Mughal soldier. A solitary Mughal soldier in a great hurry. A scout. He drew his musket and aimed at the man's back.

"You. Turn, stand. Why do you hurry?" The soldier did as he was told. Seeing the rifle, he stood silent. "Answer me, man, what business have you here?"

The soldier dropped his horse's reins and took off towards the rocks. Captain Jaswant chased him on foot. He rounded a knot of boulders and dropped upon the soldier from above. The man raised his sword. Jaswant lunged and brought him down, slashing with his dagger before the man could spring at him. Pinning him to the ground, Captain Jaswant drew a red streak across the hollow of the man's throat.

"Answer me, where do you go?"

The soldier refused to speak. Captain Jaswant put sufficient pressure to start a warm red flow from the cut. The soldier stiffened and spoke.

"You, Mewari soldier? I carry message only. Greeting from the Emperor to his son, nothing more."

"Where is the prince?"

"I do not know. I look. Emperor sent me to these hills only. I mean no harm."

Captain Jaswant drew in closer, increasing the pressure on the soldier's throat. A bit more pressure and his throat would gape open. He felt the man's tunic and found a leather purse tied around his waist next to his skin. He made a quick slit with his dagger and pulled out the damp purse. Jaswant took a few steps back, lifting his sword from its sheath to hold the man at bay while he unfolded the paper he'd found.

The message read: "My son, congratulations on your success. The Rajputs of Mewar and Marwar are to join your forces. I await as planned." It was signed: Alamgir, Conqueror of the World.

When Captain Jaswant read these words, his heart raced like a wild boar in rut. He shook his head to clear it. How close to disaster we stand, he thought. This prince, no friend to Rajputs, plotted with the cunning of a fox and colluded with his father. He must die! Jaswant silently swore.

He stripped the Mughal messenger of his clothes, shoes, sword, and horse, telling him if he fled south, his life would be spared. "If you try to go back to the prince, I will kill you before you reach him. I watch you like a desert hawk, poised to pluck you from the desert like the rat you are, ready to rip you open." He followed the man for several miles on his walk south before he galloped back to the palace to report to the Maharana.

Captain Jaswant informed the Maharana and Captain Sardar of the plot to lure Mewar and Marwar into the Emperor's hands. They set a trap of their own. They knew

Prince Akbar waited in the hills for word from the Rajputs of their support. None came – neither from Mewar, nor from Marwar. Within a day, Prince Akbar sent a messenger, one that Captain Jaswant escorted into the Maharana's durbar.

"Huzur," he said when he entered, holding the man at sword point, "you have a visitor from the prince."

"Speak," the Maharana said and walked a bit closer.

"I come with a message for you only," the man said and looked from the sword tip in his side to Captain Jaswant.

"My captain stays. Speak now or he will skewer you."

"Sir, the prince's troops grow restless. No Rajput troops have joined. Prince Akbar stayed his order to attack the Emperor. Emperor Aurangzeb remains at Ajmer with few troops but could quickly get reinforcements from Shahjahanabad where thousands camp. Your troops must join the prince now. He says time is running out. The Emperor soon marches south. Mewar must not allow this – all Rajputana must unite with Prince Akbar. He cannot attack his father's troops at Ajmer without the aid of Rajput soldiers. Peace in your kingdom requires quick action."

"Advise the prince, my informants tell me the Emperor has a small contingent of men in Ajmer and fewer than a thousand in Shahjahanabad, hardly enough to ride south to the Deccan to conquer Shambaji. I doubt the prince's motive, enlisting the aid of Rajputana against his father. He must come to me, in person, with proof – and meet the Rathore commander also. Then only will we talk about uniting our forces."

"Maharana Ji, he thought you might say that. He has no plan to come in advance, a waste of time. The Emperor plans to attack and punish Mewar for the death of the vizier. If you do not join Prince Akbar now, he will not assist you later. He prepares to march, to face the Emperor. If he wins the battle, he defeats his father's advance on you, yet he would no longer count you an ally, but an enemy."

"Understood. I take my chances. Tell Prince Akbar I await an in-person diplomatic meeting or one on the battlefield. He must decide."

"Captain Jaswant, deliver this man beyond the forest, take him the desert route for safety, so his journey hastens through the craggy hills."

"Yes, Huzur, as you command," Captain Jaswant answered, knowing the Maharana's order would set the man out in the opposite direction, to the east, not to the north where the prince's men were waiting – and the best tracker could get lost in the crags and never find his way out.

In Mewar muted suspicion and apprehension replaced days of wild speculation and battle preparation. Captain Jaswant felt a lull blanket the fortress, men poised for war but stymied by inaction. No troops had moved on Mewar or Marwar, yet Captain Sardar remained braced for siege.

Captain Jaswant patrolled the fortress domain with Captain Sardar in rounds but also took a small contingent with him to survey the surrounding forest and hills. When he spotted a lone rider raising dust in the distance, he waved his men to the trees and proceeded to rush him. He halted the man at sword point.

The rider attempted to run past him, but Mewari soldiers surged forward to surround him, dislodged him from his horse's back. Jaswant thought the horse too good for a peasant and assumed the man a spy. Searching him carefully, Jaswant found a message.

Detaining the man, Captain Jaswant took the note to the durbar hall. When he delivered it to the Maharana, Captain Sardar was present in the hall.

"Wait, both of you," the Maharana said and opened the leather wrapped paper. He read it. His face turned crimson, his hands tightened on the worn leather. He wrenched the paper free.

"This, written by the Emperor, is for his son Prince Akbar. Listen. 'I, Alamgir I, Conqueror of the World, swear to bring the Maharana to his knees for the death of my vizier. To track down the killer himself. To sew him into a live buffalo. To let him rot in the desert sun. To scorch the land so no crops will ever grow again in Rajputana. To guarantee no Rajput prince will grow to manhood. To guarantee no Rajput woman will remain to nurse her dying soldier. Send word where our forces should meet.'"

The Maharana looked at Sardar. "Brother, you forced a hornet's nest – good. Better to know your enemy than think him a friend. The prince is his father's son, no matter what he has said to the contrary. Prepare our men for a preemptive attack on the prince."

Mewar, battle-ready and with ample supplies within the fortress walls, waited while Captain Sardar and Captain Jaswant spent time away from the palace on scouting expeditions to discover troop movement and strength, often camping in the hills to spy on the Mughal camp at night. A strange idleness alarmed them – the prince's forces remained in camp, initially disquieting by its presence... then by its absence.

"Sardar, look," Captain Jaswant whispered. "They break camp – before daylight."

"Yes, I have watched them too, but they move farther north, not south. What game does Prince Akbar play? Why move troops towards his father when his father should move south towards him to unify their forces for an attack on Rajputana?"

# CHAPTER 15 – DELUGE

Devi longed to speak to Jaswant but reconciled herself to her circumstances, a captive of the zenana, plotting her escape. She awoke to a day of gray clouds drowning the distant hills and decided her day had come. With anticipation and despair she readied her riding gear. She secured the triple-blade ukku dagger to her waist, under her tunic. She ordered besan roti and garlic chutney from the eunuchs – travel food that would not go bad for days.

She quietly left unseen and disappeared into the aqueduct tunnel to begin the long walk to the lake's edge where the stable boy had tied her horse. She knew her absence would not be noticed for hours since the zenana awoke late. An entire day might pass, with luck – her presence these days rarely noticed. She longed to say goodbye to Jaswant and to the Maharana, but knew it was not possible.

Earlier when she had questioned a zenana eunuch, he informed her the captains had ridden out early from the fortress, in the darkness before dawn, the previous morning.

She carried with her several small live embers and an oil lamp to light her way, remembering the horror of stumbling down the long tunnel alone in the darkness. The shiny marble walls reflected the fire's light and made a dim amber glow. This, she thought, was the passage of her birth.

At the far end she would emerge into a new life – a life of freedom and adventure, a life in which she would entomb the past and never speak of it again.

She left the womb behind, the comforts of the zenana, her friend Mira, her husband, and her lover. As she neared the far end, the smell of rain enlivened the dank air. She extinguished her oil lamp, crawled out of the tunnel, its opening only partially covered with dirt, and emerged.

Thunder shook the hills and turbulent air grabbed her hair with unseen fingers, making it stand up wildly. The angry sky obliterated the outline of the hills. She rushed to the trees to her frightened horse. He stomped and shook with the loud crashing sky but calmed when he saw her approach. She untethered him and rubbed his muzzle with long reassuring strokes.

Large raindrops pelted the broad fig leaves above the horse's head causing the ripe purple fruit to fall to the ground. Devi gathered what she could and put them in her saddle bag. She bit one in half. The soft pinkish-purple flesh opened out like a flower. She laughed and told herself for every day of fig season, she would eat one to remind herself of the sweetness of freedom.

Devi swung up onto her horse, leaned low over the horse's withers, shielded slightly from the lashing wind, and cantered away. She kept to the trees for cover, but the storm had moved in overhead and whipped the tree branches with such force she had to dodge broken limbs strewn on the ground.

The horse shied and jumped with every explosion. Lightning struck a tree to her right. The air crackled all around her. She thought the world moved with her, nothing stationary: trees swayed, parrots hurtled through the air, wolves in the distance howled and ran in panic for cover.

She rode hard towards the river to shelter in the gorge cave. Rain, pelting down in horizontal sheets driven by the wind, stung her eyes. Her vision blurred.

Her horse lowered his head and galloped in long strides despite the biting wind. Devi tucked her head into his wet mane and gripped with all her strength, trusting his animal wisdom to guide them. Her wet tunic draped her like a layer of blue skin.

She arrived at the ridge. Below, the Meandering River roiled with frothy white water. Floating trees, snags of matted grasses, mud and debris careened down the channel, choking it where the bank narrowed until the mass exploded and swept downriver, the sound deafening.

Devi struggled to steady her thoughts, or risk her courage being swept away in the torrent also. She yelled to herself: Stay calm, think. She saw the cave, only visible at its apex. She knew the river was impossible to cross. She rode downstream along the ridge to where the canyon opened out, hoping the flow would be calmer where the large lotus blossoms grew.

The flowers, barely visible, pale brownish-pink ghosts struggling below the surface, made her heart ache. No passage here either. She remembered the exact place where she had tried to entice Jaswant to seduce her, to render her unfit to marry the Maharana. She thought, how many years have passed. That peasant girl no longer exists. She died in her youth.

Devi dismounted. This area, she knew, remained her only hope. Farther down the river narrowed, squeezed between rocky walls, water roaring. She had to cross here, above the narrowed canyon.

She chose the least turbulent section and led her horse to the churning water. He refused to enter no matter how she pulled, pleaded, and coaxed him. Every time she lured him in, he spun around and bolted out. She realized if she walked in front of him, he would not leave her, but the current could sweep her away before she could grasp his mane.

Water rose to her waist. She lost her footing, grabbed his mane and tried to swim alongside him. The current slammed her into the horse's side. She struggled, swept towards his belly. He pawed frantically at the water. Water pushed her under. With all her strength she popped back up, coughing and choking.

She was aiming for a point on the far side, fixed in her blurred sight. The bank swung out towards them. They neared it, almost in reach of the grasses, a narrow width.

Devi swam hard alongside her horse. A loud howl like the sound of an animal crushed in a trap made the horse paw the water, the whites of his eyes crescents of fear. She looked back over her shoulder. A brown wall cleaved off the canyon face into the water. She grabbed the horse's neck. The shock wave hit. He rolled, Devi with him.

Devi felt something crawl down her throat. Her stomach lurched. She turned on her side and heaved brown sludge. She heaved again. She felt someone pull her hair, drag her up out of the mud. She heaved again.

"Good, she lives. Grab the horse, unsaddle the poor beast. See if he can stand."

Devi opened her eyes but couldn't see. They oozed shut again. She felt a hand wipe her eyes. She opened them again. Leaning over her, several men pulled her upright, cleared her face and eyes of mud. She convulsed and vomited brown water. She gasped. Someone tilted her forward, hit her on the back, a sharp, quick thwack.

Devi felt as if the holy River Ganges expelled from her body, taking her spirit with it. She floated in the air, looked below to see her horse lying next to her body. Men hovered over her. She collapsed into her blue mud-covered tunic.

When she opened her eyes, she turned her head to see men rope her horse and drag him out of the muck. He lay motionless. Devi crawled to him, wrapped her arms around his mud-clotted neck and whispered: Don't leave me now. The horse convulsed. She cleared mud from his nostrils. Devi's breath became his. She inhaled. He inhaled. His belly rose and fell. She placed her hand on his matted coat.

The men yanked her clear when the horse clawed the earth with his front hooves and hoisted himself to a standing position. He lowered his head and shook from ears to tail. Mud and water flew. With large, blowing nostrils, he walked over, nuzzled Devi, her hair, her face, her arm. Devi felt life surge through her body and dispel abysmal water. She gasped. All went black again.

Devi heard one of the men say, "No wonder this animal nearly drowned." He lifted the sword. "This weighs him down like a rock." The man opened the leather satchel to pull out a wad of muddy cotton, opened it and closed it quickly. "The owner of this horse must be royalty. Send word to the palace. This peasant woman's a thief."

Devi forced her eyes open. Again he looked at the soggy cotton bag, once a finely embroidered tunic, deep rose in color, embroidered with gold thread now dulled by river mud. Devi saw him withdraw his hand as if a cobra had struck. His eyes watered. He stared at the pigeon's blood ruby-and-pearl tikka that fell from the folds, the very tikka his daughter had worn the day she married the Maharana.

He caught his breath. He stared at the bedraggled woman in the mud who stared back through half-closed lids. His eyes grew wide under bushy silver brows. He looked at the men and cried, "Send a message to the Maharana, his wife Devi is dead, my beloved daughter. This woman robbed and killed her. My daughter is dead! Return this stolen horse to the palace. Return to the Maharana what belongs to him," the old man said and hurled the satchel of goods at the messenger. "Tell him the dacoit lies dead by the Meandering River, but where my daughter lies, I do not know. I go to tell my wife."

The old man collapsed in the mud, sobbing and pounding his fist into the oozing earth. Upon rising, he spat on Devi's motionless body.

Devi listened from half-darkness, river water gurgled in her lungs, mud clouded her eyes. Her father would have known her, she felt sure.

Her mind, snared in feeble thought, commanded one thing: Escape. The sounds around her grew fainter. She heard no more.

Captain Sardar witnessed gate guards flee their posts for cover. Two men entered the gate, pleading for safe passage, but their voices, drowned by thunder and the din of hard-hitting rain on marble, rendered them unintelligible.

The full wrath of monsoon rains pelted down, flooded marble corridors, plugged up drainage holes with debris, and crashed into Lake Pichola like invasive arrows. Captain Sardar led the men under an eave to hear their news before quickly escorting them to the Maharana's chamber.

Captain Sardar found the Maharana pacing like a caged lion, back and forth, back and forth, along the marble filigree balcony. Lightning struck in jagged branches, a flashing web that netted the north end of the lake, followed by pounding thunder that slapped the marble fortress and knocked parrots from their perches under eaves.

Captain Sardar shouted, "Huzur, disaster."

"Yes, yes, I am seeing with my own eyes."

"Not the storm," Captain Sardar shouted, water leaking from the misshapen coils of his soggy turban. "Huzur, hear me. Devi...went missing. A wall of water came from the hills, taking all in its path down the river canyon. Devi's father pulled a woman from the mud. She had with her the tikka Devi wore when you married her, and these other things," Captain Sardar said, handing the muddy satchel to Huzur. "He fears Devi was drowned by the flood or killed by this dacoit and robbed of her horse and satchel. He looks now for his daughter's body by the Meandering River."

"Devi? How could that be?" the Maharana said, as white as the vicious lightning. "Not Devi, she must be here, in the zenana."

"She is not. A stable boy said he took her horse early this morning to graze by the lake, on her orders, saddle and all. No one has seen her since."

The Maharana choked. "Devi? Lord Shiva punishes me. Sardar, get Captain Jaswant from his quarters. Meet me at the stables. We ride out."

Captain Sardar ran from the chamber to find Jaswant. He almost tripped over the old sweeper crouched on his haunches out of the rain. "Old man, have you seen my Captain Jaswant?"

"Yes, Captain Ji, Captain Jaswant Ji rode from the palace like the Angel of Death chased him," the old man replied.

When the Maharana appeared in the stable entrance, the grooms jumped to his command, heard throughout the stable: "Saddle two horses, now." Grooms ran, grabbed bridles, saddles, blankets. The Maharana turned toward Sardar, his face cinched as tight as a horse's saddle. "How do you know Devi drowned?"

"I don't, Huzur. Someone did, a woman's body lies by the river. I know this only."

When the riders reached the canyon, they could see the damage done by the wall of water that had crushed everything in its path, bringing down with it trees, boulders, rubble, drowned animals and birds, and tangled snakes in branches, indistinguishable, clotted by mud.

The Maharana and Captain Sardar searched, turning over every mud-covered mound. They did not find Devi, but the tigress's yearling cub, swept from the hills, lay dead in the brown sludge. Assaulting rain forced them to the shelter of an overhanging cliff near the canyon's edge where they huddled.

"Brother, Sardar, I caused her death. Yet I loved her above all else. Since the siege I purposefully spurned her. I knew she was not happy. I sought to force her to do what I could not – to run away from her unhappiness... with Jaswant. I could not order her to leave again, I was too weak – and too hopeful she might somehow change her heart. A raven sailed past my balcony, fleeing before my falcon for its life. From that day on, I knew the curse: Devi would die here if she did not flee.

"I alienated her from the women, and from Jaswant, by keeping everyone busy with other matters, and her – busy with none. I ordered Mira, Devi's only friend in the zenana, to shun her. I sent her to her death as surely as shooting her. My curse. To live with the knowledge I killed the only one I truly loved."

"Huzur. Look at this water. You had nothing to do with this. Gods and goddesses planned her destiny, not you. We all have our paths to tread. Not because of you did she die. Jaswant will suffer. He, too, will feel responsible. He left her alone, out of allegiance to you, and out of respect for her. He wanted only that she should be well cared for.

"Not four days ago, I intervened in their misery. I told him, ordered him, to leave, to run away, to take her to a place where they could be together. I am willing to accept your wrath for my actions, yet I knew your anger would be pretense. I had realized you shunned her for her sake also, yet Jaswant refused. He said she had become distant from him, avoided looking his way, never spoke, he assumed on your request."

The Maharana looked down and sighed. "I never said a thing to her. With so many words to speak, so many thoughts, only silence and misgivings filled me."

Captain Sardar looked downstream to a low bluff over the river where a solitary rider stood like a sentinel above the rushing water. "Jaswant!" he cried out, digging his heels into the horse's side to gallop out into the rain.

He saw the rider lean far back in his saddle to descend the slippery embankment. The horse slid down on his hindquarters, stumbled, righted himself, and picked his way along the muddy bank toward something in the water. Sardar watched Jaswant leap from his horse and wade out into the water to grab a length of blue cotton... and disappear.

Sardar charged to the bluff and headed down to his brother, the Maharana following. When Sardar reached the water's edge, his horse faltered and tripped over a boulder covered in debris.

From behind, the Maharana watched his captain jump clear of his horse. The water knocked the animal on its side. Trying to pull the horse up by the reins, Sardar lost his footing and was swept into the swift current. The Maharana lost sight of him in the turbulent water.

Sardar's sword dragged him down. He struggled to release the scabbard from his belt. His hands fumbled on the wet leather. He wrenched the dagger from his waist and cut the scabbard free. He became buoyant and floated up to the surface, gasping and choking on dark water.

He struggled for the shore. He crawled out and looked downstream for Jaswant. He saw his brother afloat, not fighting the current. The water swirled past a boulder and deposited him in a shallow inlet of tangled leaves not far from another body tangled in lotus pads.

Sardar struggled through the mud to join them. Even from a distance, Sardar recognized Devi. He watched Jaswant turn Devi on her stomach and push. River water crawled from her mouth. He repeated the effort. He collapsed. Face down in the mud, Jaswant lay near her. When Sardar drew close, Devi, digging in the muck with her elbows, dragged herself to Jaswant to clear mud from his mouth.

Sardar yelled, "Breathe into him."

Devi tried to slap Jaswant but had no strength. Sardar watched her clear his throat with a finger and yank his head to the side. Sardar gave him a hard slap between the shoulder blades. Murky water and mud oozed from under his tongue. Jaswant gasped, spat, inhaled, and sputtered to clear his throat. He opened his eyes to see Devi beside him and Sardar leaning over him.

Someone shouted, "Sardar Ji, Sardar Ji" as a small boat approached, and Sardar, too weak to lift his head, heard a voice say: "I am coming. Here, climb in. We must be getting back before the sky opens again. You could drown out here. Very dangerous this monsoon. All night rain, all day rain, I am never seeing such water."

Sardar Singh looked at his old friend and nodded. The ferryman helped him into the boat first. Then the American guests climbed in. Sardar looked from Jaswant to his wife in bewilderment. He replied to the ferryman, "Yes, yes, rains coming with force of many years." Turning from the American couple, he whispered to the ferryman, "Hold silence on this matter. You know how management is about... about our guests."

The ferryman, averting his eyes from the bedraggled couple, nodded to Sardar. "Yes, Ji, I am not wanting to lose my job until the rains are here to stay, when we return to our fields. What do you say, Sardar Ji? What crops we will have. Good I came. You three almost drowned. Why in Pichola, Ji? No matter... I am speaking no word. Our guests are speaking no word to management also. Please and thank you."

Jaswant said, shaking mud from his hair, "What happened, Sardar?"

The ferryman broke in, "Flashflood, sir."

The ferryman's chatter went on and on while he steered them across Lake Pichola. Jaswant and Ciprianne paid little attention. Despite the morning's warmth, Ciprianne could not stop shaking. Sardar Singh interjected "Yes, yes" occasionally to keep the ferryman going. Sardar Singh needed time to sort out his own disturbed thoughts, but he found it impossible. He wondered at the Americans in their Indian clothes, bewildered and wet, mud oozing from their leather sandals, silent.

"We cannot let the other guests see us like this. Take us to the kitchen dock," Sardar Singh told his friend. The ferryman let them off, advising Sardar that he was going home to rest since the rains had brought cancellations.

Sardar Singh escorted the couple along the servants' hallway to the rear of the kitchen and from there to the gardener's storehouse behind their suite. Glancing around to make sure no one watched, he opened the side balcony door to the suite and the couple slipped in unnoticed, except for the trail of mud on the wet marble terrace.

From inside, a deep voice said, "Come." Fearing management had discovered them, Sardar pushed ahead to enter the sitting room first. Jaswant and Ciprianne following close behind.

Sardar called out, "Who is there?"

"I believe we have business with you, Captain Sardar. Your impulsiveness presented quite a problem." Sardar Singh glanced round the sitting room. The stained glass lamp sat on the carved teak table, as usual. The portrait of the elderly Maharana hung in its assigned place; the settee with red velvet cushions, positioned to look out at the gray lake, remained just as before.

"I do not understand how to justify what you did," the man's voice stated.

Sardar Singh turned sideways to see the Maharana seated on a large, cushioned chair with teak claw feet. Next to him stood his sister, the mural woman with small even teeth.

"Devi," Mira spoke. "My brother is not angry with you, with any of you. We have come, not out of malice, but because we need your help."

Ciprianne ducked her head to her chest and covered her ears with muddy hands. She squeezed her eyes tight. When she opened them again, the Maharana and Mira looked at her in wonder. She gasped, "How are *you* here, *now*?"

The Maharana spoke. "Do not waste effort on how. Let us merely accept. You must help us. In doing so, you help yourselves."

"We can walk out that door," Ciprianne shouted, "and be in the courtyard, and go to the front desk, and check out, and leave this palace forever!"

"True, but hear us out. Then decide. I have not come for you. I come for something else. Tell me, brother Sardar, why did you behead the vizier? Your real reason?"

"He meant to harm you, Huzur," Sardar replied with respect, feeling himself not here and now but there and then. "I knew when I saw his troops, when I heard their campfire gossip. Who, more than I, Captain of the Guard, responsible for your safety, should have acted?"

"He had not that intention. He came on a mission from the Emperor, as he said, to enlist the support of Mewar. His men, a moderate force en route south to the Deccan, came fully armed for their own protection, to negotiate a peace with Mewar kingdom, fearing we would unite with Shivaji's successor, Shambaji, in the south, and fearing what Prince Akbar might do."

"I did not believe it so simple, Huzur. With battle elephants?"

"Yes, prepared only. The vizier feared Prince Akbar and suspected him a usurper. I had struck a secret pact with Prince Akbar. Emperor Aurangzeb had ordered the prince to subdue the clans of Mewar and Marwar. He took advantage of the plan to foment an uprising against the Emperor. Your killing the vizier sped everything up. Prince Akbar struck the vizier's forces at our gates to demonstrate his loyalty to our pact. He covered it up, sent word to his father that a contingent of Marathas from the south had inflicted the wound. No one was the wiser, at least, not for a while. That gave Prince Akbar time to organize his revolt, with the help of Mewar and Marwar.

"No one knew I had contact with the prince. At least, in that he kept his word. So the Emperor blamed Shambaji for the uprising, at first. We were ready to march with Prince Akbar's men when Captain Jaswant intercepted a message from the Emperor congratulating his son on drawing us into a trap. Word had gotten back to the Emperor that the Rathores of Marwar and the Sisodias of Mewar had forged an alliance against him, to assist Prince Akbar in his bid for power."

"The Emperor's forces met the prince's near Ajmer?" Sardar said, thinking that impossible.

"Prince Akbar ran for his life. His troops suffered many casualities. He escaped to the south, to Shambaji's protection.

"Now the Emperor's troops bear down on us, to destroy us for assisting the prince's plan to overthrow him."

"What action do we take, Huzur?" Sardar said as if he could cross back over to aid his ruler.

Turning to Devi, the Maharana said, "I have come to ask for your help, Devi, not only for me – but for your son."

Ciprianne's eyes bulged, "What son?"

"Sired by Captain Jaswant. You would protect him, would you not?"

"Naturally I would," Ciprianne replied, "but I have no memory of a son."

"Not long after the flash flood, an elderly gypsy woman hobbled to the palace gate demanding an audience. She told the guards she knew where Geeta, my missing wife, lived. I met with her. She informed me how you had helped Geeta escape."

"Yes, I did. I remember – Geeta, unhappy and scared, saw me leave the zenana and followed. I could not turn her back. I hid her with a village family and returned to help you. I arranged a marriage for her. Forgive me."

"I made a mistake bringing her to the palace. I had no time for her – and little interest. The triple-blade dagger of ukku steel. I must have it."

Ciprianne stepped back, visibly shocked by the Maharana's easy forgiveness of her treachery, of how she had dishonored him. She bent forward, hung her head in disgrace. A quick jab made her straighten up. She tugged on her wet, clinging tunic. She lifted a corner of the tunic, reached in, grabbed the hilt, pulled out the triple-blade dagger and handed it to the Maharana.

The Maharana studied the workmanship. "It is as she said."

Jaswant spoke up. "What, Huzur?" "The gypsy. She knew the legend of this dagger. It belonged to the Emperor himself. He stole it, of course –pilfered it when he pillaged Afghanistan, war booty. Very ancient craftsmanship. Finest metal ever forged. Sikander, Alexander the Great, the Western world calls him, heard of this metalwork in Greece. On his march to Peshawar in 326 B.C.E. he looted a stash of these weapons destined for Damascus.

"Emperor Aurangzeb succeeded in procuring many weapons of this metal. Their art had been lost for over a thousand years, yet the blades remain as sharp as newly forged. As a gift, and to secure the allegiance of his most trusted generals, Emperor Aurangzeb gave daggers, such as this one, when they promised an oath of undying support – a most precious gift for both the giver and the receiver. The vizier outsmarted him, exchanged his dagger for the Emperor's without anyone noticing.

"According to the gypsy, the Emperor had awarded the vizier one of these prized daggers and pledged he would make him governor of Rajputana. The vizier had a weakness for hookah and beautiful women – something he kept hidden from the Emperor, knowing it an abomination to Aurangzeb's strict faith. He crossed the gypsy's path years before Captain Sardar severed his head.

"A band of gypsies had come to entertain the vizier with song and dance while he camped for a night in the desert. He enjoyed the young dancing women with silver jingling anklets. They made dark passionate eyes and offered him potent opium while their nimble fingers stripped him of his possessions. When he awoke, the gypsies had departed with his cherished possession, the famed triple-blade ukku dagger, and four prize Arabian horses.

"The gypsies traveled towards Sindh. Along the way, they met a humble man, a metalsmith, who traded them a deer and a boar he had cured, and metal tools, as well as a wagon – all for that one dagger. The gypsies gladly traded, knowing immediate death was the punishment for stealing from the Emperor. He asked for information where he could get more metal of its kind. He lived in a small village not far from the shadow of Guru Sikhar Mountain."

"The village," Ciprianne said. "I remember it. Treasures lay hidden in a hut of the farmer's cousin. The farmer presented them to me when I asked for Geeta's marriage token."

The Maharana turned the weapon in his hand, grasping the two engraved handles slowly. He studied the seam where the two blades opened to allow the third, an inner blade, to thrust out. He saw a small inscription chiseled in Greek letters: Μέγας Αλεξανδρος – Alexander the Great.

"This is the dagger, Emperor Aurangzeb's prize, switched by his trusted vizier, the man meant to be the governor of the Rajput kingdoms under the Emperor's command. It belonged, at one time, to Alexander the Great – of inestimable value, for many reasons."

"Huzur, a great treasure no doubt, but what good does this do now? It's a museum piece only," Sardar Singh said.

"Now depends on then," the Maharana replied, the pearls on his turban swinging gently side to side as he looked over his shoulder. "When I return with this treasure, present it to the Emperor, inform him his own son, Prince Akbar, gifted it to me when he came in secrecy, dressed as a peasant, to secure my support for his revolt, using this dagger he had stolen from the vizier to seal the pact, the Emperor will believe his son killed the vizier.

"That will secure my standing as not having conspired against him, innocent of collusion with his errant son. Thus Mewar eludes the Emperor's wrath. With the vizier dead, his own son on the run to join up with Shambaji, and the Emperor longing to push south into the Deccan, I believe I can save Rajputana. Otherwise he will descend on our lands, destroy all in his way."

"Can you trust him, Huzur?" Ciprianne asked, disbelief in her tone.

"That remains to be seen. I shall bargain for our sovereignty with this dagger, Alexander the Great's, a legend, and demand he leave our temples alone, repeal the tax on non-Muslim men, and disallow forced marriages of Mewari women to Mughals.

"I believe he will see the wisdom in leaving us in peace to focus on his battlefront to the south in the Deccan. I hope Shambaji, as clever as his father, inflicts a deadly wound to the empire."

Sardar Singh spoke up, standing erect and expanding his chest with force.

"Huzur, I stand with you, whatever the punishment for my actions. I shall follow you back, assume my role, Captain of the Guard, and fight our enemy. You dispense my punishment then only."

"Nonsense, brother Sardar. I did not come for you. I do not wish you there again. That time has passed."

"Huzur, I never meant to cause you, or anyone, harm," Ciprianne said, turning to Mira with tears in her eyes. "If I can help, I will."

Jaswant stepped forward and shouted, "No! What's done is done. How could we effect change in a distant time, a distant place?"

"What is done is never finished, Captain Jaswant. We attempt to make ourselves forget. Events are not isolated in a sea like lost islands. The past exists in the present in all our actions. Even you suffer as a result of your past, now, in the present."

Jaswant's brow knitted, his face electrified with heat, turning his golden-brown skin to glowing fired brick. "Not possible."

"Your child, Captain," the Maharana said, glancing at Devi. "I refer to your child."

Jaswant stared at the Maharana like a predator ready to pounce on its prey. Sardar moved to intervene when the Maharana continued, "You have forgotten the curse an old woman spoke in ignorance? Queen Devi will suffer and pay with barrenness, now and forever."

Ciprianne looked at Jaswant with the stricken look of one ripped open, revealed. "Oh, God, you mean I have miscarried because... because of this? An old woman's curse in a long ago time?"

Sardar shot the Maharana a damning look. He understood the Maharana had struck a deadly blow when Ciprianne's husband walked over and wrapped her in his arms.

"By giving me this dagger," the Maharana said, "you give me the chance to save our kingdom from the crushing assault of the Emperor's wrath."

"Take it, I don't want it! I never wanted it for myself," Ciprianne said, sobbing.

"We will not return to you again, if all goes according to plan," the Maharana said and stood to leave. "You will know the outcome. There will be a sign, a very obvious one."

Mira walked to her sister and embraced her, "Hush, Devi, do not cry. We want the best – for us all." She kissed her on the cheek and stepped back behind her brother.

The Maharana led her into the mural room and shut the door behind them.

Sardar Singh, Jaswant and Ciprianne remained – stunned, wet, and shivering with unnatural cold in the dimly lit sitting room, shocked into silence. A new wave of black monsoon clouds rolled in from the far end of Pichola Lake and exploded overhead. The doors rattled.

Jaswant walked over and opened the heavy wooden door to the empty bedchamber. They witnessed a white crane rise from the Meandering River and disappear into the mural's rain-swollen sky.

# CHAPTER 16 – HARVEST TIME

Sardar Singh waded in the heavy rain. Each drop seemed like circles of mirrorwork falling around him, reflecting off other drops until the entire sky became a constellation of flashing gray discs that clouded his vision – with joy. He lifted his face to greet the huge drops, let them run down his beard and seep down his tunic, unconcerned about rivulets of mud soaking into his tan loafers.

It felt justice to him – first the absence of rain that had robbed him of farming and now the torrents of mud from high meadows to nourish his starved fields. The Creator and the Destroyer worked his plan for Rajasthan, that Sardar Singh knew.

Water dripped from the limp, soggy folds of his turban, but he did not care. He told himself he would never again complain of any inconvenience caused by water, not even a raging flash flood, because he now knew even a sinister event could bring life.

Life without water was not worth having. Water without knowledge was incomplete. And water – whether past or present – is full of potential, the continuing thread that binds present to past.

He stood watching the lake drink volumes of rain. The level had risen to cover the palace foundation, plus some – something that had not happened in years. The palace now looked the ephemeral swan he knew her to be, mistress of the lake, mother of imagination.

The choking and sputtering ferryboat disturbed his contemplation. He saw the small boat struggle to cut through the whitecap waves and arrive at the palace dock.

"Sardar Ji, jump in. I cannot stop the engine for fear she will not start again. You are my last passenger of the day. Then I go home. Jump."

"Thank you, friend," Sardar Singh said as he gingerly stepped onto the boat's hull. He quickly sat down to avoid the wake catching up.

"Pichola Lake rejoices. She dances, a warrior goddess with veils," the ferryman said, smiling.

"Let us hope she will carry us in her arms to the far shore, old friend," Sardar Singh said.

"She will, she is most forgiving. Our prayers are answered! Sardar Ji, we may soon plant our fields and return to the honor of our land and farming."

The boatman's words filled Sardar Singh with joy. He thought of his lovely daughters, his dear wife, and his aging parents – with renewed hope. He knew he could care for them now. The rains – a sign, a blessing.

The gods had admonished him for his past deeds, yet they had not destroyed him: he had been washed clean. His grief, his disgust, his anger, all cleansed. When he entered his small home, his daughters rushed to greet him. His wife served him hot chai with cardamom and black pepper and a fresh roti spread with sweet buffalo milk butter, something he had not tasted in a long while – to honor him.

He put on a fresh kurta pajama suit and relaxed with his parents, children, and wife by the light of the oil lamp. The smell of curry spread throughout the small house. When his wife called them to dinner, Sardar Singh sat amazed by the dishes on the table.

He knew they did not have the money for this sort of feast and pulled his wife aside to question her. She told him provisions had come as a gift earlier in the day, brought by a market boy on the request of a Sikh man, as a surprise. Sardar realized its source. He had not seen the Americans before their early morning departure that day, something that filled him with sadness – and gratitude. What to say? Sardar felt he owed them, not they, him.

All Rajasthan danced in the rains for thirty days. The desert bloomed in bright colors, not seen for many years. Sunshine and cloud bursts marked the days. Once cracked dry earth now yielded tender green shoots. Long dormant rivers, reborn from brown shadows, became lively turquoise ribbons. Lake Pichola drank her fill, the waterline on the palace found its natural mark. The white marble palace looked like a celestial being hovering on a mirror of sky and cloud.

Sardar Singh relished every sign of life returning. He planted and tended his fresh shoots as they grew into dense fields of millet. He no longer bemoaned the early morning hours he worked at the Palace Hotel because afterwards he tended his crops, knowing it only a matter of time before he could return solely to farming.

He set aside dowry money for Asha, his eldest daughter, on this, her nineteenth birthday, to give her a proper marriage. The chosen boy pleased him, a good boy from a farming family. He felt pride. He could do his duty, hold his head up, make right the wrong he had carried deep within him, the secret weight that shouted when he prayed. A terrible image haunted his days, overwhelmed his nights, interrupted his prayers. The scene burned his heart, scalded his mind, and festered in a deep pit that threatened to consume him. Sardar strove every day for nineteen years to find peace. None came.

With every seed he sowed, every plant he tended, every harvest he reaped, he sought forgiveness. Sardar realized his hope lay in caring for his family, in dedication, in honor, in working hard. Every time Asha approached him, her sweet smile, her kind eyes, her gentle voice made his mind race back to the morning of her birth. His mother-in-law and the midwife would handle it. He would be away working the fields, as planned.

A shout reached him. He lowered his sickle. A cloud blocked the sun making the golden millet gray. The midwife ran to him shouting, "Ji, a girl, come. Your mother-in-law took ill. You must do the duty."

Sardar ran to his house, burst through the door, saw his wife on her birthing bed with a tiny baby tucked into the crook of her arm. "Wife, I must. A girl." He reached down and lifted the baby from his wife's grip. Her eyes, full of pain, pleaded with him. She said nothing. Sardar looked away.

The midwife stepped forward to take the infant, but Sardar pushed past her and left the house with the baby balanced on his forearm. He walked to the rear courtyard where the milk cow stood under skimpy shade of the acacia tree. He placed the baby girl on straw, trying to avoid looking at her.

He shouted to the midwife. "Bring the supplies." She approached with the items. "Put them down. Leave. Attend my wife and her mother."

Sardar reached over for the wad of cotton and placed it into her small hand, prying open the delicate brown fingers clasped to the soft palm. He spread the fingers of her other hand and put a pinch of jaggery, brown sugar, in the palm. The baby made no cry.

Sardar mumbled, "Spin the cotton. Eat the sweet. Next time send your brother to this family to keep." He crouched over her and scooped her up in his large, calloused farmer's hands. The baby regarded him. He looked into her black eyes, as dark as night. Sardar winced and looked away. He lowered her tiny body into the cool earthen pot. She didn't cry. Tears collected in his eyes. The baby's warmth radiated up into his hands. He felt heat flood his face. He wiped the wetness from his cheeks. He slid the baby from the cold pot and brought her to his chest. He rocked back and forth holding her. The midwife approached. He shouted at her to leave him.

Over and over these nineteen years, the scene had appeared before him. The joy of his life, Asha, firstborn, named for hope, changed him. Her gentle smile reminded him of the goodness he almost extinguished and the debt he owed. Her kindness drove Sardar to work hard to deserve her love and respect, something he knew she would never know, something she would never have believed. Her birth. His decision.

With renewed confidence Sardar Singh strode across the recently swept floor of the Jharokha Café to close out his shift's earnings. He glanced up when a reception clerk came to deliver a message: Sardar Singh is wanted at the lotus pool terrace.

Sardar Singh arrived at the pool to see a stranger walk up and hand him a brown paper package tied with a single string. Taking it, he saw his name scribbled across the front in Hindi. The man said, "She sent this for your daughter's wedding."

Sardar Singh twisted the graying hairs of his mustache briefly as he stared at the package. "This woman, who is she? Is she here?"

"No, Ji. This came to me by way of the railroad with instructions to give it to you."

Sardar Singh regarded the messenger's cleanly pressed synthetic Western suit that hung loosely on his diminutive frame, his polished overly large closed-toe shoes, and asked, "Where do you live?"

"Me? Delhi only."

"The woman gave you this in Delhi?"

"No, Ji, in Udaipur station only. I work for the railroad. She paid me well to wear fine clothes and deliver this package to you. I had two days' furlough from my regular route, so I agreed. I borrowed these clothes. They are very fine."

"American, is the lady American?" Sardar Singh said with growing apprehension.

"No, Ji, proper Hindu lady. I think I have seen her before, somewhere, the bazaar possibly. Her smile, I remember – fine white teeth like small square pearls."

Sardar Singh started to speak, but the man hurried away towards the lobby. He let him go. He wanted him to fade away as if the interchange had never happened. Yet in his hand the brown package called to him, taunted him. He slumped into a chair in the late afternoon light. Cooing pigeons strutted along the corridors outside the bar; guests mingled on the terrace.

He knew it wouldn't look right for staff to lounge like a foreigner, yet his body felt like lead. His feet wouldn't move, his lungs found it difficult to inflate. He realized when he took a large gasp that he had not been breathing. He sighed. Exhaling, he saw his life leave him, his dreams disperse in motes dancing in the oblique light.

Beyond the terrace wall, the setting sun danced orange on the placid lake like it had since the brunt of the monsoon rains had abated. Sardar Singh untied the string and opened the brown paper. He lifted from the box the very same peacock blue sari he had once given the hotel desk manager. He ran the scarf, embroidered with pure gold threads, across the back of his hand. In the folds of the gossamer silk he felt a heavy object – a small package wrapped in embroidered cotton, a faded rose colour.

He lifted out a gold mirrorwork wedding set. A tikka of tiny gold mangoes and pearls on a long chain for the head ornament. Gold filigree domed bell earrings with dangling pearls and rubies. Three yellow-gold bangles. A nose ring the shape of a lotus blossom with petals of enameled glass around a central ruby. All ancient, traditional Rajasthani work – that he knew. Priceless. Sardar pondered, What to do?

Sardar blinked and put the jewelry back in the cotton covering so no one would see. He looked up and spotted a white crane lift off from the near bank and sail across the setting sun, its belly feathers glowing yellow-gold like the jewelry in his lap. His heart raced, sweat wicked into his turban.

He rewrapped the sari and jewelry neatly in the package and marched back across the lobby to finish closing out his shift at the café. When he handed over his keys to the night manager and turned to cross the lobby for the front entrance, a loud voice shouted his name. He stopped abruptly, fearing the worst.

"Sardar Ji, come here," the reception desk manager said. "I have a letter addressed to you."

Sardar Singh warily approached the very man to whom he had given this sari so many weeks back. He saw a peculiar look in the man's eye, an accusatory glare.

"Sir," Sardar Singh said in a hushed voice, "sir, I must ask... I have wondered... What became of that blue sari the American woman discovered?"

The reception desk manager, taken off guard, narrowed his eyes, looked this way and that, before answering. "Sardar Ji, I did as I said. I turned it in to the Department of Antiquities at the old palace. Why do you ask?"

Sardar Singh gave a nervous laugh. "No reason, sir. I suddenly remembered it, having seen a guest on the terrace in the very same color, that unmistakable peacock blue. It is funny how memory works, the scent of a spice bringing back an image of one's mother, the color of a sari bringing back... well, it made me think of... you know."

"Yes, Sardar Ji, I fully know. I am happy to report we have had not one bit of trouble from Sajjan Niwas Suite since the Americans left. A blessing. Not only was that ruinous to our guests' well-being, but as you saw, dangerous for the murals, and perilous for our jobs. What with that woman scratching the precious paint away – well, we are indeed lucky the upper management never came to know.

"In fact, I do not believe I ever congratulated you on your handling of that delicate, uncomfortable situation. Since I am unable to thank you on behalf of my superior, let me alone show my appreciation. You saved our jobs and our honor." He took from his pocket a thick roll of rupee notes and thrust them into Sardar Singh's free hand.

"Sir, I cannot accept this."

"Sardar Ji, it is not for you. As a father, I was most happy when my daughter made such a suitable marriage. I have heard you, too, found the right boy for your eldest. My present to the young couple, something to put with her dowry. That is all. I refuse any rejection. You dishonor me with the thought. Take this gift for your daughter only. After all, she is like a daughter to me. We are brothers, are we not?"

Sardar Singh knew that by the manager invoking him as brother, he would insult the man severely if he refused. "Thank you, Ji. On behalf of my daughter, I thank you. Namaste."

"Namaste, brother, namaste," the desk manager said.

Sardar Singh hurried across the marble tiles to the front door. He waited for the ferry and thought of the Americans, hoping the package in his hand would not spoil their memory. He reveled in the quiet knowledge that at one time, in his own way, he had made a difference. Just as now. He intended to make a difference in the lives of his family.

Armed with that thought, he had worked his fields during the early morning and early evening hours while continuing at the hotel, tirelessly and with joy in his heart. But this package, he feared, might end all that. If all was well, a sign should not have come. But what could this be if not a sign?

His ruminations were cut short by the sputtering approach of the ferry. His friend waved him over with a large grin on his face. "My friend, namaste, I have news."

Hearing this, Sardar Singh's heart sank further. He wanted no more news. This day, too full of it. "Tell me another time. I am weary."

The ferryman pulled alongside the dock and motioned him in, speeding off before the next group of guests could reach the dock. "I'll be reported for that," he said with a chuckle. "I had to speak to you alone, out here, with no ears to hear my words. Do you remember that odd foreign couple I pulled from the flood with you?"

"Naturally."

"It is rumored the American woman had found a precious sari in her compartment."

"Is that so?"

"Yes, Ji, the sweeper told the vegetable boy who told the cook who told a clerk whose son told me. Have you heard of this?"

"No. Tell me."

"The desk manager whisked away the sari and didn't report the woman; at least, that is what the clerk said. She was never arrested."

"Correct, they returned to United States of America," Sardar Singh replied in a lackluster tone.

"That sari was very ancient, a treasure. Some weeks later, it appeared in Jaipur at a carpet and antique dealer's. It is said he paid lakhs of rupees for it.

"Listen up, brother! People say it is the same sari the Maharana's favorite wife wears in the portrait he had painted of her before the Mughal invasion, just before she ran away, maybe died, the one hanging in..."

"Why do you bring this up?"

The ferryman continued, foaming at the mouth, spittle dripping at the corners of his moustache from excitement. "They say she died, or ran away with gypsies, no one knows which for sure. Peacock Lover Queen, that is her name. The barren Peacock Lover Queen. Surely you know of her!"

"Yes, yes, I have heard the ballads at Diwali when the gypsy minstrels come to town. Who hasn't."

"Almost as beautiful as Queen Padmini, I believe. She broke the Maharana's heart and fled to the hills with the sari, never to be seen again. There she bore a son to her gypsy lover, obviously no barren queen! Years later, her son, on his wanderings in the Aravalli Hills, met Prince Ajit of Marwar, and they became friends. When General Durga Das restored the young prince to his throne, he made that gypsy a member of his army."

"The story must be wrong. The Peacock Lover Queen was barren. She had no children, that is what barren means."

"That is not how the ballad goes."

"No matter, what is your point, old friend? I am tired and we are nearing shore."

"Recently that sari was stolen from a museum in Jaipur, on loan from the carpet dealer for exhibit. There are security police here in Udaipur looking for it. There is a huge reward for information! 101,001 rupees! I could work sixteen lifetimes and never see that much. Everyone looks for it."

"Why do you tell me this?"

"Why else? So you look also. You may find it yourself," the ferryman said with a broad grin, his lips pulled tight at the edges into a net of fine lines.

"And where would I look for such a thing?" Sardar Singh said, trying to regulate his erratic breathing.

"Why in the Sajjan Niwas Suite, of course. If once there, it may reappear. You see the suite daily, keep your eyes open."

Sardar Singh forced a muffled laugh and clapped his friend on the back. "Yes, yes, I will look and if I find, you will be the first to know."

Sardar Singh disembarked and walked home with an unsteady gait. The package and the unopened letter tucked securely under his arm weighed him down like lead. When he entered his home, he walked to place his turban on the table and sit in the small courtyard behind his house.

The rainfever bird cried incessantly, "Rain fever, rain fever, rain fever", even after darkness hushed the other birds, and the crickets and frogs had begun their chants. His wife brought him tea but kept her distance when he didn't speak to her. She returned to the kitchen.

He thought and thought about his situation, tried to understand what it meant. He had very valuable, historical, stolen property in his possession. That meant jail. But why had the mural woman done this to him? All had been well for some months. Was this a sign of distress? A message from the Maharana?

Sardar Singh did not know what to do. The Americans had left with no word. He could not contact them, he knew, nor would he want to, yet Sardar now found himself in great peril. If the investigators from Delhi discovered the errand boy from the bazaar, they might also discover him. Was it more reasonable to destroy the package and contents? Turn them in? Plead innocent? Explain a story no one would believe? He realized he must consult the one person he could: the desk manager. He had taken the sari before. He could take it again, forever.

Sardar Singh passed a fitful, sleepless night, and arose to dress in the blackness of approaching dawn. When his wife inquired if he were ill, he said he had to catch the first ferry since a large tour from Germany was due and the desk manager needed his help. She got up to prepare hot chai and a roti with curds for his breakfast and watched him walk out into the early morning coolness.

But Sardar Singh did not walk towards the ferry. He walked to the compound wall that enclosed the desk manager's bungalow and waited by the guarded gate for him to come out. The man was startled, seeing the hotel waiter sitting on his haunches by the night watchman.

"Sardar Singh, is there a problem? Why have you come for me?"

"Sir, let us walk together so we do not disturb the sleeping."

They walked the dirt path that wound past the houses near the railway station before Sardar Singh stopped the man. "Sir, we have a great problem. Do you remember the sari from the Sajjan Niwas Suite's hidden cabinet?"

"Of course."

"It has appeared, again," Sardar Singh said, handing the package to the desk manager. The manager carefully opened it and looked inside. His eyes grew wide with fear when he saw what lay before him.

"How? How could this be? The very sari, and...a gold wedding set. Where did you get it?"

"A stranger delivered it to me, yesterday only. I thought you had sent the sari to the Department of Antiquities."

The desk manager faltered and replied in a weak voice: "I did. I know nothing of this, or the jewelry."

"I discovered in the outer flap of the package an unsigned note, written in Hindi. It says: Replace in Sajjan Niwas Suite mirror cabinet. Do not delay.

"Sir, do you play a joke on me?"

"No, never would I. We face jail for this. It is no joke. These are very valuable, very rare items. We must do as instructed. You take the jewelry set, and we will replace the sari. Done."

"No, Sardar Singh, I will not take the set, and I will not replace the sari. This is your responsibility. The package came to you, did it not?"

"Yes."

"So, it is for you to do."

"No."

"Stubborn man, will you help me then? We can get into the suite this morning – it is not booked – and replace the treasures before anyone should come."

Sardar Singh agreed with a nod. The two men hastened their pace to catch the first ferry. Sardar Singh felt relieved when he saw it was not his good friend who worked the ferryboat this day. They rode in silence across the tranquil lake and disembarked, lingering outside until the boatman pulled away.

They followed the kitchen hallway to the far courtyard. Sardar Singh stayed behind the garden wall while the desk manager opened his desk and got the suite key.

When they entered the dark suite with heavy velvet curtains closed, it smelled of musty sandalwood. The two men walked to the gilded mirror to begin the delicate work of scraping back the mural plaster to reveal the thin line of the cabinet door. They had only to pull lightly and the cabinet door swung open.

"Sardar Singh, I want you to know – well, I apologize for the trouble this has caused you. I do not know why it reappeared, or who is seeking it, but I will, on point of death, never reveal that you and I replaced this sari and the wedding set. On that I swear to Lord Shiva."

"And I will forever keep this secret."

Having made their pledge, they replaced the package on the cabinet's shelf and carefully closed the door. They looked at one another in the light seeping in around the curtains. Sardar saw they both had the same question on their lips. What now?

"How do we repair the mural unnoticed?" Sardar Singh said.

"We leave it as is. That is all," replied the desk manager. "Quickly, we must be leaving unseen."

They abandoned the suite before the hotel staff arrived and assumed their posts, each going his separate way to prepare for the day's duties.

Sardar Singh enjoyed counting silver utensils before his shift that morning. It assured him of routine, a welcome routine, normal life. They tallied exactly.

He greeted guests, explained the buffet and à la carte specialties, and soon relaxed into his work. For a brief moment he regretted his daughter not having the gold wedding set, yet he knew it would have been a finger pointing at him. No one of his caste could afford such jewelry. Everyone would have talked. He would have been labeled a thief and his honor taken from him. For what? For gold? Nothing was worth losing one's honor for, of that he was sure. He had done it once and suffered for it. He could provide a wedding for his daughter with his meager farmer's income and his workman's wage – honest money, the best blessing.

Sardar Singh questioned why the package had come to him. What did it mean? Was he to pay for lifetimes for the deed he had committed in the past for the sake of his Maharana? Was that not honorable? Or had it led to tragedy, and the package brought that message.

When a waiter approached and told him the front desk manager requested him, his large hands ran cold. He walked with a brisk step to the lobby where he spotted an elegant gentleman in a silk tunic suit flanked by two men in military uniform standing with the desk manager.

"This is the man of whom I spoke, sir," the manager said talking to the gentleman. "He was the first to reach the

Americans' room when the lady discovered the hidden cabinet."

Sardar Singh felt his heart skip a beat, wondering if the man would think he had stolen the sari. He remained quiet.

The man said, "I have been told the American woman was unwell, mentally unstable, is that true?" He stared straight into Sardar Singh's eyes without a hint of emotion.

"Yes, sir. The heat affected her. May, too hot for a white woman."

"Would you recognize the items if you saw them again?"

"The sari, peacock blue, yes sir. A special dye, sir."

"Is that all the woman found?" the elegantly dressed man asked.

"Yes, sir. As far as I know."

"And what did you do with it?"

Sardar Singh considered protecting the manager but realized the man was in no way sparing him, so he said, "She gave it to me. I turned it in to the manager."

The desk manager, without looking at Sardar Singh's face, denied his claim. "He did not. I never saw the item."

The man in the silk suit said, "Is that so? Somehow a sari of similar description came to Jaipur and was sold – and later stolen. We have come here to discover if the two are one and the same."

Sardar Singh hesitated and then spoke up. "You will have to see for yourself, sir."

"You have the sari here, now?"

"I know where it is, in the very cabinet of the Sajjan Niwas Suite where the American found it. I will take you there, now."

The desk manager hurried along, trying to keep up with Sardar Singh's sweeping strides as he marched the marble corridor to the suite, but the elegant man came between them.

Sardar Singh felt as if he were walking to his execution. Determined the desk manager should not cast the blame on him for the missing – and somehow recovered – sari, he resolved to tell all. Brothers, he thought... No brother of mine!

He led the men inside. The curtains were pulled open, the lake glimmered in the soft morning light. The bed-chamber door stood ajar, its air conditioner murmured in the corner. Sardar Singh walked to the cabinet and halted abruptly. Looking askance, he saw the mural woman with small square teeth smiling in recognition. He looked away. He avoided her.

"This is it, sir, the cabinet the American woman discovered. As you can see, it..." A soft gust of wind wafted in from the sitting room, the fresh aroma of sandalwood and rosewater filled the suite. He felt along the cabinet's edge but could not find the opening. "I thought it was open. We repaired it after the incident, but it should be open," he exclaimed, confusion evident in his voice.

"Let me see," the elegant man said pushing closer. "There is no seam in this plaster. It cannot open. A mirror only! Is this a joke? Do not play me for a fool."

"No, sir, it opens. If you will allow me..."

Sardar Singh withdrew a small pin from his turban and scratched along the edge of the mirror. Tiny bits of painted plaster fell to the ground. He traced around it, over and over, until a shallow seam appeared. He wedged his fingers in the crevice and gave it a quick jerk.

The door of the cabinet swung open slowly to reveal several shelves built into a wooden frame. On the top shelf lay a peacock blue sari, on the second, a gold wedding set entwined in a faded embroidered scarf. The men gasped. The desk manager stepped back, ready to run. Sardar Singh stood silently, awaiting his death sentence.

The gentleman lifted the objects from the cabinet. "This is it! This I saw in the museum in Jaipur. I would recognize that work anywhere. How odd it should be here. I am not at liberty to discuss this case, but let me say, sir, there is a handsome reward for its recovery. That will be determined by the investigation. Should you be found innocent in its missing, a reward will be granted you – and the desk manager."

The desk manager spoke up, his words catching in his throat. "Please...sir...I did nothing. My friend here, Sardar Singh, deserves...er...all credit or...well, for its recovery. I had no hand in it, I assure you."

Sardar Singh glared at the manager and said firmly, "Sir, I am a man of honor, willing to accept the outcome."

"Yes, yes, so I have heard from the woman who hired me. Just her words, 'a man of honor'. She said you protected the treasure."


Time passed. No one mentioned the treasure. It seemed no one knew about its recovery, not even hotel management. Sardar Singh enjoyed the satisfaction of not seeing the desk

manager again. He left his post saying he had to return to
Gujarat to tend his dying mother. He never returned.

Sardar Singh passed his days in the Jharokha Café and
his long summer evenings in his fields, until one evening
a knock came at his door. His wife came running into the
field to fetch him. Seeing her so agitated and nervous, he
assumed the worst. He took one last look at his beautiful
fields of grain glowing red-orange in the evening light and
turned to meet his fate, happy that he could remember his
farmer's life at its best – harvest time.

After the mysterious man in the silk suit left, his wife
reappeared from the kitchen and found Sardar slumped
under the betel palm tree in their courtyard, sobbing. He
handed her a cloth bag, full of rupee notes.

She looked at him as if he had committed a crime and
would now go to jail. Wiping his eyes, he laughed: "For
our daughters' weddings. I was given a reward. I found a
treasure at the hotel and turned it in to the authorities. This
is my reward: 101,001 rupees. A sign, a blessing. All is well.
I am forgiven. All our daughters will enjoy their marriages
and we can expand, buy more farmland."

His wife looked at him in disbelief, then opened the bag.
She gasped, cried out and slumped to the ground.


Harvest time came and went. Sardar Singh welcomed the
coolness. December reverberated with the happy sounds of
drums and horns in his daughter Asha's wedding procession.
Family and friends lit the road with torches. They walked
to the temple to offer prayers for the couple. Sardar Singh

led the procession with the gait of a man assured, content with life, at peace.

Sardar Singh no longer worked for the Palace Hotel after that harvest. He bought more land and grew busier than ever planning elaborate irrigation systems for his fields. He showed such promise that others came to him for advice, which he freely gave.

His old friend the ferryboat captain came by on occasion to catch up with Sardar Singh's news, to study his crops, his irrigation system, his seeds. One day he came with something more – a letter addressed to Sardar Singh that had arrived at the Palace Hotel reception desk.

Sardar Singh studied the envelope carefully before opening it. He stared at the colorful stamp of a duck in the corner. He lifted the note and read the Hindi script:

"Dear Brother, we had a son June 7th. You must know that made us happy. All is well. Your sister 'Devi' sends her love. We will come visit next year. We named our son Sardar in your honor. All the Best. Namaste. Jaswant Singh."

Sardar Singh turned the small photograph over in his hands. He pointed to the baby with milky skin and black hair and said to his friend, "My nephew! May the gods bless."

# IN THE 1600s...

Aurangzeb Alamgir, "World Conqueror," reigned in India for forty-nine years from 1658 to 1707. He came to power by imprisoning his father and having his four older brothers either beheaded, imprisoned, banished or all three.

He had no love of the arts, especially music; destroyed Hindu temples, taxed the peasant farmers heavily, and waged war relentlessly to extend the Mughal empire.

He detested the people who opposed him, especially the Sikhs who gave safe haven to Aurangzeb's brother Dara, his rival, and the Marathas of the Deccan, who mounted the most effective war against him led by their leader Shivaji and then carried on by Shivaji's son Shambaji.

In 1680 the Rajputs of Jodhpur (Marwaris) formed an alliance with neighboring Udaipur (Mewaris) – clans that had often warred between themselves but now united to fight against Emperor Aurangzeb. They declared themselves free from his sovereignty. Emperor Aurangzeb answered with an army under the command of his son Akbar.

His son declared himself emperor but had to flee his father's wrath. He went south to the Deccan where the Marathas, now led by Shivaji's son Shambaji, sheltered him. From there he fled to exile in Persia and never returned.

Shambaji, captured in 1689, was tortured and then murdered for his insurrection.

Aurangzeb's empire began crumbling, too unwieldy to manage with so many adversaries. He died in 1707. The Mughal Empire fell after the Indian Rebellion of 1857-58 when its last ruler, Emperor Bahadur Shah, was put on trial by the British for treason.

The Mughal Empire reached its greatest extent under Aurangzeb's rule. The empire extended from present-day Afghanistan in the north to the southern tip of India, excluding Tamil Nadu and Kerala, and east to Bengal.

# ACKNOWLEDGMENTS

Many thanks to the "team" who inspired and guided me on this journey. A creative endeavor is never a solo event.

In chronological order of input:

Crystal Williams, friend and first reader who, with little acquaintance with the land and culture, provided succinct perspectives and captured pesky errors trying to hide in the text.

Janet Switzer, "joie de vivre Janet", who approached the story with amazing enthusiasm and let me see it anew through her eyes, imbued with our mutual love for India.

Anthea Guinness, editor extraordinaire, whose knowledge of India, its customs, languages and subtleties enriched the story's accuracy. Her editing skills, only surpassed by her passion for publishing books, made it all real.

Two I have yet to meet:

Carol White, artist of book design, understood the feeling of the story I had hoped for but hadn't verbalized.

Andrew Johnson, photographer, captured the beauty of the shimmering Lake Palace Hotel in Udaipur that graces the cover.

One I knew well:

Ranjit Gill, interpreter and escort, who shared and enhanced the journey, himself a wonderful story teller.

# ABOUT THE AUTHOR

Dyan Dubois, author and visual artist, resides in California but considers India her second home. A Fulbright scholar and academic, she now focuses primarily on writing and painting, enjoying the diversity of world cultures, people and stories that link our global human family.

# BREAK THE TREND

A London publisher once said, "People will beg, borrow or steal a book, but not buy."

**Choose to be a buyer! Don't lend** your copy to all your friends – order two copies of this book **today** and give them away.

**This is your chance** to stand with all of us – the writers, artists, editors and designers associated with the no-profit Salt River Publishing company.

www.SaltRiverPublishing.com
*Publisher discount available at the estore*

SR

# SALT RIVER BOOKLIST

## Global Library Books
+ Janice Fletcher, EdD – *Teach with Spirit: A teacher's inward journey guide*
+ Anthea Guinness – *The inner way: A mystic anthology of songpoems, stories, reflections*
+ Anthea Guinness – *Wake up! if you can: Sayings of Kabir with reflections and mystic stories*

## Tuppany Books
+ Shanan Harrell – *Stumbling towards enlightenment: A Yoga 101 collection*
+ Rosemary Rawson – *Coming of age: Notes from the front line of aging*
+ Elley-Ray Tsipolitis – *Butterfly kisses: Quotes for daily motivation and renewal*

## Pocketbooks
+ Anthea Guinness – *Dawn has come: Songpoems of Paltu*

## Beyond Borders Books
+ Dyan Dubois – *Rajasthan suite memory*

New Moon Books for children

+ Village Voices series – *I am the rainbow, With my hands, Color in the book, In my dreams...*

**Independent Publications** *Salt River assistance with editing, book design, composition, cover design*

+ Rosemary Rawson – *Dark bread and dancing: The diaries of Sue Rawson*
+ Chloe Faith Wordsworth – *The Fundamentals of Resonance Repatterning,* and ten other Resonance Repatterning practitioner sourcebooks
+ Chloe Faith Wordsworth – *Spiral up! 127 Energizing Options to be your best right now*
+ Chloe Faith Wordsworth – *Quantum change made easy: Breakthroughs in personal transformation*

SR

www.SaltRiverPublishing.com

*Publisher discount available at the estore*

# COLOPHON

**Typefaces:** Garamond Premier Pro (designed by Robert Slimbach), Moravian (designer unknown)
**Software:** Adobe InDesign
**Book Design:** Carol White of Salt River Publishing –
   *email:* carol@saltriverpublishing.com
**Composition:** Anthea Guinness of Salt River Publishing
**Cover Photo**, used with permission: Andrew Johnson
**Cover Design:** Carol White of Salt River Publishing –
   *email:* carol@saltriverpublishing.com
**Printer:** createspace.com
**Printing method:** Print-on-Demand (POD) digital printing
**Paper:** Library quality
**Binding:** Perfect binding

SR

www.SaltRiverPublishing.com

# SALT RIVER

Salt River Publishing believes in encouraging artists and publishing professionals to come together and reach their empowered "Yes!"

Salt River was established as a no-profit publisher for two reasons:

To help writers, translators, poets, graphic artists and photographers bring their work into publishable form and let them make 100% of the profit on their book sales.

And to promote, for free, the expertise of any publishing professional whose services an author might need when they have a book in the making.

We publish books that inspire, encourage and entertain, including children's books and books that deepen the understanding of mysticism.

Do you have one?

SR

www.SaltRiverPublishing.com

## READER RESPONSE
## TO SALT RIVER BOOKS

"So many problems are spiritual in nature. And healing often involves finding meaning, purpose and spiritual uplift. The right words at the right time can turn a life around. Therapists and practitioners can point the way for clients who are seeking meaning; writers and artists have an opportunity to share in that work. Thank you, Salt River."